Territories of the Psyche

Territories of the Psyche:
The Fiction of Jean Rhys

Anne B. Simpson

TERRITORIES OF THE PSYCHE
© Anne B. Simpson, 2005.

First published in 2005 by
PALGRAVE MACMILLAN™
175 Fifth Avenue, New York, N.Y. 10010 and
Houndmills, Basingstoke, Hampshire, England RG21 6XS
Companies and representatives throughout the world.

PALGRAVE MACMILLAN is the global academic imprint of the Palgrave Macmillan division of St. Martin's Press, LLC and of Palgrave Macmillan Ltd. Macmillan® is a registered trademark in the United States, United Kingdom and other countries. Palgrave is a registered trademark in the European Union and other countries.

ISBN 1–4039–6613–3

Library of Congress Cataloging-in-Publication Data

Simpson, Anne B., 1956–
     Territories of the psyche : the fiction of Jean Rhys /
Anne B. Simpson.
          p. cm.
     Includes bibliographical references and index.
     ISBN 1–4039–6613–3 (alk. paper)
          1. Rhys, Jean—Criticism and interpretation. 2. Psychological fiction, English—History and criticism. 3. Rhys, Jean—Knowledge—Psychology. 4. Psychology in literature. I. Title.

PR6035.H96Z865 2005
823′.912—dc22   2004050530

A catalogue record for this book is available from the British Library.

Design by Newgen Imaging Systems (P) Ltd, Chennai, India.

First edition: January 2005

10   9   8   7   6   5   4   3   2   1

Printed in the United States of America.

Permissions ✍

This book is for Ben.

Divinity must live within herself
Passions of rain, or moods in falling snow;
Grievings in loneliness, or unsubdued
Elations when the forest blooms; gusty
Emotions on wet roads on autumn nights;
All pleasures and all pains, remembering
The bough of summer and the winter branch.
These are the measures destined for her soul.

—From Wallace Stevens, "Sunday Morning"
Typescript copy included among Jean Rhys's
personal papers, McFarlin Library,
University of Tulsa

Contents ✍

Acknowledgments ↩

This book has developed through many years of thought and discussion, and I owe numerous debts of gratitude. To begin, I would like thank California State University, Pomona, in particular the offices of the vice president and the dean of the College of Letters, Arts, and Social Sciences; the Faculty Center for Professional Development; and the Department of English and Foreign Languages, for providing assistance in the form of grants and release time from teaching that enabled me to work consistently on this project. I thank the staff of the McFarlin Library of the University of Tulsa: Milissa Bukart and Tim Anderson for their indefatigable efforts, and Lori N. Curtis, Head of Special Collections and Archives, for her expertise, guidance, and very tangible support while I was consulting Jean Rhys's papers at a preliminary stage in my research. Lois Wallace of the Wallace Literary Agency extended generous and much-valued help on my behalf as I navigated the waters of Rhys's several publishers.

I thank my teachers at the Southern California Psychoanalytic Institute for providing the inspiration of a dynamically engaged psychoanalytic community receptive to a wide range of analytic paradigms. I am indebted to Marvin Osman, who read a chapter of this book in draft form and made valuable editorial comments; to Harvey Weintraub, who shared clarifying accounts of the symptoms displayed by victims of sexual abuse; and to the members of Harvey Weintraub's analytic consultative group of the spring of 2001, who gave illuminating feedback, drawn from their own therapeutic work, on passages from *Good Morning, Midnight*.

I give special thanks to Alan Karbelnig, who has modeled the creativity of psychoanalysis as a form of art and has been mentor, colleague, and friend from the tentative beginnings of this project through to its conclusive moments. My appreciation goes to Helen Nedelman for sharing a nuanced interpretation of Kleinian theory and practice that deepened my engagements with the material. Conversations with Terry Jordan helped refine my understanding of primitive phenomena explored in these pages, and I thank her for instances of illumination. I am thankful also to Matthew Simpson, who offered perceptive and sensitive responses to a portion of this manuscript.

Finally, to my husband, Ben Patnoi, to whom this book has been dedicated, I am grateful in a space that lives beyond the words.

1. Introductory: Jean Rhys and the Landscape of Emotion ᗩ

The big idea—well I'm blowed if I can be sure what it is. Something to do with time being an illusion I think. I mean that the past exists—side by side with the present, not behind it; that what was—is.

—Jean Rhys, *letter of February 18, 1934*

Jean Rhys wrote four of her five novels in the period between the two world wars; she lived for some time as an expatriate in London and Paris; and her fiction is notable for its stylistic experimentation on multiple levels. Until recently, however, she has not garnered the critical attention or the reverent following accorded other Modernists of her day. Despite the perspicacity with which all of her narratives record the lives of the disenfranchised and interrogate the conditions of subjectivity, even readers who have become Rhys enthusiasts tend to privilege her last novel, *Wide Sargasso Sea*, which was published almost three decades after the others and is usually celebrated at the expense of her earlier works.

It is not surprising that *Wide Sargasso Sea* would appeal to contemporary audiences, for its positioning as self-aware "prequel" to Charlotte Brontë's nineteenth-century narrative *Jane Eyre* offers up a bouquet of poststructuralist delights. Rhys's most famous work depends upon and yet forever alters the prior text—*Jane Eyre* is never the same upon rereading, after one experiences the critique of imperialism mounted by *Wide Sargasso Sea*—for Rhys's novel problematizes the hierarchies of "originary" and "secondary," "colonizer" and "colonized," "subject" and "object" in modes of analysis that resonate in the current critical climate. Yet the novels that Rhys wrote at mid-century make powerful and unforgettable claims as they evoke the primitive states of emotional life. These narratives, in turn, place *Wide Sargasso Sea* within a new kind of interpretive frame.[1] The span of Rhys's development shows her continuous reworking of preoccupations that were with her from the start. Over many years, in the painstaking refinement of her aesthetic, she summoned again and again a vision of the psychic terrain as a wild and frightening place whose borders were uncertain and where time stood still. How she came to this vision, and her achievement in finding ways to communicate it in her sparingly selected words and in the spaces between those words, are the subjects of this study.

In spite of her dedication to mapping her perceptions and sharing these with the others who read her work, Rhys thought of herself, in her personal life, as someone who would always be misunderstood. This conception informed her bearing in the successive environments that she felt she always bordered. Born in 1890 in Dominica, a small island in the West Indies, Rhys felt marginalized on several counts: because she was living in a multiracial population marked by strong antagonism toward the lingering imperialist presence, and she was white; because she was brought up in a late-Victorian culture shaped by powerfully masculine values, and she was a woman. Most intimately, she felt isolated within her own family; she was distrustful of her rivalrous siblings, attached just tenuously to her depressed father, and both afraid of and alienated from her punitive, unavailable mother.

The autobiographical sketches in *Smile Please* in addition to the fuller biographical treatment in Carole Angier's *Jean Rhys: Life and Work* clarify that Rhys was adrift in the world from the start. She had been conceived to compensate for the loss of a little girl who had died nine months previously (Angier 11), and so she was born into an atmosphere of mourning—a depressed domestic environment that did not really change, as Rhys recollected, through her childhood and early youth. In a telling vignette that describes the feelings of loneliness and self-hatred, and also the defiance, that were with her from an early age, Rhys recalled the arrival of two dolls from England, gifts from a relative, and of how she longed for the dark rather than the fair one (Rhys herself was fair; the rest of her family, dark). Her younger sister, however, appropriated the dark doll and Rhys was told, over protests, that she ought not begrudge her sister her happiness and should feel content with the fair doll that had been allotted to her by default. Instead Rhys took this fair doll into the shadows and smashed its face with a stone; in the ensuing domestic upset she herself didn't understand why she had done what she had done, "Only I was sure that I must do it and for me it was right" (*Smile* 40). Later, after sobbing about it in the arms of a great-aunt, Rhys began to mourn for the doll and made plans to bury it ceremoniously. This episode models in miniature Rhys's lifelong sense of the insignificance of her own needs as measured against others' wishes; her ensuing envy, jealousy, and rivalry; her inarticulate and terrific rage; her remorse over the reflexively alienating behavior that was to characterize so many of her interactions; and yet, despite it all, her compassion for herself and her determination that whatever she did, "I must do it and for me it was right."

Her accounts of her family reveal a culture of sadness and a tendency to hold intimacies at a distance. Her father came from a deprived emotional background, the son of an Anglican clergyman who had neglected him and favored his elder brother (Angier 8). When he traveled from Wales to Dominica and set up practice as a doctor, he adopted a way of life that kept him busy but also remote, as he dispensed a sort of distracted kindness toward his children, flirted playfully with women other than his wife, and spent money improvidently, without regard for the anxiety this provoked in everyone around him. The coral brooch that he gave young Rhys and that was a favorite among her things was crushed in their last embrace, as she boarded a boat bound for England. Rhys's response was characteristic: "I had been very fond of it; now I took it off and put it away without any particular feeling" (*Smile* 93–94). This cutting-off of feelings in the attempt to disavow painful connection with others would characterize Rhys throughout her life whenever confronted by wrenching loss; it was a defensive mechanism that she recognized when she saw it in herself and other people, and she could write about it with disarming perceptiveness.

Of her mother Rhys recollected a woman of mixed background, the descendant of a Scottish slave-owner and his Hispanic wife; she was a white Creole who loved babies, particularly black ones, but apparently not the little girl who was growing up before her eyes. Rhys mused, "Was this the reason why I prayed so ardently to be black [. . .]?," voicing her early sense of her own hopeless inadequacy (42). She came to find her mother frigidly inaccessible. She was unreceptive to kisses and generally disapproved of Rhys's behavior, sometimes resorting to physical punishment. From early in life Rhys made a despairing conflation of her mother, God, and books: she imagined that God "was a large book standing upright and half open and I could see the print inside but it made no sense to me. Other times the book was smaller and inside were sharp flashing things. The smaller book was, I am sure now, my mother's needle-book, and the sharp flashing things were her needles with the sun on them" (27). Both books, of God and mother, excluded Rhys, and thus she was kept away from the sources of power; further, the mother's sharp, flashing book suggests the mother's sharp, flashing look, the critical, wounding gaze that is trained on an unloved child. Rhys experienced her mother as so distant emotionally that eventually she came to seem like someone with whom Rhys could have virtually no connection and, characteristically, she retaliated with her own withdrawal. In *Smile Please*, she reports, "I stopped imagining what she felt or what she thought" (46). The stern, principled distrust of the weak that her mother voiced would be countermanded by Rhys's ever more determined alignment with the vulnerable as against those who hold the power. Other than setting herself up in opposition to her mother, she had for all intents and purposes done with conscious affiliation with her by the time that she left Dominica. She had adopted a sense of her own liminal status that was to shape both her self-awareness and her work for succeeding decades as she became the author of her own books and found power, of a kind, in this way.

When Rhys moved to England at sixteen, to pursue her education first in a regular secondary school setting (as was not unusual for white children from the colonies) and later in an acting academy, she carried with her the conviction, as she expressed this once in an interview, that she never managed to "get into the sacred circle. I was always outside, shivering" (Vreeland 221). She eked out an existence in England in the semi-disreputable occupation of a chorus girl after her schooling abruptly ended, apparently because of her lack of conventional talent as an actress as well as her family's dwindling funds. Later she occupied a similarly uncertain social placement in Paris, her loneliness intensified when her first husband was arrested and extradited for a series of petty crimes. It was her attunement to the experience of marginalization that so impressed her first literary mentor, the influential reviewer and critic Ford Madox Ford, when he was shown Rhys's work by a mutual acquaintance in Paris who had seen and liked Rhys's manuscript-diary (the narrative that came to be entitled *Triple Sec* and that would form the nucleus of her later novel, *Voyage in the Dark*). Describing the impact of her fiction, Ford noted "her profound knowledge of the life of the Left Bank—of many of the Left Banks of the world," places delineated more by psychology than topography, by an atmosphere of sadness and deprivation that distinguished the inhabitants (Preface 23). Ford had edited both *The English Review* and *the transatlantic review*, which made a point of publishing diverse, up-and-coming talents who had been unrecognized previously but came to light in literary circles thanks to Ford's support. His patronage of young writers was consistent and perceptive, and he tutored Rhys in paring down her prose, illustrating but not editorializing, imitating French models, and eschewing melodrama (Angier 131–35). A piece of her manuscript-diary was published in the *review*'s last issue; and it was Ford who devised for the former Ella Gwendolen Rees Williams the pseudonym Jean Rhys—the two names adopted, respectively, from her first husband, who used the nickname Jean; and her father, whose middle name of Rees was restored to its Welsh spelling. She was thus positioned within a line of masculine influence that she would learn to modify as she began to claim her own voice.[2]

By this time Rhys and Ford were sexually enmeshed in a complicated situation that reverberated in both their marriages, as documented by Rhys's fictionalized account of the situation in her first published novel, *Quartet.* Most pertinently, however, despite Ford's support and advice, and despite the presence of the many other aspiring writers who circled around him, Rhys continued to think of herself as alone. She barely knew Hemingway and chose successive, one-on-one intimacies that almost always ended badly over inclusion in the group life of the literati in postwar Paris. In a letter written in 1964, Rhys dismissively recalled the expatriate milieu: "The 'Paris' all these people write about, Henry Miller, even Hemingway etc was not 'Paris' at all—it was 'America in Paris' or 'England in Paris'. The real Paris had nothing to do with that lot—As soon as the tourists came the *real* Montparnos packed up and left" (*Letters* 280).[3]

As the defensive tone of her statement suggests, Rhys had a far-ranging suspicion of social circles; this was accompanied by a keen awareness of how conventions of every kind exert pressure on the individual to mask genuine feelings with contrived forms of outer display. From the first, her fiction demonstrated her concern with inner states of experience as this paralleled, always, her distrust for external show. The phoniness of much outward presentation, the unforgivable sin of socially conditioned behavior, formed the target for her most scathing attacks. Her protagonists characteristically respond to the vicissitudes of human relations by learning to distrust the mouthings of conventional expression and feel, as their sharpest reality, how deeply other people can wound them. Their habituated expressions of suspicion and their sometimes more stark demonstrations of fear create resonances at the heart of Rhys's work. These are complicated, however, by her unfailingly honest perception: that a grim take on life's offerings may not make an unparalleled claim of truth but rather invite further scrutiny precisely because it is a response to having been badly hurt.

Rhys's candor in accepting that a profound legacy of pain may cause the self to misperceive aspects of others does not diminish the power of her vision, which presents, with compassion, how the warping of individuals' lives connects with the warping of their outlooks and expectations. Her sense of the characters' self-imposed alienation as well as their alienating activities is offset by her awareness of their tragic loneliness and reflects Rhys's own self-identifications, which shaped, on the one hand, her wary and hostile interactions with the people she met and, on the other, their readiness to exclude her from communities of various kinds. By the time she published her last novel, *Wide Sargasso Sea,* in the 1960s, she was living reclusively in a remote corner of Devonshire, her old age characterized by successive days of drinking and hangovers (Athill, Introduction xiii). In these final years, despite the growing critical recognition of *Wide Sargasso Sea*, the unaccustomed financial success it brought her, and the concern of those who considered themselves her friends, Rhys felt in her darker moments, of which there were many, that she was existing as she had throughout her life—as the consummate outsider. "My Day," a brief autobiographical account of this period, records the wish for self-enclosure that served as one well-worn strategy of response: "Wouldn't it be marvelous," she suggests to herself, "if I had room for several trees and at last could live in a forest, which has always been one of my ambitions." The memoir goes on to capture with evocative indirection the feeling of isolation shadowing her in a singular, paradoxical, and stubborn companionship. Recalling a "very frightening ghost story" of a "solitary woman," she describes its chilling moment of truth when, having "just turned the key and shot the bolt for the night [. . .] she hears a voice behind her saying: 'Now we are alone together' " (*My* n. page).

In the insistence throughout her oeuvre on the unassailability of her protagonists' union with unhappiness, Rhys offers finely honed portraits of individuals who are accompanied by a persistent sense of grievance that can never be assuaged. The aggrieved mood and Rhys's sense of life are closely linked, for it is when they are acknowledging the feeling of pain that her characters live their selfhood fully. Underscoring the power of her own melancholy, she establishes that she is committed to finding a way to give sadness a voice, to let it speak without compromise, in her most memorable creative work.

*   *   *

Rhys's ability to evoke the depths of emotional experience in her writing was not the product of any academic understanding of the theories of Freud, which, insofar as she was exposed to these, she disputed. In her Black Exercise Book, one of several unpublished notebooks in which she kept memoirs, observations, first ideas, and preliminary drafts for some of her fiction and poetry, she recorded her encounter in adolescence with a family friend who introduced her to sexual life by narrating a series of increasingly explicit sadomasochistic adventures in which she functioned, in fantasy, as his sexual slave (Thomas 65–66)—an experience that would form the kernel of her story "Good-bye Marcus, Good-bye Rose," to be discussed below. As an adult, browsing in Sylvia Beach's bookstore in Paris, she came across a psychoanalytic study that disputed claims by women of a certain kind (presumably sexual hysterics) that they were victims when younger of seduction by older, fatherly figures. The limited insight and failure of vision in such analytic positioning were patently clear to Rhys on this occasion. Although it seems likely that she had seen some variant of Freud's refutation of the seduction theory,[4] there is no evidence that she read Freud himself and certainly no sign that she had any strong grounding in his work or that of his successors. When her fiction does directly reference analysis, it is to serve the purpose of ridicule: for example, Sasha Jensen of *Good Morning, Midnight* recalls a former employer whose discourse style was rambling and irrational and who moved mindlessly from topics like pricey restaurants to the treatment of one's social inferiors to psychoanalysis and such comments as "Adler is more wholesome than Freud, don't you think?" (168). Freud is thus offered up as fodder for the small-talk of the socially banal. Aside from using psychoanalysis to show the superficiality of characters she disdained, Rhys apparently found Freud irrelevant. Although later in life she was under court order to see mental health practitioners because of her increasingly antisocial behavior—and she experienced them as sympathetic and understanding (Angier 446)—her formal exposure to psychoanalytic premises appears to have been almost nonexistent. Nevertheless her fiction reveals an interest, always, in sharpening her focus to reveal the emotional core of her characters, the inner lives that determine their perceptions and responses to the others they encounter.

Rhys's work reflected a different kind of interest in emotional life than that offered by the more forceful personalities in European aesthetics of the 1920s and 1930s who were documenting the blasted lives of disaffected individuals. The metaphors that were deployed by influential Modernists to describe the wounds suffered by the generation that survived World War I did not engage Rhys's imagination. Jake Barnes of Hemingway's *The Sun Also Rises* carries his castration as a trophy, signifier of the failure of a young, heroic striver to compete with the brutal machinery of Euro-American warmongers. In a classical psychoanalytic frame of reference, as determined by Freudian concerns with male development, Jake stands as the Oedipal son of the infamous filial rivalry, thwarted in his efforts to surpass those who are stronger, and therefore cut to the quick, the thematics of castration anxiety literalized in his broken body. This masculinist rendition of the trauma suffered by modern individuals was widely appealing to the readership of Hemingway's day and to successive generations of audiences who have been conditioned to think via the patriarchy, with a consciousness shaped by male perception. This mode of awareness elides the recognition of another kind of wounding, one implicated deeply in more primitive experiences of alienation. It was to the vexed dyad of mother and child that Rhys returned, in her fiction, again and again. This brings us to the template upon which Rhys constructs the life of her protagonists. Even those Rhysian narratives that inscribe the triangulated dynamics of the "family romance" are built upon earlier modes of infant relationship to a maternal body that is experienced as forever withholding. Her short stories from the early collection overseen by Ford, *The Left Bank* (1927), sound the first notes of this interest; and it appears at the very end of her life, in the last stories she published in magazines and two final collections, *Tigers Are Better-Looking* (1968) and *Sleep It Off Lady* (1976).

The *Left Bank* sketch "Mannequins" offers a preliminary Rhysian view of the condition of daughters who have been allowed to drift along without any maternal guidance. The models whose lives the story documents struggle to support themselves in an impersonal urban atmosphere that values them only for their looks, for the types they present as they step in and out of dresses for a privileged clientele. Overseeing Anna, the heroine, is a "helpful and shapeless" old woman, the dresser whose "professional motherliness" stands in for genuine concern (*Collected* 21); she occupies the place of the missing mother, the ghostly reminder of the nurturing that Anna, as well as the other young mannequins, need and do not have. Like many of Rhys's protagonists to come, Anna finds herself lost in the bewildering corridors of a huge establishment that tropes the vastness of the social world; and as she seeks connection with others she finds only girls who have become masked automatons, "practising rigidly" their expected social roles (22). They act according to "genre," competing with one another and finding comradeship just briefly when aligned against their common enemy, "the *Mère* Pecard" mother-substitute (24). Then they are out on the floor, isolated and on display, subject to the consuming gaze of customers who see them as mere extensions of the clothes they wear. When Anna leaves at the end of her first day of work and returns to the streets of Paris she feels, appropriately, that "now she really belonged to the great, maddening city [. . .]" (25–26). What Rhys has delineated in this brief story is the condition by which a motherless child is cast into a world populated by rivalrous and greedy others, lost until she begins to learn how to masquerade and conform to social expectations of her. It is a "maddening" experience—an experience that makes one mad—insofar as it denies and then deprives the individual of her subjectivity. Within this short narrative exploration of the betrayal and dehumanization of women, Rhys is already displaying the depth of insight that characterizes her treatment of the same material in later stories and novels.

Another early story, "Learning to Be a Mother," directly confronts the vicissitudes of mother–infant connection as it describes the experience of a pregnant woman who has come alone to a large, frightening maternity home and finds herself surrounded by women "already crazy with pain" (55). When her infant is brought to her just after his birth, the heroine can think only of how ugly he is and how much she herself needs; her sense of intense deprivation is brought to the fore as she peevishly asks that he be removed and that her own thirst be slated. "What lies people tell about maternity!" she thinks bitterly, as she listens to the screams of a woman in the room next door (58). It is only in the final moments of the story that she is able to feel a stirring of affection for her child; and even then it is colored by narcissistic projection, as she sees that his eyes are like her own and her speculation, "Perhaps that is why he looks sad—because his mother never has kissed him," directly follows from her own wish, "I must kiss him" (59). In an atmosphere of Gothic horror appropriate to the subject matter, Rhys describes the dark side of the unclear distinction between mother and baby, as the mother who herself needs mothering sees only her own deprivation and desire in her child and is unable to recognize this other's needs. The terror of abandonment, as felt by mother and in turn communicated to baby, is a feeling-state to which Rhys would return later, in more fully developed stories and novels, with similarly unsettling vividness.

These first narratives, written by Rhys at the beginning of her career, delineate two ways of being in the world. There is the way of her protagonists who feel, as one *Left Bank* character puts it, that " 'very strong emotion is an excuse for anything [. . .]' " (82). Alternatively, there is the way of the "civilized," those who respond, always, with condescension and contempt; as a representative character in an early story thinks, "Balance. When people lack Balance there's really nothing to be done" (46). Rhys is passionate about those with very strong emotion, however trying and impossible they become—and she is distrustful of the balanced, however responsible and upstanding they seem.

However, the symbiotic linkage between her heroines and their adversaries is one of the complexities of social life that Rhys does not shirk. Her late story "Till September Petronella," written when she was in her seventies, recounts the disastrous holiday of a young woman and her admirer, companioned by his friend and the friend's mistress, in the countryside. Despite the apparently artistic complexion of the group—the narrator's young man is a painter, his friend a music critic—they are rivalrous and jealous with one another; the men align against the women and the women compete; and finally Petronella flees it all to return to the city. She is aided by a local farmer who picks her up along the road, buys her a train ticket and some chocolates, and then unctuously intimates that she become his lover once back in London. Her thoughts as she looks at herself in the mirror of her train compartment reflect a defensive self-absorption shot through with hostility toward the knowing faces presented by the social world:

> "Cheer up," I said, and kissed myself in the cool glass. I stood with my forehead against it and watched my face clouding gradually, then turned because I felt as if someone was staring at me, but it was only the girl on the cover of the chocolate-box. She had slanting green eyes, but they were too close together, and she had a white, square, smug face that didn't go with the slanting eyes. "I bet you could be a rotten, respectable, sneering bitch too, with a face like that, if you had a chance," I told her. (144)

One of the more intriguing questions raised in this moment is whether Petronella is condemning the outside world for its disingenuousness or accusing herself of her own hypocritical potential, or both. The line between self and other is indistinct, as throughout much of Rhys's fiction, alerting readers to the collaborative processes that ensure that an outsider remain in the margins not only because of her own "oddness" in the eyes of the group but because of her expectation of mistreatment by them and her projection of disavowed anger. In a vicious cycle, those others then proceed to confirm her grim suspicions of the self-serving brutality of human nature. The blurriness between "us" and "them" reproduces a primitive level of experiencing when clear boundaries are not established and identity is unarticulated. It speaks to a time before processes of compartmentalization and labeling have taken hold: a pre-Oedipal realm of perception, in which infant and mother are together yet apart, enmeshed but not whole.

Movement toward a more clearly Oedipal set of problems is always offset, in Rhys's fiction, by attentiveness to how triangulated domestic interactions of a later developmental stage build upon already-established, early modes of response between mother and child. The story "Good-bye Marcus, Good-bye Rose" (published in 1976) describes a twelve-year-old girl's attraction to a handsome elderly man, a Captain Cardew, who has come to stay for the winter on the small West Indian island where she lives. He flatters Phoebe by engaging with her as if she were an adult, and she is continuously reminded by the grown-ups around her that it is a privilege to be treated so well by such a distinguished old man. Thus he proceeds, abetted by those who have stressed how very kind he is, to lure her into taking a series of long, isolated walks with him. After an initial, astonishing grope at her breast, he settles into the seductive narration of sexually charged stories, "ceaseless talk of love, various ways of making love, various sorts of love. He'd explain that love was not kind and gentle, as she had imagined, but violent. Violence, even cruelty, was an essential part of it" (287). Although Phoebe is alarmed by these tales, she is also deeply compelled to listen; and she determines at once that there is no point in telling anyone about what is happening because she is certain not to be believed.

The young girl's victimization by an older man with whom she feels complicit because of her sense of how fascinating he is reproduces an incestuous Oedipal relation in which a daughter's evolving sexuality is exploited by a powerful, charismatic father to serve his own ends. Her certainty that no one will believe in the exploitation is a characteristic response of the incest victim, especially when she is conditioned by maternal figures to think that she is blameworthy. In Rhys's story, the Captain's wife begins to harbor an aversion to Phoebe when she becomes aware of the volatile situation that has developed. His remark to his wife, "it was quite true that the only way to get rid of a temptation was to yield to it," clearly references his own behavior; and yet it is the young girl, not her husband, who is the target of the wife's anger. Responding to an innocuous compliment from Phoebe, she voices her displaced outrage: " 'What a really dreadful little liar you are!' " The wife's alignment with husband against young girl reproduces a nightmare version of the family romance in which the child's experience is dismissed and condemned. The story goes on to suggest that the woman's unfair judgment of Phoebe replicates a foundational experience of misperception by her own mother, "a silent, reserved woman" who now starts to observe her "in a puzzled, incredulous, even faintly suspicious way" (288). This withdrawn, disapproving reaction is at a far remove from the protectiveness that might be expected from a mother who feels concerned above all for her daughter's welfare; the maternal response speaks instead of a misattunement in the dyad of mother and child that predates this malign Oedipal scenario and that has now been reactivated.

After the Captain and his wife leave the island, Phoebe is confirmed in a sense of her own wickedness:

> She was sure that now they had gone her mother would be very unlikely to question her, and then began to wonder how he'd been so sure, not only that she'd never tell anybody but that she'd make no effort at all to stop him talking. That could only mean that he'd seen at once that she was not a good girl—who would object—but a wicked one—who would listen. He must know. He knew. It was so. (288–89)

The story ends on a note of innocence lost, as Phoebe reflects that she will never be like the older girls she knows who talk happily of marriage because she will never be good enough to deserve wedlock. Most significantly, she will no longer compose lists, as they do and as she once did, of the names of her future children. At this final moment the narrative takes an ironic turn: "The prospect before her might be difficult and uncertain," as Phoebe reflects, "but it was far more exciting" (290). In proclaiming her own unconventionality, the heroine takes up the position of the "other" against the norm, a position that is adopted by Rhys's many protagonists. In renouncing her own prospective children, she also firmly closes the door on any identification with the maternal; eschewing motherhood, she symbolically turns her back on the disappointments of pre-Oedipal life.

*   *   *

Despite Rhys's distrust of psychoanalysis as she knew it, and despite the necessity for a reworking of any strictly Freudian model when describing her presentations of psychological states, psychoanalysis as a body of thought still offers the most powerful theoretical paradigm to date for exploring the complexities of emotional life as these are expressed in literature as well as life. In a study of a writer's achievement, it is important to begin, however, by acknowledging the limitations of both psychoanalysis and literary criticism when thought of as disciplines that may be "applied" to one another. As Shoshana Felman has pointed out, in all such thinking there is an implicit Hegelian equation that posits one term as master, the other as slave; one privileged, one subordinate. Thus we might say, as she argues, that literature exists as a focal point for interpretive activity; that psychoanalysis as a discipline provides the means for performing interpretation; the literary is implicitly reduced, the psychoanalytic inflated (5). (These value-judgments may be reversed, of course, depending on whether one's primary affiliation is to literature or to psychoanalysis.) As literary critics know, psychoanalytic approaches to texts tend to seem naïve; interpreting at the level of what seems obvious, treating characters as if they were "real" people without regard for their textual function, what psychoanalytic critiques often seem to miss are the peculiarly "literary" qualities within a text, among which, as Felman notes, is irony. Literature, Felman claims, alerts us to the fact "that authority is a *language effect*, the product or the creation of its own *rhetorical* power: that authority is the *power of fiction*; that authority, therefore, is likewise a fiction" (8). I would modify this statement to suggest that literature has come to seem this way to us in light of the poststructuralist dismantling of truth-claims over the past several decades. The self-conscious awareness of the literary as meaning-making, and the sense of an excess within the text that allows for the deconstruction of authorship and authority, is literature as literary critics of today choose to know it; and this variety of knowledge will be supplanted, in time, by another version of what litera-ture is and does. Nevertheless, Felman's insistence on the specifically literary as it is often overlooked in psychoanalytic interpretations is an important corrective, explaining in part the discomfort that classical psychoanalytic accounts of texts and their authors may produce in contemporary readers who have been trained as students of literature.[5]

However—and this literary critics do not always recognize—psychoanalysis of the twentieth and twenty-first centuries has also become increasingly subversive about its own explanatory paradigms and power structures. The prevailing notion of the analytic scene, in which the patient lies prone and vulnerable in submission to Herr Doktor's stern mastery and deftly pruned interpretations, has been so embraced by the popular imagi-nation as to acquire a truth-status quite at odds with its parodic flavor—and this although Freud himself, as well as early followers, could be notably less contained and more volatile, in addition to having a much more fluid sense of boundaries, than is usually allowed.[6] Certainly the initial case stud-ies do promote some sense of Freud as the authority giving interpretive "truths" to his analysands, who listened, with varying degrees of credulity, appreciation, and dismay, to what they were being told about their uncon-scious motivations. (His famous patient Dora was so horrified by Freud's insistence on her unclaimed sexual desire—and by Freud's bullying demand that she accept his views—that she left treatment. To his often overlooked credit, Freud devoted considerable time and effort to trying to understand why she had left and how it was that the analysis had taken this turn ["Fragment"].) Recent psychoanalytic approaches, as diversely practiced by those influenced by the British "object relations" school, by "intersubjectivists," and by "self psychologists," have in common another model of analytic engagement, one that stresses dialogue between two sub-jectivities. Such dialogue disrupts the Hegelian opposition and hierarchy and recognizes that for exchange to occur in analytic discourse, a paradox must be acknowledged. As intersubjectivity theorist Jessica Benjamin argues, "Recognition is that response from the other which makes mean-ingful the feelings, intentions, and actions of the self. It allows the self to realize its agency and authorship in a tangible way. But such recognition can only come from an other whom we, in turn, recognize as a person in his or her own right." Only in such a "mixture of otherness and together-ness" can the analysand come to recognize the analyst as both similar to and different from herself—and vice versa (12; 15). While contemporary ana-lysts vary in the degree to which they disclose information to their clients, they have in common a more loose and relaxed model of self-presentation than posited by classical analysis, one that acknowledges how truths about themselves, and often truths of which they are unaware, will be revealed in the analytic exchange. Thus there is tacit agreement that their "authority" as such is a fiction, perhaps one that is useful for both therapist and patient at times, but one nonetheless subject to continual revision during analytic encounters, as the transference and countertransference progress.

One frustration for the analytic community as it has watched literary criticism deploy psychoanalytic theory is the seeming single-mindedness of the recurrent use of Freud and his most direct descendant Lacan, with little regard for the many other analytic figures who have revolutionized the profession over the past century. Lacan's interest in the construction of symbolic systems is understandably congenial to those in literary studies whose own discipline focuses attention on language use and textuality. His explanation of human development, rooted as it is in Freud's notion of Oedipal dynamics, also has the appeal of the somewhat-familiar. As Lacan posits, the child turns from an undifferentiated sense of fusion with the maternal body to an increasing awareness of its otherness in itself, its non-self-identity with the apparently unified being it sees in the mirror; and its entry into the substitutive but reassuringly sense-making Realm of the Father, where words give names to strange experiences and authority is conditioned on the use of the word, privileges masculine experiences of loss and, in turn, masculine ideals of control, as these have been articulated for centuries in Western culture.

Continental feminism, in a line of development that parallels the evolution of alternative analytic models, notes that Lacan's emphasis on women as spaces of loss for men may be supplanted by another paradigm of human growth and symbol-making. Hélène Cixous describes what she calls the feminine experience, with "feminine" here standing in for the nontraditional as well as more literally the non-male, by describing a type of writing that defies conventional categories and hierarchies between people. Using a language that is remarkably similar to Benjamin's intersubjectivist discourse when she discusses the paradoxical interplay of self and other, Cixous comments:

> To admit that writing is precisely working (in) the in-between, inspecting the process of the same and of the other without which nothing can live, undoing the work of death—to admit this is first to want the two, as well as both, the ensemble of the one and the other, not fixed in sequences of struggle and expulsion or some other form of death but infinitely dynamized by an incessant process of exchange from one subject to another. ("Laugh" 1,459)

Similarly, Luce Irigaray, in reconceptualizing the female imaginary outside the realm of the defining male gaze, advocates a recognition of multiplicity within the self as a thrilling, a liberating, abundance—a fascinating supplementarity within one's subjecthood and not an occasion for the exercise of control or the adoption of rational, sense-making activities to help one compensate for some kind of incoherence. " 'She,' " argues Irigaray, describing that which happily escapes traditionally patriarchal strategies of discourse, "is indefinitely other in herself." Further,

> One would have to listen with another ear, as if hearing an "other meaning" always in the process of weaving itself, of embracing itself with words, but also of getting rid of words in order not to become fixed, congealed in them. For if "she" says something, it is not, it is already no longer, identical with what she means. What she says is never identical with anything, moreover; rather, it is contiguous. It touches (upon). (29)

Irigaray calls for a different kind of interpretation of a different kind of language: for an open acknowledgment of that which is allusive and suggestive, of that which reverberates with meanings, without recourse to a system that would either produce hard-and-fast explanations or fall into mourning over the impossibility of putting experience precisely in the form of words. She sees another kind of activity as the site of possibilities within both the writer and reader who are willing to view language as process rather than product—as a beginning of thought, rather than an end.

While both Cixous and Irigiray are specifically concerned with feminine experiences as these are recuperated from masculinist conventions and framed in a celebratory way, I would like to argue that many of their insights reverberate in psychoanalytic discourses other than those of Freud/Lacan—discourses that have in fact been of crucial importance in the modern age. For example, the triangulated family romance that captured Freud's imagination and privileged masculine experience and modes of sense-making has receded from view in most psychoanalytic circles. The shift of interest, by the middle of the twentieth century, to an earlier condition of human existence, one that is less clearly differentiated and concerns mother and infant as they participate in nonverbal modes of communication, may be ascribed in part to the archaic wish for a state of merger that has occurred in our intellectual climate as a response to an increasingly isolating and chaotic modern culture (Loewald 773). In particular, the work of Melanie Klein displaces Freud's preoccupation with the Oedipal rivalry between father and son by reclaiming the significance of the maternal–infant pair of the earliest moments of life experience; along with this reclamation is a profound respect, in the work of Klein and her successors, for the cadences of connection and misattunement that shape infant experience, in a place that resonates without words.

Klein disputed Freud's insistence on the male scenario as paradigmatic for all human development; she took issue with the fact that the mother was relegated to the role of mere catalyst for action, and she argued that Freud's conception of the Oedipal triangle as coming into place at the relatively late state of toddlerhood implied, incorrectly, that earlier experiences were of little count in personality formation. In contrast, Klein placed emphasis on the infant's experiences of its primary caregiver, usually the mother, and the degree to which these determine later intrapyschic awareness as well as interpersonal behavior. With her colleague Joan Riviere, Klein also examined the states of envy and jealousy as these shaped and were in turn shaping of mother–child dynamics, with attentiveness to how feelings of rivalry could result in a spoiling not only of one's desired others but of every ensuing psychic experience. Those under Klein's influence at mid-century such as D. W. Winnicott and Ronald Fairbairn, as well as more contemporary successors like Christopher Bollas and Donald Meltzer, have found much that is too stringent in her theory. What they share, however, is an appreciation of how Klein's radical reformulation of Freud relies, first and foremost, on a recognition of the importance of earliest infancy; and a sensitive awareness of primitive states of being characterizes the work of this so-called object relations variant of analysis, despite notable differences among the practitioners.

The work of Klein and her others is, therefore, of particular relevance in traversing the landscape of Rhys's fiction. The Rhysian text demonstrates ways in which the mother–daughter pair characteristically serves as the source of subsequent misadjustments in adult life. The pre-Oedipal dyad is thus especially important in understanding the fundamental, often preverbal states of awareness and reaction that Rhys's heroines express. They enact a primitive mode of engagement with the world that often baffles readers, even as it proves compelling. It is precisely the heroines' inability to function within more sophisticated modes of development reliant on symbolic making that leaves so many of Rhys's audiences in the dark, struggling to make sense of something that eludes rational explanation of the Oedipal kind.

Here theories of pre-Oedipal life prove particularly salient. But object relations theorists can make arguments that seem strange or downright perverse on one's first exposure to them, as the analysts discuss, variously, infantile mechanisms of splitting and paranoia; a dark envy of the mother's imaginary internal contents; murderous feelings of hostility and aggression toward her as well as toward perceived rivals of the baby; the early desire to incorporate the other's entire body by biting into and devouring it; the terrifying infant fear of the vengeful parent's retribution—to name just a few of the assertions that are explored in these pages. Of readers who find themselves particularly skeptical when confronted with Kleinian-derived ideas that seem blatantly non-commonsensical, I would ask the same willingness to suspend disbelief that allowed for the initial reception of Freud's notion of the unconscious as well as the tripartite division of ego, id, and superego that informs his account of the personality: ideas that have now become such staples of Western thought, paradoxically, that any challenge to them is met by the same sort of resistance that greeted the airing of his early views in his foundational work. My interest is to see how and if we may find new lenses for appreciating a writer's power if we consider the insights of influential analysts who have been overlooked in literary circles.

The theorists who follow Klein most closely, and whose work will be enlisted throughout this study, tend to emphasize ways in which the infant mind projects her own states of being onto sites in the external world. In instances in which the role of actual parental behavior in contributing to a child's perceptions is underestimated, Kleinian theory has been the target of persuasive attack. For those in the analytic community who are familiar with the horrors of child abuse (see, e.g., Alice Miller), any tendency to blame the child herself as the source of her own misfortunes is misguided, at best, and enabling of abusers, at worst. Rhys was at no pains to spare *soi-disant* caregivers from penetrating critiques through the course of her fiction. Despite her acknowledgment of emotional mistreatment, manipulation, and neglect, however, her work most specifically records the subjective views constructed by her protagonists—the ways in which their expectations of others are determined by their own longings and terrors. Thus an analytic approach that stresses the processes by which mental images, or imagos, are shaped and refined proves especially illuminating in a record of the powerful feeling-states of Rhys's successive heroines.

An awareness of pre-verbal states of primitive life is also useful when considering Rhys's formal choice as a self-conscious stylist who was concerned, always, to reduce her prose—to cut relentlessly, so that she could convey as much as possible in the fewest words and rely on implication rather than direct statement. Although she loved "beautiful words" (*Smile* 60), she shared with some Modernist contemporaries the concern to orchestrate moments of silence with powerful effect. In response to a comment by David Plante, the novelist who helped her organize the auto-biographical material for *Smile Please*, that " 'there's a sense of space around your words,' " she concurred: " 'Yes [. . .] I tried to get that. I thought very hard of each word in itself' " (*Difficult* 53). As a result of this considerable economy, the quiet that surrounds the words in her fiction often gives them heightened meaning. At times her narrators and characters fall completely silent; their lack of speech creates a reverberating muteness, recalling the symbolically loaded question posed by the protagonist of her story "The Sound of the River": "The river is very silent. [. . .] Is that because it's so full?" (*Collected* 237).

Rhys's speakers withhold information because of their own confusion, their need to suppress or repress, or their temporary reversion to moments of experiencing that are infantile in nature. They also demonstrate, despite their keen sense of isolation, a profound need for connection with the other who witnesses their stories; and again and again they enlist the second-person pronoun to invoke the collaborative efforts of readers in arriving at a sense of what has been omitted from the page. The Rhysian invitation to "you," as I demonstrate, can be used with varying intentions: to find a somebody to empathize with one's emotional distress; as the reflection of an incompleted selfhood and the lack of conviction that an experience can have meaning unless it is passed through the consciousness of another; and in creation of a sense of comradeship that may mediate against personal agency or primary responsibility for one's actions. Rhys's narrators, her female protagonists, and her male characters may all, in turn, make use of "you"—not in speaking to others in their fictive worlds but in direct exhortation that the reader join them in creating potential meanings.

The meanings, however, often remain elusive, which recalls Irigaray's notion of how words may be contiguous, may "touch upon." At key moments in Rhys's narratives, her reader is enjoined to imagine possibilities rather than settle into a fixed and certain understanding of what has been felt or experienced by a character. In this way the audience participates in a kind of interaction that replicates the complex tasks involved in psychoanalytic "working-through," as analyst and analysand collaborate in acts of telling and retelling. The analyst must be able to listen attentively to the *un*said of the speaker's discourse, forming ideas about how to voice this unsayable but also keeping them provisional and being willing to release them if other ideas float up into the analytic space. As Freud put it, the analyst should attempt "to surrender himself to his own unconscious mental activity, in a state of *evenly suspended attention*, to avoid so far as possible reflection and the construction of conscious expectations [. . .] and by these means to catch the drift of the patient's unconscious with his own unconscious" ("Two" 239). What Freud referred to as a free-ranging associative process that allows not only analysand but also analyst to hold in abeyance the need to "make sense," while the unconscious processes of two individuals find modes of connecting, also conditions the reading of Rhys's work; her audience is enjoined to entertain first one possibility for understanding, then another, in entering the amorphous atmosphere of her characters' emotional lives. The refusal of closure that is a marked feature of the "conclusions" of her narratives actually reproduces the strategy used throughout a given text, when omissions and partial statements allow for multiple explanations that often coexist, as do the elements of a dream, whether they seem to cohere or blatantly contradict one another. Rhys demonstrates that in the life of emotion, words only, at best, approximate and suggest. As a character in her story "The Lotus" comments, " 'That's the torture—knowing the thing and not knowing the words' " (212). The thing at the heart of the Rhysian text is *feeling*, and this occurs on a nonverbal plain that the reader is invited to inhabit once she steps within the pages of the narrative.

In this way, despite the grim outlooks of Rhys's heroines, the shady motives of those who surround them, and the tragically foregone outcomes that are effected, her work offers readers an experience that is powerfully affirming insofar as it insists on creative engagement. In his study *Playing and Reality* D. W. Winnicott describes the importance of creativity for psychological health:

> It is creative apperception more than anything else that makes the individual feel that life is worth living. Contrasted with this is a relationship to external reality which is one of compliance, the world and its details being recognized but only as something to be fitted in with or demanding adaptation. Compliance carries with it a sense of futility for the individual and is associated with the idea that nothing matters and that life is not worth living. In a tantalizing way many individuals have experienced just enough of creative living to recognize that for most of their time they are living uncreatively, as if caught up in the creativity of someone else, or of a machine. (65)

Rhys's fiction rejects compliance and the machine. Her protagonists may buckle under after fits and starts of rebellion, but her reader cannot do so. The very provisionality of her language-use enlists the energetic awareness of her audience. To read a Rhys narrative is to join her in the act of creation.

*   *   *

In accordance with the psychoanalytic paradigms that this book enlists, the sections of my discussion proceed in recognition of the attention Rhys gave to pre-Oedipal and Oedipal dynamics, respectively, rather than by following a strict chronology of the publication of her works.[7] As the novel was the primary genre in which she chose to write, this study also places emphasis on her longer fiction despite the many fine short stories she composed.

The first two novels to be addressed, *Voyage in the Dark* and *After Leaving Mr. Mackenzie*, both highlight the vicissitudes of earliest infancy. Although *Quartet* was actually Rhys's first published novel, I have placed it here as my fourth chapter, followed by a study of *Good Morning, Midnight*; for in both cases she is building upon a primitive, pre-Oedipal foundation in a more pronounced engagement with the Oedipal relations of a subsequent developmental stage. The last chapter of this study addresses Rhys's final novel, *Wide Sargasso Sea*, as it proves the culmination of her lifelong interest in psychosexual development and addresses both pre-Oedipal and Oedipal issues in a complex interweaving of thematic concerns.

Because the theories of Klein, Riviere, Winnicott, and others may be unfamiliar to students of literature, I have elected to explain them as they are relevant in successive chapters, with particular concern to move from discussing the theory to modeling how it might encounter (and how it might fail) a literary text. Works by Freud and Lacan have proved most useful in those parts of the study that confront Oedipal issues most directly; and I have reviewed their key premises, again as they are pertinent, when Rhys's material called for it. Further, insights by contemporary theorists who are presenting their work in the latest issues of psychoanalytic journals and by analytic practitioners with whom I am in personal communication, as they have reported observations derived from sessions with their analysands, are incorporated where warranted into these pages. My concern throughout the volume has been to balance the interests of literary critics with the claims of psychoanalysis. I have tried to respect the premises of each discipline by not oversimplifying their arguments but rather presenting key assertions in a language that speaks to members of both communities, in their shared concern to explore the fascinating varieties of emotional experience.

Finally, it is my hope that this study inaugurates terms for considering the work of Rhys anew. If she was once a marginal Modernist, she may now be counted among the major figures of twentieth-century art. The fraught conditions of psychic experience, the dense layers of feelings within the individual, are expressed in both the words she chooses with such care and the silences that resonate so fully in one Rhys narrative and then another. The body of her work speaks to a determination that even when, as one character puts it, "words haven't been invented" (*Collected* 237), the life of the emotions will always be honored.

2. *Voyage in the Dark*: Propitiating the Avengers ✍

Each personality is a world in himself, a company of many.

—Joan Riviere, "The Unconscious Phantasy
of an Inner World Reflected in
Examples from Literature"

This exploration of Rhys's novels begins with *Voyage in the Dark*, the first long narrative she drafted and the first to sound the complex rhythms of mother–child relating as these are orchestrated in the phantastic[1] life of infancy. Although the story of Anna Morgan ostensibly recounts her entry into adult femininity in progressively sexualized and ultimately demoralizing affairs with various men, beneath the text is another story, one that records a child's powerful and consuming need for her mother; the desire to incorporate her mother, and then others, into herself; and the terror of retribution for such voraciousness. In charting the process by which a mask of femininity is crafted, Anna's narrative throws into relief an infantile strategy serving interrelated functions: compensating the hungry daughter for her missing mother by attracting men to fill the empty space within her, the mask also deflects recognition of her sources of aggression so that she may be absorbed into the larger social body, no matter what the cost.

Anna's experience illustrates the primitive stages of female development as explicated by object relations theorists Melanie Klein and Joan Riviere, whose emphasis on the mother–infant dyad stressed preverbal, unsayable experiences of horror that continuously play on the emotional registers of the psyche in the course of later life. Although Klein's work is much more fully articulated than Riviere's and has earned its deserved place in major analytic theory of the modern age—and it is to Klein that this study will recurrently turn as Rhys's own evolving aesthetic is examined—I begin here with salient insights offered in several influential essays that Riviere composed in the middle decades of the twentieth century. For it is in her canny observation of the art of masquerade, as this addresses one aspect of female experience, that Riviere illuminates those conflicts that are central to Anna Morgan's story.

Voyage in the Dark is disarmingly accessible by contrast to the two novels that Rhys had already published by the time this narrative saw print in its final form. She had in fact been reworking the text for many years; it was the product of much more labor than its apparently effortless prose would suggest. First it was composed as a diary in a set of notebooks that accompanied her throughout Europe in her early travels; then it became a manuscript that she allowed a reader, Mrs. Adam, to edit and rearrange before submission to the appraising eye of Ford Madox Ford; and finally it acquired the form in which it appears today as *Voyage in the Dark*, when Rhys was unhappily compelled to change the ending of the narrative to accommodate an editor who wanted her to "give the girl a chance" by suggesting that Anna survive the abortion that concludes the text.[2]

The deliberation of Rhys's approach to her material is highlighted nonetheless in the published novel, which bears witness to her decision to diminish real-world events and understate action so that the protagonist's sense of isolation and her need to hide may be brought into relief. The narrative offers a first-person account of the development of an apparently naïve heroine who has recently arrived in England from an island in the West Indies and learns through her work as a chorus girl and a series of traumatically wounding relationships how to become progressively less genuine, open, and vulnerable as she creates a mask of feminine display. The interiority of Anna's experience is what matters, and Rhys attunes her reader to the frustrating inadequacy of words as expressions of this experience by using her language sparingly, with a disciplined compression. Anna's diction as she narrates is simple and understated, with a reliance on descriptions of physical sensation and minimal self-awareness about what is happening to her. Rhys positions herself at some distance from Anna by establishing the partiality and inadequacy of her protagonist's understanding. Anna uses the tag line "when it was sad" throughout her story as a marker of inevitable, recurrent periods of her life without, however, being able to diagnose her feeling beyond offering brief speculations. She is sad because "something about the darkness of the streets has a meaning"; she is sad as "the sparrows [start] to chirp" (57; 74). Such vagueness and lack of insight are juxtaposed with the particularity of Anna's record of physical suffering, of which she is acutely aware.

The reader is thereby conditioned from the opening pages to make sense of Anna's emotional experiences in a way that Anna cannot; Rhys establishes an approach to early phantasy and trauma in a seemingly pellucid, objective presentation that actually makes significant demands on the attention of the audience. In its apparently artless capacity to engage, and the fact that such artlessness reflects the unsophisticated style of its heroine, who is chronologically the youngest protagonist of the four novels Rhys composed in the interwar period, *Voyage* serves as a fitting introduction to the experimental approaches and recurring preoccupations of her mature fiction.

The opening of the narrative establishes both the discourse style of its speaker and the thematics of repetition and alienation that will be elaborated in the course of the textual journey. The novel proffers an initial vision of rebirth to describe Anna's arrival in England, but it is presented immediately and paradoxically as a birth into death, as Anna starkly comments, "It was as if a curtain had fallen, hiding everything I had ever known. It was almost like being born again" (7)—a response to the entry into an apparently new world that is actually a space of loss. This vision is repeated in the conclusion of the text, when, after a mishandled abortion, Anna records, "[. . .] the ray of light came in again under the door like the last thrust of remembering before everything is blotted out. I lay and watched it and thought about starting all over again. And about being new and fresh. And about mornings, and misty days, when anything might happen. And about starting all over again, all over again. . . ." (188). Anna's "fresh" vision, associated with the death image of "the last thrust of remembering," reiterates the opening implication that beginnings are predicated on grief, that what is apparently new is in fact a repetition of entry into deadness.

For an explanation of such a perception—why the new would reenact the old, a beginning reproduce an ending—the complex, associative processes of infant experience merit exploration. As both Klein and Riviere, as well as their later followers, observed, a baby perceives the first "other" in her life in pieces; the mother/caretaker drifting in and out of her view is unintegrated, as yet, into the whole of a separate human being. The infant accordingly develops phantasies of her own ability to summon and control these pieces at will. Because the primitive mind is initially undifferentiating, without a sense of boundaries, the movements of the maternal parts—or "objects," to use the terminology of object relations analysis—are imagined as continuous with the baby's own movements, needs, desires, and fears. The infant phantasy world is shaped by the sense of omnipotence: any actions by the child's objects are for all intents and purposes products of her own design. The more consistent and available the objects, the more the infant is blissfully reassured in the phantasy of her success. The more tenuous and provisional the objects, the more the infant is confirmed in horrifying phantasies of her own soiling and destructive state of being.

Rhys establishes, through implication, that Anna perceives her mother as absent from her youngest life; Anna makes sense of this absence, which would be otherwise inexplicable, by viewing herself as omnipotently capable of damage. But to feel that she has destroyed the object of her deepest need is, in turn, to accede to a horrifying awareness: that she is utterly alone. The awareness itself must be defended against. No explicit description is given of the mother of earliest childhood, the very lack of commentary forming a statement about how much this absence resonates through subsequent stages of her experience. The text is preoccupied with young women who hunger (the chorus girls of Anna's acquaintance) as well as substitute maternal figures (the servant Francine, the stepmother Hester, and a series of landladies in English lodging houses). The recurrence of needy and needed feminine figures speaks to the enormity of the space that Anna struggles to fill.

Her actual mother is only referenced briefly. In one recollected episode Anna insists to her stepmother that her mother was not "coloured" although Hester always implied otherwise (65); her need to rise to defense against any attack against her parent reveals her warding-off of an acknowledgment of her own angry feelings toward her absent mother. In another instance her mother's funeral is obliquely recalled as Anna lies beside Walter, the older man who has become her first lover, and the warmth of his body summons the memory of another, more remote, experience of warmth: *"Of course you've always known, always remembered, and then you forget so utterly, except that you've always known it. Always—how long is always?"* (37). This elliptical passage characterizes the discursive style of the text, which relies on repetition of language ("you've always known, always remembered [. . .] always known [. . .]. Always—how long is always?") and matter-of-fact phrasing ("of course") to suggest inevitable yet inexplicable returns. It is a narrative approach that undermines certainties with unresolvable questions ("how long is always?"); and, in relying on the second person ("you've always known"), it makes a direct appeal to the reader to engage in sensemaking activities. Anna's memory of another warmth dates to a primitive experience, something deeply embedded in her psychic inventory. She establishes that she will recall this experience during apparently new encounters, so that beginnings are a species of returning, and the reader is entreated ("how long is always?") to uncover the mysterious sources of her sadness. Her forgetting "so utterly" speaks to her need to forget; the insistence that she's "always known" what she's forgotten points to the ineradicable quality of some feeling she has that lingers in the margins of awareness.

The length of "always" is, as the narrative cryptically suggests, both forever and nevermore. Her mother's warmth is always with her, but it is never with her; its presence is always tantalizingly recollected, but its loss is always traumatically reinvoked. Rhys presents the textual clues to explain Anna's sense of abandonment when Walter eventually dispenses with her after he has tired of her, and she imagines how she would talk to him about her feelings. In this passage, the third to reference her mother, Anna does not directly articulate any of her anguish to Walter. She remains characteristically silent, underlining the fact that it is an inner territory of object relations that has the largest claim on her, so much so that her interactions in the "actual" world of people are necessarily partial and inexpressive. Contemporary analyst Michael Balint, developing his insights from the legacy of Riviere and Klein, among others,[3] describes a pre-Oedipal, two-person psychology that may produce a "basic fault" in the individual that cannot find expression in words. The person who is characterized by a basic fault, Balint theorizes, is beset by the sense that something within her is all wrong and needs to be mended, and that what is wrong has been caused by the fact of another having terribly let her down. Further, she has a heightened need to assure herself that she will not be let down again. Although such an individual may appear to be intact, the right mix of precipitating factors may reveal "a sudden irregularity in the overall structure, an irregularity which in normal circumstances might lie hidden but, if strains and stresses occur, may lead to a break, profoundly disrupting the overall structure" (*Basic* 21). Significantly, this person experiences most of her strongest feelings at such a primitive level that the very keenness of her need not to be disappointed is met, pathetically, by inarticulateness; her desire cannot be expressed to anyone who is not also attuned, extra-verbally, to the rumblings of the basic fault.

Anna's silence demonstrates her reversion to this fundamental level, while the words she uses to think to herself proclaim a restraint that she would will into being, to keep the fault within her hidden: she pictures herself speaking "very calmly." Yet she also imagines a statement that in its reliance on the hyperbolic potential of language signals the catastrophic dimensions of Anna's pain. Internally, she tells Walter, " 'The thing is that you don't understand. You think I want more than I do. I only want to see you sometimes, but if I never see you again I'll die. I'm dying now really, and I'm too young to die.' " Indicative of the depths of this experience, the words remain within; as if believing their expression would court further disaster, Anna chooses hiding in muteness as her only recourse from the one who has let her down.

As the thought continues, Anna gives fragmented form to the sources of her inadequacy and trauma: ". . . The candles crying wax tears and the smell of stephanotis and I had to go to the funeral in a white dress and white gloves and a wreath round my head and the wreath in my hands made my gloves wet—they said so young to die . . ." (97). Her certainty that the loss of Walter will lead to her death implies that she has already experienced a loss that led to her sense of annihilation; the immediate association to a funeral, most probably her mother's (since she would have been "so young to die," while Anna's father survived and remarried), conflates the disappearance of the maternal figure with Anna's own imagined demise, so that the infant's lack of differentiation from her object is symbolically evoked. The ellipses preceding and concluding the funeral paragraph speak to the unsaid of this text, the injunctions that reader produce meanings where they are not given in words on the page; also established is a kind of circle of inevitability, so that the "beginning" of the paragraph follows from a mysterious ending, the "ending" leads to a mysterious beginning; and the effect of the whole is to suggest a cycle of return, always, to death.

Anna's preliminary thought, unexpressed to Walter—" 'The thing is that you don't understand. You think I want more than I do' "—emphasizes that her desire is not as great as he might imagine. This gives the lie to what in fact textures infant longing—insatiability. It is not possible for the hungry baby to want moderately, or to want just what is appropriate. She desires the whole world.[4] This desire takes shape in phantasy as the voracious wish to devour the object, to incorporate it literally by exerting an imaginary omnipotence. It follows that the more precarious the object, the more violent the desire; the more loss threatens, the more terror consumes. Riviere's work on the infant's profound fear of loss is explored in her investigations of the phenomenon of envy, which determine that infantile phantasies to possess something that the other is perceived to have and indeed to possess that other, as well, are based on the early, oral, stage of erotic longings ("Jealousy" 111). Sadism and desire are handmaids here, the wish to claim and completely devour the object a response to the terrifying fear of abandonment. As Riviere argues,

> All fears are intrinsically related to the deepest fear of all: that in the last resort any "loss" may mean "total loss"; in other words, if it persists or increases, loss may mean loss of life itself and unconsciously any loss brings that fear nearer. All fears come back to the fear of death: to the destructive tendency that might be called the capacity for death in oneself, which must be turned outward in aggression if it is not to work out in and on oneself.

The double-bind created when one propels destruction toward outside objects is that their demise is thereby, in phantasy, assured and, as a result, the infant's own sense of impending destruction, the specter of a complete loss of being, is intensified. Riviere reaches the conclusion that "the fear of death" motivates, finally, the voracious appetites and wounding impulses that characterize some forms of human behavior ("Unconscious" 314).

Anna's early convent schooling provides an illustration of abandonment-as-death that both resounds on the registers of her first experiences and anticipates those that are to come. Left at boarding school by her father, who went to England and returned with a new wife (both deserting Anna and, symbolically, betraying her dead mother), Anna is tutored by the nuns to link primitive states of being with dying. Mother St. Anthony, Anna's surrogate parent during this period, instructs: " 'Children, every night before you go to sleep you should lie straight down with your arms by your sides and your eyes shut and say: "One day I shall be dead. One day I shall lie like this with my eyes closed and I shall be dead." ' " Reversion to sleep and the vulnerability that comes with loss of consciousness thus associates with annihilation; most significantly, Anna recollects this lesson after her first sexual experience with Walter, so that intercourse and orgasm—"the Little Death," as she thinks of it—also evoke the potential for her own obliteration (55–56). The closer one comes to one's naked desire for the other, the nearer at hand is death. It follows that the desire itself is felt as alarmingly dangerous and malign.

A constellation of psychic factors provides some explanation for Anna's most persistent symptomatology, her feeling of coldness, as if the warmth of life is being taken from her. Her emotional pain is rendered in concrete, physical terms that suggest that the broken heart produced by perceived abandonment robs the body of its vitality: "[. . .] in my heart I was always sad, with the same sort of hurt that the cold gave me in my chest," she comments early in the narrative; later on, to Walter's request that she stop looking sorrowful, she thinks, "My chest hurt"; later still, that a feeling "came out from my heart into my throat and then into my eyes" (15; 24; 127). The alignment of coldness and chest pain stresses that the emotionally isolated Anna is always in proximity to death; that loss of the beloved is complete loss of both self and others, with whom one is fused and as yet undifferentiated, as in infancy.[5] When Anna muses, in a parenthesis, "No, nothing can be as cold as life" (154), she describes the death-like reception she has felt from the object world and also by implication the wish to be in a place before birth, before coming into the frigidity of existence and being confronted by the per-ceived menacing intentions of others. The parentheses express the marginal-ity of her experience as against the self-importance of the objects that surround her, as her thought offers one more textual instance of the conflation or confusion between metaphors of birth and death.

The central trope in *Voyage* for the condensation of life and death is Anna's abortion. Notably, the episode is preceded by her ingestion of assorted over-the-counter "remedies" that will result, she thinks, in a baby who is monstrously deformed. Thus she has already equated, in phantasy, the state of infancy with horror; the unwanted child is shaped into a terrifying image that speaks nonverbally of her dismay over her own neediness and desire. For to be a baby who wants so much is to become, in Anna's imaginary configuration, disfigured and disgusting. While pregnant, she dreams of being on board a ship, where her imagery of "dolls of islands" on "a dolls' sea" again suggests her own return to a state of childhood (164); and when she dreams that a coffin of a child is opened before her to reveal "The boy bishop [. . .] a little dwarf with a bald head," she perceives that she ought to kiss his ring, symbolically signifying her fealty to the world of infant experience and perception. This boy bishop, significantly, is also "like a doll," and as he assumes a sitting posture the imagery commingles the living and inanimate, human and doll, baby and corpse. Anna's next dream-thought is the question, " 'What's overboard?,' " which characteristically remains unanswered and thus enjoins the reader to participate in producing a response. Her ensuing comment about "that awful dropping of the heart" (165), which assumes the reader's understanding of what "that" must feel like, universalizes the condition to which the dream gives voice and thereby tacitly expresses the wish for understanding from some imagined witness, to counter the unbearable sense of isolation in which Anna is enclosed. Her wording, for all its indirection, nevertheless suggests the answer to the question of what is overboard: that it is her heart that has been dropped and with it the longing that has been unmet; further, that death has been assured as she has been tossed away by a mysteriously absent other.

Anna's actual visit to an abortionist repeats the patterning of abandonment throughout the narrative. Although she pleads to have the procedure stopped if she cannot tolerate it and elicits the abortionist's promise "as if she were talking to a child" that she will discontinue the operation at Anna's request, she is ultimately betrayed; the abortionist actually proceeds to the end despite Anna's desperate entreaties (177). Thus Anna, presented here as child to the older female figure upon whose reliability she depends, is symbolically dropped so that the business of death may proceed. The abortion is completed and the annihilation is effected. It is altogether fitting that it is not her baby's death but her own that becomes Anna's focus as she walks back out onto the London streets: "[. . .] I was afraid of the people passing because I was dying; and, just because I was dying, any one of them, any minute, might stop and approach me and knock me down, or put their tongues out as far as they would go" (178). Here once more the infantile perception of abandonment is projected into an object world that is perceived as filled with potential violence. At the very least, as Anna imagines, her demise will elicit others' mockery; her waning life, their hostile mirth.

The imagery of dying life or living death and the dream-images of dolls, doll-islands, and a doll-ocean that have led to this moment in the narrative are elaborations of its central metaphoric preoccupation: with the inauthentic, with the conforming, with masks and masquerade. As Anna is born again into experiences that evoke her primitive awareness of loss, and as she feels the death within her while moving in a world made up of others who have no autonomous reality, the narrative produces and reproduces images of affectless states and woodenly unreal, imitative presences.

The environment of England itself suggests inauthenticity and lack of originality. Anna's recurring complaint about the country is that all the streets and houses look the same, stressing conformity as the order of the day; spontaneity is curbed by gardens that are "walled-in" (9). Artifice rather than nature presides: the city of London feels no sun, rather "a glare on everything like a brass band playing" and inside, for example, in the restaurant where she dines with Walter, there is a fire "like a painted fire" (41; 24). The artificiality of the environs is stressed in street names— Walter's urban flat is ironically located on "Green Street" (49)—and interior decor, with Anna's lodging house room graced by artificial pineapples on the molding. Anticipating Rhys's rendition of Edward Rochester as he will appear years later in *Wide Sargasso Sea*, the stiffly correct Walter, who walks with hands enclosed in pockets as if to suggest both his secretiveness and masturbatory self-interest, imagines that he would find the West Indies " 'altogether too lush' " (54). In this comment on the freely vegetative world from which Anna comes, Walter offers a model of an altogether different kind of citizenship in another kind of country, with England and its inhabitants vigilantly enforcing the status quo of artifice and subterfuge. Rhys thus makes a subtle yet pointed comment on colonial versus colonized nation-states, the one with an overweening desire to control and the other with an ethos that seems threateningly untamed. However, her insight into the shaping of the psyche suggests conditions that cut across the ideologies of nations, speaking to fundamental and ubiquitous psychological mechanisms. *Voyage* indicates that in spite of Anna's unrootedness she has *never* felt at home, and that her awareness of the need to hide comes from ancient fault-lines within her that are simply reactivated in the landscape of England. The country and its people are apt focal points for Anna's resentment as she looks out onto a world from which she already feels that she must hide. Given her vexed relations with an absent maternal figure, Anna's own aggression must be held at bay and a demeanor must be found that will elicit social approval if she is to survive in a environment that she perceives to be dangerously malicious.

Living with the fear of annihilation, Anna constructs patterns of behavior to provide her another means, in addition to silence, of hiding her unacceptable strivings. The behavior she chooses arises as does a reaction formation, in apparently direct opposition to primitive phantasies: she elects a seemingly cultivated mode of dispensing goodwill in contrast to her elemental, ravenous desires for others, as they are most fundamentally conceived. As Riviere describes the infant's attempts at omnipotent satisfaction of needs, the sadistic desires to attack and fully ingest the first objects in sight, she elaborates that these objects are identified, initially, as the aspects of another that are available at the most basic, biological level, which is all that the infant mind can process. After the first stage of infancy, when objects take shape as the mother's breasts, the dawning perception of another presence brings with it a shift to wishing to incorporate, through attack, that which epitomizes this other's physical reality, as well—that is, prototypically, the father's penis. In referencing the masculine, the penis and its symbolic equivalents are the figures that Anna's narrative most consistently registers, while her accounts of femininity incorporate a range of anatomical features still identified, nonetheless, in an iconic way. Anna's behavior toward both men and women suggests the terror that accompanies infantile desires to ingest, when the child is visited by the frightening possibility that phantasied attacks will incur harsh punishment. As Anna's actions illustrate, the specter of retribution by the parents who have both in phantasy been mutilated must be encountered and in some way managed if the primitive being is to ensure her own survival.

The infant's proclivity to project her own instinctual aggression outward and then fear the reprisals and violence of aggression returned is at the core of Riviere's interpretation of infancy, on which this account of Anna relies; like Klein, Riviere acknowledged but was apt to underplay the role of actual caretakers in descriptions of childhood phantasy, so that the parents who may in fact be abandoning and punitive are not the focus of her theory. While I cannot fully subscribe to this psychological model, insofar as parents do in some instances seriously fail their offspring—and Rhys's work certainly suggests real lack and loss at the center of Anna's childhood—Riviere's work does justice to the complex interplay in the child's insatiable longing, urge to incorporate her objects, rage at frustration of desire, and omnipotent fears that this consuming greed and anger will give rise to vengeful, murderous behavior directed back toward the self.

For a girl, as Riviere argues, there is fear of the mother's vengefulness because she has in phantasy been twice harmed: directly, by the daughter's biting; and indirectly, by being robbed of that which represents the father, his penis. Demonstrably placating behavior, accompanied by the suggestion that it serves as a cover for hostility, is conveyed through Rhys's narrative in Anna's attempts to help women over whom she has first established, in her own mind, distinction and power. Toward her roommate Maudie, Anna cultivates a sense of distance predicated on Maudie's defectiveness; Maudie's smile reveals a missing tooth, as if her own orality has been punished and she has been left maimed as a result of her hunger, and Anna squarely registers her sense of superiority: "Every now and then she would giggle a nervous and meaningless giggle. When I remembered living with her it was like looking at an old photograph of myself and thinking, 'What on earth's that got to do with me?' " (43). However, when she encounters Maudie later in the narrative and sees that she is financially adrift, Anna offers her money and thus both confirms her own elevated position and presents an appealingly benevolent aspect of herself for the other's view.

Throughout the narrative Anna tries to distinguish herself from all of the chorus girls, disavowing the vulnerability that connects her to them as well as her aggression. Her internal comments are uniformly disparaging; for example, Ethel, who will become another roommate, "looked just like most other people, which is a big advantage. An ant, just like all the other ants. [. . .] She was like all women whom you look at and don't notice except that she had such short legs and that her hair was so dusty" (106). Notably, even Ethel's minimal distinctions—her legs and hair—are cause for critical comment. These observations suggest Anna's investment in her own specialness, of background and of character: that it is important to signal her uniqueness and by extension her privilege. At the same time, her hatred is masked in apparent compliance to Ethel's regulations about the rent and directives that Anna learn the art of manicuring, a semi-respectable form of prostitution that will keep the money coming in. Anna again wards off possible hostility directed toward herself, for her own pre-sumed power, by seeming to accede to another woman's wishes.

The relationship between Ethel and Anna, which is one of the most volatile of those delineated in the narrative, hinges on a confusion of needs and projective processes. As Rhys presents them, each of these women is arrested in infantile object awareness, viewing any other female in intimate range as one with whom supremacy must be established and from whom gratitude must be culled; the other woman represents, as well, a figure to whom favors must be dispensed in the attempt to mask a deep and primitive rage. As Ethel, like Anna, enacts the infant daughter's role in response to the other close female as someone who must be propitiated, Rhys achieves, through duplication, an emphasis on the psychic states of insatiability and terror. With the progression of the narrative, Ethel becomes, in her own neediness, increasingly demanding; neither appreciating nor understanding Anna's behavior, of seeking approval from a wide variety of outside sources, Ethel feels that her own magnanimity has been rebuffed and turns against Anna with the very aggression that Anna has tried to fend off. Here Ethel illustrates how an angered girl may revolt against the person who seems to have failed to appreciate her goodwill gestures; she becomes like a patient of Riviere's: "[. . .] if gratitude and recognition were withheld, her sadism broke out in full force and she would be subject [. . .] to paroxysms of oral-sadistic fury, exactly like a raging infant" ("Womanliness" 98). In her fury, Ethel violently reviles Anna and sends a slanderous letter denouncing her to another chorus girl, Laurie, upon whom Ethel will refocus her longing gaze. Noting Laurie's way of walking, of wearing her clothes—" 'Now, that's the sort of girl I should want if I were a man [. . .] that's what I call smart,' " Ethel comments (141)—she illustrates Anna's own desire for a woman as the focus of primary erotic longings, even as the aggression of her unmet wishes toward Anna has fully emerged into view.

Although Laurie's good looks and savviness cause admiration, she too is subject to Anna's evaluative and diminishing response, with its source in the infantile exertion of phantasied power. Laurie's hennaed hair is attractive, as Anna assesses, but she is overly made up, and in close-up her masked qualities are not effective but outworn, overused, and grotesque: "She seemed very tall and her face enormous. I could see all the lines in it, and the powder, trying to fill up the lines, and just where her lipstick stopped and her lips began. It looked like a clown's face, so that I wanted to laugh at it. She was pretty, but her hands were short and fat with wide, flat, very red nails" (123).[6] Demonstrating a callous approach to living, an approach that Anna defines herself against, she leads Anna into compromising situations, setting her up on a double date with men who expect her to be the "tart" that Laurie appears to be; and the help that she offers, finding an abortionist and calling a doctor when the aftermath of the operation proves disastrous, all go to demonstrate her unsentimental, rather brittle pragmatism. Anna's perceptions and the perceptions of others whom she elects to record frame Laurie as promiscuous and world-battered (Walter's cousin Vincent notes that Laurie " 'really is pretty. But hard—a bit hard. [. . .] They get like that. It's a pity' " [174]). Her experience makes her of value to Anna, who does rely on her assistance, but more suggestively it provides Anna with a way to diminish the worth of this other woman.

In addition to serving as a target for Anna's veiled hatred, Laurie, like Ethel, functions as a warning for potentials that Anna should not realize, in this instance offering the grim illustration of what will happen when feminine ability is too clearly on display, is not sufficiently disguised. Laurie's case as "hard" woman deserving of pitying judgment from the Vincents of the world points out that such a version of the female will assuredly earn the condemnation of men. In primitive perceptions of the type that Anna registers, all men in turn stand in for the first male, the father, confronted with his daughter's power. Riviere's argument that a daughter learns to pacify the mother whom she has in phantasy besieged carries as its corollary the notion that the girl must also find a way to pacify the potentially enraged father, whom she believes she has robbed of masculinity in her attacks on the penis. A mask is devised to placate the male, a womanliness constructed that accommodates and appeases; the appearance of femininity functions as a mode of coping with the tensions arising from a fear of masculine vengeance. Soliciting male approval in the form of sexual favor, such a woman earns a doubled reward: she is confirmed in her attractiveness while concurrently keeping at bay any resentment a man may feel about her own abilities. "Obviously," Riviere writes, in the passage that my chapter title adapts, "it [is] a step toward propitiating the avenger to endeavour to offer herself to him sexually" ("Womanliness" 93). The so-called femininity functions here to hide strivings for power as well as divert possible punishment for such strivings.

As a contrasting, ominous portrait of what becomes of the woman who has seized phallic power in dramatically open display, Rhys presents the episode of "Three-Fingered Kate," a movie that Anna and Ethel watch together. Anna describes the film:

> On the screen a pretty girl was pointing a revolver at a group of guests. They backed away with their arms held high above their heads and expressions of terror on their faces. The pretty girl's lips moved. The fat hostess unclasped a necklace of huge pearls and fell, fainting, into the arms of a footman. The pretty girl, holding the revolver so that the audience could see that two of her fingers were missing, walked backwards toward the door. (108)

The gun tropes phallic power as it has been claimed by this thieving heroine, but the price that stealing masculine aggression exacts is imaged by the missing fingers that suggest a symbolic castration for unacceptable strivings. When Three-Fingered Kate is apprehended and the theater audience claps loudly, Anna and Ethel are given tacit instruction in the social condemnation that results from direct female attempts to seize control. Later

Anna is told that the actress playing the role was " 'a foreigner' " (109), enforcing her own identification with and fear of the woman who has tried to grab what she wants and faced a violent, mutilating punishment.

But transcending cultural borders, and thus speaking to Rhys's concern with a kind of universalizing female psychology, Anna recalls from her childhood stories of subversive West Indian women: "obeah-women who dig up dead people and cut their fingers off and go to gaol for it—it's hands that are obeah" (163). The use of present tense for remembered events signifies, as it will throughout Rhys's oeuvre, the living reality of an individual's history: for Anna, the possibilities of a primitive state continue to exist as she fantasizes robbing "fingers," or phallic power—and then, inevitably, paying the social price. Tellingly, Anna is fearful of the obeah-women she so vividly remembers.[7] Their black magic expresses the potential aggression of womanhood that she feels she must whitewash, or hide, by obliging behavior.

The narrative offers a further instance of the punishment that directly aggressive femininity will elicit, most particularly from men. After Walter announces that he is leaving Anna to go to New York, she grinds her cigarette on his hand, figuratively attempting to castrate him, in an action for which he never forgives her. The moment of violence marks the end of the relationship; it is an act from which nothing can be recovered. A woman's direct claiming of power will not result in a transfer of power but rather is prelude to abandonment. Looking at a bracelet that Walter had given her, Anna slides it onto her hand as if it were, in her words, a "Knuckle-duster" (148). Yet it is never used for fighting or even self-defense; it remains, in fact, just an ornament, metaphoric of Anna's socially determined passivity and her loss, once again, of a longed-for object.

The jealously guarded power of masculine forms of aggression is highlighted throughout the novel. In one instance, Anna observes two boys engaged in sadomasochistic play. The larger child binds and kicks the smaller, the little boy demonstrates vulnerability by crying, and the big one prepares to kick him again; then Anna notes, "[. . .] he saw I was watching. He grinned and undid the rope. The little boy stopped crying and got up. They both put out their tongues at me and ran off" (75). In sight of the female, violence as well as victimhood between males is hidden so that aggression may be redirected toward the woman, who now plays the role of outsider to the united masculine pair and is thus put firmly into place. She cannot be one of them. The episode in turn evokes a childhood memory in which Anna's sleeping Uncle Bo revealed "long yellow tusks like fangs [that] came out of his mouth and protruded down to his chin [. . .]" (92). When he awoke, as she recalls, he put his false teeth back and addressed her benignly. Nevertheless Anna was traumatized into an immobile silence; and the lesson learned, that wolves lurk in sheep's clothing, bears the stamp of an insouciant and ubiquitous but extremely forceful masculine economy.

Ultimately *Voyage* presents social control where it traditionally belongs: quite literally in the hands of men. The doctor who comes to take care of Anna after her botched abortion has hands that "[look] enormous in rubber gloves." The large fingers signifying phallic prowess, and his distance from Anna—he will not touch her directly, skin on skin—speak to the order of things in the social milieu and a reminder of Anna's position as a woman. She is prone,[8] her apparent helplessness the expected feminine posture; and as he neatly sums her up (" 'She'll be all right. [. . .] Ready to start all over again in no time, I've no doubt' " [187]), his words recollect the pattern of inevitable return that has textured the entire narrative.

Given the pointlessness of direct attempts to seize power, Anna learns the female guises that are acceptable modes of self-display. The substitutive maternal figures in Anna's story provide illustrations of how one may present one's femininity to the world: through the art of masquerade, through an apparent yet calculated artlessness, in behaviors that are practiced with varying degrees of success by the older women she observes. Her stepmother Hester speaks in "an English lady's voice" that Anna finds condescending and affected; it is "[t]hat sort of voice," Anna comments, assuming the reader's complicity in disparaging the transparent pretenses that Hester adopts (57). Hester fails in her mask of femininity, as revealed in Anna's observation that Hester "began to stroke her upper lip, as if she had an invisible moustache" (58); noting the behavior that Hester has not been able to suppress, Anna records Hester's unconscious but visible desire for possession of masculine power.

Anna implicitly demonstrates her contempt as she wills herself not to become like Hester, because her affectations, her masking of hostility, are only partially successful. Anna remembers that from an early age: "[. . .] I hated being white. Being white and getting like Hester, and all the things you get—old and sad and everything. I kept thinking, 'No. . . . No. . . . No. . . .' " (72). Here Hester's "whiteness" equates with vulnerability, with being too easily seen and read because of her maladroit posturing; her sadness is on display for the perceptive to notice, and her attempts to hide are ineffectual. In her decision to break off communications with Hester, Anna disowns connection with this particular model of womanhood.

In apparent contrast to white Hester is black Francine, the cook from Anna's childhood home. She appears at first glance to offer a type of womanhood that has no need of masquerade, as she gives spontaneous expression to her appetites and partakes in a sensual, unselfconscious way of being in the world. "Her teeth would bite into the mango and the lips fasten on either side of it," Anna comments, "and while she sucked you saw that she was perfectly happy." However, the liberated potential of the behavior is immediately qualified: "When she had finished she always smacked her lips twice, very loud—louder than you could believe possible. It was a ritual" (67–68). That taking pleasure in the satiation of desires is transformed into "ritual" suggests that even here mechanisms of containment are invoked, female expression curbed. The woman, always aware that she is on display, must accordingly stage even her most gratifying experiences to suggest that she can harness desire and behave in a tamed, habituated, and unthreatening way.

Francine and Hester are therefore not as different as they at first seem. Anna recollects that Francine, like Hester, could be sad, with her sorrow apparent even in her lighthearted songs. They both engaged in activities to mask the sadness and differ primarily in the degree to which Anna subjects them to criticism. Finally they also shed light on her own desire and her own evasions. Anna holds to her memory of Francine as maternal figure as a way of recollecting Hester's rivalry with her over Anna: during an illness in which she had spoken persistently and deliriously of Francine, Hester responded by actively wanting Francine dismissed from service. The scene places the two surrogate mothers in direct opposition as competitors for Anna's attentions, thereby inflating her importance and also converting her own aggression into aggression leveled by one woman toward the other, by Hester toward Francine.

Anna's anger within an object world of defective and defaulting mothers who cannot model femininity, and the projective processes that she unwittingly enlists, recall the lack of distinction between infant and her objects, the unclarity of borders in primitive psychic life. As Riviere contends, the hatred of the subject toward her objects can feel, in phantasy, the same as hatred or ill-will directed from objects toward the subject ("Unconscious" 323). Illustrations of hatred directed outward but perceived as coming in, as attacks, appear in Anna's responses to the numerous landladies who also, like Hester and Francine, substitute as maternal figures. One after another is disparaged for her self-interest, her judging of Anna, her inability to understand. These landladies are continually presented as the emblems of British hypocrisy who condemn girls of the chorus for the lives into which the girls feel they have been thrust; Anna, Maudie, and their associates persistently complain about the restrictions the landladies try to impose and the sneering they perceive from these older woman who disapprove of the single girls for their carryings-on. Their ogling glances reveal, to Anna, that they actually achieve a vicarious thrill from the way the girls conduct their lives; and they are ingratiatingly opportunistic in the presence of those whom they perceive as powerful and wealthy (men like Walter, for example), even as they demean the girls who trade on masculine favor and upon whose rent they depend.

In counterpoint to these portraits of the landladies who oversee the temporary "homes" that Anna and the others inhabit is the brief presentation of a woman who works for Laurie as housekeeper, whom Laurie patronizingly refers to as " 'Ma.' " She is discovered asleep in Laurie's kitchen in a self-enclosed posture, arms around head. Laurie's bitter remark, " 'She's always going to sleep on me. I'd fire the old sod tomorrow only I know she'd never get another job' " (117), symbolically gives voice to the disappointed daughter who chooses condescension as her means of control when feeling afflicted by a maternal figure who cannot be relied upon. As such, the incident is as revelatory of Anna's tendency to find ways to deflect anxieties about hostility toward the mother, as it is of Laurie's own strategies of self-containment.

The rage of the daughter and the horror at the damage this rage may inflict is produced in Anna's recollection, late in the narrative, of an old woman of her island home whose face was partially destroyed by the infectious tropical disease, yaws: "I suppose she was begging but I couldn't understand because her nose and mouth were eaten away; it seemed as though she were laughing at me. I was frightened; I kept on looking backwards to see if she was following me, but when [. . .] I saw clear water I thought I had forgotten about her. And now—there she is" (152). The figure is shaped, in memory, by the daughter's shame over wanting; although the woman was probably begging and therefore in need, Anna interpreted her mutilated expression as mockery. She thus expressed back Anna's near-phobic response to her own desire. Recollection of this woman also gives Anna opportunity to fantasize about the retribution that awaits women who devour, with the yaws-woman's eaten-away mouth troping, through displacement, a punishment for Anna's own insatiability. Further, the figure embodies Anna's doomed sense of entrapment: she cannot escape this memory, which means that she cannot forget her profound longing for and hatred of the mother whose warmth first was and then was not there.

As further comment on the social imperative to secure violently needy and unacceptable feelings from sight, Rhys offers a vignette about the use of costumes as armament for female survival. In the preliminary stages of Anna's relationship with Walter, he acts as substitutive maternal presence, providing care for her when she is ill; she thus begins to learn that a woman may turn to men rather than other women to compensate for basic, unmet needs. He also supplies her with money, which she uses to buy herself clothes from the shop of the "two Miss Cohens"—their doubleness serving to underscore their function as maiden women initiating Anna into the first rites of adult femininity, a state that Walter will later exploit. Clothing her "as if [she] were a doll" (28), dressing her as she puts her arms into the air, these women as cultural emissaries refashion Anna into a mannequin existence. The doll reference implies two related conditions of being: both a reversion to the state of helplessness, as in childhood, and the adoption of an inauthentic, constructed self to meet the social requirements of female life. When she leaves their establishment Anna notes, "The streets looked different that day, just as a reflection in the looking-glass is different from the real thing" (29), stressing how the externally unreal world reflects her own artificiality when she clothes her living being in the image of hapless womanliness that the culture expects to see. Not coincidentally, she has trouble breathing and becomes increasingly ill after this episode. Anna's foray into the feminine causes an initial regression that Walter addresses as a primary caregiver might, again coming to her rescue with a supply of food and also a doctor. However, after her recovery Walter has waited long enough: exacting the price of her virginity, he tutors Anna in the lesson that sexual rewards must be given to palliate the male, who is the only one who will provide for her; and her entrance into womanhood as masquerade is effected.

Anna's self-consciousness about how she appears, about her presentation to the world, is manifested as she continuously watches herself as another would and ultimately becomes her own primary spectator. Her self-observation is increasingly obsessive: after she has been first approached by Walter, Anna reports rather casually, "I watched myself in the glass over the mantelpiece, laughing"; but after his preliminary sexual advance to her the self-scrutiny intensifies: "I walked up to the looking-glass and put the lights on over it and stared at myself. It was as if I were looking at somebody else" (13; 23). These episodes suggest a progressive splitting motivated by Anna's growing sense of how to manipulate her self-presentation in relation with others.[9] When women do not do this artfully, as she learns, they are reviled: a brief sojourn with Walter, Vincent, and Vincent's lover Germaine goes badly, not just because of Germaine's dissatisfactions but more specifically because she generates the feeling in both men that she has moved beyond her proper place of feminine subservience. As if in response to the implicit warning this offers to Anna about how she should conduct herself, she records her awareness about the way she must manage her feelings as she poses before the mirror. When Walter informs her that he is to leave shortly with Vincent for an extended overseas visit, she is working to hold her reactions in check; without responding to Walter, she peers more closely at the mirror, "Like when you're a kid and you put your face very near to the glass and make faces at yourself" (84). The anger expressed not at the other but in "faces at yourself" indicates that her primary relationship is with herself and the inner object world; further, now that her subjectivity is actively removed from outer view, at least for the moment, she is learning to "face" relationships by hiding from them.

In the postabortion delirium that concludes Anna's tale, she dreams a memory of the West Indian celebration, Masquerade, that puts the final punctuation mark on her narrative of desire, aggression, and subterfuge:

> [. . .] the masks the men wore were a crude pink with the eyes squinting near together squinting but the masks the women wore were made of close-meshed wire covering the whole face and tied at the back of the head—the handkerchief that went over the back of the head hid the strings and over the slits for the eyes mild blue eyes were painted then there was a small straight nose and a little red heart-shaped mouth and under the mouth another slit so that they could put their tongues out at you. [. . .] (185)

The masks of the women contrast with those of the men, the former much more elaborate constructions that disarmingly suggest the benign and loving, with their "mild blue eyes" and "heart-shaped mouth[s]." The female strives to perform the masquerade of innocuousness beneath which an entire world of feeling hides; but for the reader of this passage there is no mistaking the hostility that the mocking tongues, thrust through the other, second mouths, resonantly express. Recalling the little boys who stuck out their tongues at Anna and the people on the streets whom she imagined, after her abortion, sticking "their tongues out as far as they could go" (178), the Masquerade women offer protruding tongues to trope their hatred and aggression. In real life, however, women must never make hideous faces that others can see; if the tongues appear at festival time, this is by special dispensation. As a spectacular event, Masquerade provides a safety valve for expressing otherwise unsanctioned behavior, thereby serving the larger purpose of social containment by offering women—very briefly—a license that does not attend everyday existence in the social world.

Anna has learned and relearned the lesson that her longing mingled with her aggression must be masked by feminine disguise. Coming to measure her value in terms of her attractiveness to men, she assures herself of a position within the bedroom. The bedroom functions, ostensibly, as a sanctuary from the maternal as she puts herself in the father's arms; it is actually the site for regression to a primitive state of erotic desire, with her seeking of male attention recalling the search for another warmth, from a female object. The bedroom just happens, conveniently, to service the male imperative that a woman's "place" be lying down, as the daughter acting servant to the father punctures her own vitality and turns into a mannequin or a doll in his presence, like most other women. The danger that her hunger represents to the male and, behind him, the woman whose nurturing Anna forever needs, results in the choice that she render herself prone. In doing so she effectively disguises her longing and, to echo the narrative's opening line, she is "born again"—even as she annihilates herself into nonexistence. But Rhys was passionately engaged in exploring the impulse of continuous return; and thus *After Leaving Mr. Mackenzie*, the novel to which this study now attends, provides further expression of the daughter's compulsion to find, again and again, the mother who is not there.

3. *After Leaving Mr. Mackenzie*: The Search for Maternal Presence ➤

[T]here is no instinctual urge, no anxiety situation, no mental process which does not involve objects, external or internal; in other words, object relations are at the centre of emotional life.

—Melanie Klein, "The Origins of Transference"

After Leaving Mr. Mackenzie offers an austere yet resonating treatment of a pathology conditioned by loss, as Rhys continues to investigate the inner world of the child whose mother is irrevocably out of reach. While protagonist Julia Martin wanders across a ravaged landscape, from Paris to London to Paris again, geographic dislocations serve as external markers of her vacillating internal states. Although she enacts her distress in successive relationships with men—she is a woman, like all other Rhys heroines, who depends on male favor for her survival—at the center of this text lies the ailing body of the mother, whose physical sickness tropes the emotional malady of her relationship with her daughter. Rhys's consideration of the mother–daughter pair as source of subsequent misadjustments in adulthood invites a reading of pre-Oedipal connection as the dominating paradigm for human intimacy in this early work, published in 1930. Rhys also inscribes in this narrative a different kind of Modernism, one that is distinctively inflected by feminine concerns and the attempt to replicate maternal–infant modes of communication, in its injunctions that author and reader unite in cocreation of the text.

In its nuanced attunement to primitive states of feeling, the analysis of infantile object relations—most notably, as modeled by Melanie Klein, D. W. Winnicott, Ronald Fairbairn, and their successors—offers a way to revision this novel's powerful effects.[1] Although the rare psychoanalytic critical treatments of Rhys's fiction do not deploy the strategies of object relations theorists, it is in the deep understanding of the perceptions, desires, frustrations, and terrors of earliest existence that this novel, like *Voyage in the Dark*, makes compelling claims.[2] The work begun by Klein and composed more or less contemporaneously with Rhys's novels at mid-century, work then modified and revised by those under Klein's influence, is particularly salient here. For in evoking the desperate yet inarticulate qualities of those who demonstrably lack ontic status, Rhys replicates, in symbolic forms, the nascent states of human life.

It is this earliest condition of being that forms the template of Kleinian theory. Deriving her initial observations from Freudian assertions about the instinctual drives, Klein posits that the infant reacts to frustration with aggressive phantasies,[3] which, as seen in Chapter 2 of this study, the child imagines to be all-powerful. The baby lives in a state of desperate need of her first object—paradigmatically, the mother's breast, a piece of a whole that cannot yet be realized by the child's developing perceptive apparatus. In order to preserve her own love, the infant, in phantasy, splits this off from her hate. In turn, she also splits the breast in two: there comes to exist "a good part and a bad part," an all-nurturing breast and a denying breast (J. Mitchell 20). The good breast is imagined as fully giving, and will in conditions of health be introjected; thus the infant has her first positive experience of a now-internalized object. The bad breast, on the other hand, is felt as frustrating and internalized accordingly. Furthermore, it is dreaded for its destructive potential.

I am most interested in the aspect of Klein's work that conjures up this phantasized bad breast, for it has direct bearing on the inner world of Julia Martin, as Rhys conceives it: a world contoured by her own tremendous need. Julia's condition illustrates the overwhelming desires of infancy as these give rise to the phantasy of bad objects. The proliferating pieces of aggression that Julia locates in everything and everyone surrounding her demonstrate how a baby's desire for complete oral incorporation of the mother—to fully devour her body and break this up, as she does so, into smaller and smaller pieces—endows the fragmented bad breast, the bits she imagines she has created, with her own hostility. This hostility having been directed outward now into the breast, the result of these phantasied attacks is to cause the breast fragments to appear as "actually dangerous," as persecutory and likely to consume the infant, to "scoop out the inside of its body, cut it to pieces, poison it [. . .]" (Klein, "Contribution" 262).

The bad breast is also, however, partly created by the actual breast that fails to meet the infant's desire; and Rhys is at pains to explore this real deprivation in the portrait of Julia's infantile relation with her mother, as it is reproduced in the mid-section of the novel. Here Rhys, like Klein, is recognizing that outside sources do have some influence on the developing baby's unconscious. For if the ravenous infant, imagining a good "feed" that will satiate him, is offered a breast from which the baby can experience repletion, he is reinforced in the sense that his object can be trusted to meet his desire because the infant's own goodness is all-powerful. On the other hand, if the baby remains hungry and without satisfaction from a breast that is unable to satiate his need, the infant is confirmed, in rageful phantasy, in the view that the bad breast will be destructive to him. The child will feel, too, that he is more bad than good, his love very weak in contrast to his experience of his hate (Segal 4).

From the opening scene of the narrative, *After Leaving Mr. Mackenzie* establishes through a spatial metaphor its protagonist's inclination, as a result of her own sense of desperate lack, to split the world into objects that are all-good or all-bad. The hotel where Julia lodges in Paris has the grim atmosphere of all lodging-houses in the Rhys oeuvre—it is "a lowdown sort of place"—but its rooms surprise Julia by their cleanliness (9). The two perceptions, of the malign and the wholesome, are placed in proximity to one another and yet are not integrated in any way that would produce a coherent experience of the environment. Julia's infantilized state of victimization is enacted by other inhabitants of the hotel: both the landlady and an upstairs tenant have the look of the ravaged and the clinging behavior of those who have been beaten down by entities more powerful than themselves. The specters of these women reproduce Julia's own spectral life as she ekes out her existence and suffers from the whims of the entitled; the latest abandonment, by her lover Mr. Mackenzie, is simply the most recent in a sequence of abandonments by all of the objects of her need: mother, father, sister, and uncle. Thus, in Part I of the novel, hostility and distrust dominate: as Julia baldly puts it, " '[. . .] I hate people. I'm afraid of people' " (42). Nevertheless, the aggression is disavowed, as Rhys demonstrates ways in which it may and must be split off from conscious awareness.

To reinforce the metaphor of splitting, *After Leaving Mr. Mackenzie* produces and reproduces the image of two uncanny, unknowable female figures. Paired women are featured in the texturing of this novel, as symbolically highlighted at the outset by the sign over a cinema that Julia visits with a new, would-be suitor, Horsfield. The narrative's description of "the Jewish twin-triangles" (43) defamiliarizes the Star of David by the emphasis placed on its doubled shape, which in turn evokes associations of a multiplied feminine pubic region: Jews and women are thus aligned as outsiders in the prevailing cultural hegemony. The novel creates pairings of women throughout—mothers and daughters, sisters, and homoerotic friends—to interrogate whether or not meaningful relationships between women are possible. When undifferentiated, elusive "twins" appear, their peculiarly enigmatic quality reproduces, by virtue of their eerie unreality, the unknowable components of the primitive intrapsychic world. Julia observes at discreet moments a succession of female duos who variously dissolve from sight at a restaurant; exclude her from mysterious intimacies when she visits her Uncle Griffiths's house; and even appear at her mother's funeral, although Julia neither recognizes them nor is able to make contact before they vanish into the interstices of the text. The heavy freight of meaning accorded these apparently diaphanous and always inaccessible figures is evident when Julia, wandering through the fog of London, passes another figure, "the ghost of herself," who drifts by "coldly, without recognizing her" (67–68). The indistinct world of detached selves, coming only partially in and out of view, etches wide distances between Julia's states of feeling, and her split-off rather than synthesizing perspective.

External reality repeatedly lends credence to this protagonist's inner states, as she lives in an environment that will neither nurture nor sustain her. In the melding of inner and outer worlds, Rhys illustrates another Kleinian premise, that of "projective identification." This differs from a classical notion of projection insofar as it incorporates the concept of an object who responds, for good or ill, to both positive and negative aspects of the infant that attach to her. The maternal object that feels the impact of the baby's aggressive "bits" and is unable to tolerate these may accentuate the baby's anxieties by mirroring back to the infant a pathologically heightened rendition of the original phantasies. The infant's terrified response to the world is reinforced (Ogden, "Schizophrenic Conflict" 517), a point that Rhys exemplifies in presenting Julia's unhappy projective identification with an identified repository of her aggression, as well as her unabating psychic hunger. The situation is mapped spatially once more; in this instance, on the wallpaper of her Paris room, where a bird of imposing size, "sitting on the branch of a tree, faced, with open beak, a strange, wingless creature, half-bird, half-lizard, which also had its beak open and its neck stretched in a belligerent attitude" (10). The uncanniness of the "strange" creature facing the open-mouthed bird bespeaks its role as a projection of an unclaimed self, as does the "wingless" state that suggests it cannot function freely on its own, but is, rather, the incarnation of phantasy. The creature's in-between state, "half-bird, half-lizard," underscores its fragmentation; it exists in pieces rather than as a whole. Offering its open mouth to the large bird facing it, it enacts hunger; its belligerence, in turn, expresses hostility. The impossibility of satiation is underscored in the wallpaper's rotting trees and unnatural-looking growths. The fungal environment containing oddly configured elements demonstrates that illness rather than health prevails as no sustenance can be taken in by one being from another.

Julia's perceptions are diametrically opposed to those of the fortunate baby who, imagining that he has placed parts of his aggression inside the mother as a way to achieve control over both her and himself, feels the object respond by accepting and processing his bits of hatred. The aggression is thus modified by the mother, who helps the infant feel it as less threatening; the baby can then reintroject this in a form whereby it feels acceptable, with a salutary effect. Conversely, the sad outcome of projective identification with a misattuned primary object is observable in the adult person who is filled with the dread of persecution and can only see others in binary opposition: as those who persecute versus those who do not. A state of true understanding of any object as a coherent whole, with its own complex character of virtues and deficiencies, is rendered impossible.

Klein termed the state of relentless fear and aggression the "paranoid-schizoid" position. The consuming hunger of an anxiety-filled baby who perceives only the bad, fragmented breast is expressed, in *After Leaving Mr. Mackenzie*, in the horrifying insatiability that Julia experiences in Parts I and III as well as most of the intervening Part II; nothing and no one can make her feel replete. And her characteristically paranoid-schizoid mode is fueled by the fear that her own rage, affixed to external objects, will turn back upon her and tear her asunder.

While love and hate are split apart in the paranoid-schizoid position, as Klein envisions this ("Notes" 298), it is, in effect, aggression that reigns supreme. This hostile, split, and distrustful state is Julia's predominating condition; and accordingly the world as she experiences it is populated by malevolent figures whom she abhors and fears. Her paranoiac perception of Mackenzie and his lawyer is reinforced in the collusion of these powerful men: Mackenzie has hired this lawyer for the precise purpose of doing his dirty work, to pay her off and so ensure that she stop making demands of any kind. Like the other men in the text, Mackenzie has the circumscribed worldview of a self-elected victim, suspecting, for instance, that Julia's sweetness is a ruse for manipulating him and, in his fear that she will launch an attack, impotently and unrealistically feeling his own helplessness: "[. . .] as it might have been in a nightmare, he could not do anything to stop her" (34). Both Mackenzie and her next lover, Horsfield, illustrate the degree to which projection may come to the fore in romantic object choices. Julia enacts the internally divided state that each man himself possesses; both are drawn to her in an effort to renounce their own hostility by locating it outside of themselves.

The tenor of Mackenzie's relationship with Julia is masochistic, as he allows her to be the carrier of aggression: a letter he writes to her and desperately wishes to retrieve after the end of their affair contains a provocative phrase stating that he would enjoy positioning himself with " 'my throat under your feet' " (28), indicating his fantasized subservience and her mastery. These positions he later disclaims, suggesting thereby a refusal to witness his own hostility. When the aftermath of their relationship finds him "thrust[ing] his chin out in an instinctive effort to relieve the constriction" (32–33), his rebellion against what she has represented is explicit.

Horsfield also uses Julia as a vehicle for inner conflict, for in his own paranoid-schizoid mode he repeatedly expresses his distrust of humanity, thinking, for example, that whenever it is that " 'you are tottering, somebody peculiarly well qualified to do it comes along and shoves you down. And stamps on you' " (49). Notably, he first sees Julia in a looking-glass, as she squabbles with Mackenzie, implying that she will serve the function of mirror to himself. Because both Horsfield and Mackenzie eventually turn away from Julia as her neediness increases, Rhys offers the suggestion that they are too damaged themselves to recognize Julia as a person in her own right even if they are capable of empathizing with her briefly. Overall, both of them, in failing her, reproduce the negating object world of her earliest memories.

Julia's reactions to the treatment to which these men subject her are notably inarticulate: her first significant interaction in the narrative occurs when she hits Mackenzie angrily and only subsequently offers brief, verbal commentary on her disgust with him. Julia's choice to act first and then, parenthetically, voice her rage typifies her presentation throughout the text and sanctions a reading of her behavior as situated, chronologically, in the stage of pre-verbal infant response. All heightened moments in the novel are dominated by Julia's silence as well as the absence of textual interpretation: in the one instance when the reader is to assume that Julia is about to have intercourse with Horsfield, for example, Horsfield finds her blankness unreadable,[4] and the narrative becomes mute, a literal break on the page acting as visual signifier for the silence. The force of Julia's desire is expressed with words only later, as Horsfield is about to leave, when she curtly reminds him, " 'You promised to stay with me' " (153). In its entirety, this episode suggests that the vulnerability arising from desire for fusion with a needed object is so threatening that it demands repression; words occur only as an afterthought, and then in the familiar zone of aggressive rebuke.

The opening chapters of the novel present a Julia who seems incapable of health-sustaining introjection because all of her objects are felt to be contaminated by her own projected hostile impulses; she relates to the external world as a space filled with angry others seeking revenge, and it becomes impossible to take in anything nurturing or life-affirming from these others (see Klein, "Notes" 304). She is a damaged person who seems to have no psychic fluidity, for although she may be in some ways keenly sensitive to external factors, she cannot observe these factors in a comprehensive manner, with clarity. Yet the untenable quality of Julia's existence helps to explicate the positive shift that Rhys structures, at the end of Part I, away from a paranoid-schizoid mode. In "The First Unknown," as the chapter concluding this section is titled, Rhys darkly references a stranger who makes aggressive overtures to Julia on the street (her world is filled with predators); more resonantly, however, Rhys suggests that the trip Julia is about to undertake—to London, where her mother languishes—is a journey into an unknown space. This unknown does not signify the "never known" but rather suggests the "once-known," then lost, object of first attachment, as will become evident as Part II unfolds. In planning to revisit what she has lost, Julia demonstrates that she is still striving for what Klein calls "a full capacity for love" ("Contribution" 271).

The import of Julia's venture is signaled symbolically when a woman in the boat train takes a pill from "a box of Mothersill's remedy" and swallows it; the trip to the mother who is ill may remedy Julia if she can simply find the right antidote for her ailment (61). In an effort to recuperate the remote, beloved object, Julia is beginning to work toward what Klein terms the "depressive" position. According to Klein, the developing psyche arrives at a point of being able to tolerate both good and bad feelings for the object; the splitting apart of valences of feeling that characterizes the paranoid-schizoid position now becomes ambivalence, as the subject experiences mixed feelings toward the object in the depressive position. However, the infant is beset by severe guilt because the object loved is also the object hated, and as a means of diminishing this guilt there is a need to make reparation toward the mother who has been violently attacked in phantasy ("Contribution" 265). This development of a depressive position, predicated as it is on some recognition of the infant's object as a whole person capable of being hurt, leads the baby "to realize the disaster created through its sadism and especially through its cannibalism, and to feel distressed about it" (269).

In the course of her narrative Rhys intuits, as did Klein, that vacillations between positions characterize all psychic strivings; that one does not simply progress, in a linear fashion, from one state to a "better" one and therefore Julia cannot easily shift into a depressive mode without any backward movement. Motion between the two conditions, paranoid-schizoid and depressive, occurs, in Klein's view, continuously throughout life; from the time that the individual first experiences the horror of having empathy with objects it has hurt, defensive movements back into paranoid-schizoid space occur whenever guilt becomes too difficult to bear (271). Thus in London, where the mother whom she has neglected lies dying, Julia's perceptions are colored by the paranoid-schizoid lenses that she so often wears. Upon her arrival, she is struck first by its atmosphere, which duplicates the menacing yet sad, paranoid-schizoid space of Paris: a clock near her Bloomsbury lodging "struck each quarter in that aggressive and melancholy way [. . .]" (67). This perception of the sinister dominates the opening of Part II even as she moves toward the sick bed and the possibility of a new beginning.

In her initial visit to her mother, the moment of peace that Julia experiences (the first and only such moment in the novel) offers the hope that she may achieve, through healing gestures, blissful reassurance of her mother's survival. Julia offers the entreaty, " 'Oh, darling, there's something I want to explain to you. You must listen.' " But the fragile desire is defeated as the mother stares at Julia in nonrecognition and then faces away, to begin wailing. In response to Julia's wish for forgiveness, the sought-for and clearly damaged object negates the child's need; the text starkly comments, "Nothing was there" (98). When the passage ends with the mother herself reduced to helpless, infantile cries, the daughter's desire is effectively bracketed and movement into a depressive mode is impaired.

The depressive position is complex and, as Rhys shows, it can be achieved only with the tacit cooperation of the maternal object. An infant journeying in this direction, experiencing a new awareness of the mother as a whole rather than as something split into parts, is additionally alerted to his own terrible impotence as someone who is utterly dependent. Hanna Segal describes how the tenor of anxieties changes when the infant moves from the paranoid-schizoid to the depressive mode. Rather than fearing that bad objects will attack him—the terror of paranoid-schizoid experience—the depressive baby is alerted to the possibility that his aggression may have demolished his good and much-needed object. This situation produces new, refined responses of loss and mourning over an object relationship that the child fears he has irrevocably damaged (55–57). In emotionally healthy circumstances, the mother's actual survival acts as a tonic for the baby's anxieties, curbing his sense of destructive phantasies as all-powerful and helping the baby to note "the limits of both his hate and his love," which enables him to achieve realistic interactions with the outside world (61).

But in situations of ill-health, recuperative attempts prove futile. Julia's efforts to achieve reparation are, from the start, vexed and thwarted. Alerted to Julia's plan to ameliorate the damaged relationship with her mother, her sister Norah warns that their mother is incapable of response and will not recognize her visiting daughter, just as she no longer recognizes Norah. Shortly after Julia experiences the unusually soothing bedside moment, her mother again stares at her; but this time Julia registers her parent's "recognition and surprise and anger" as Julia imagines being questioned about why she has returned and if it is to serve the purpose of mocking her mother. The mother's fantasized interrogation causes Julia to make the claim that her mother obviously " 'does know' " her (100)—in effect confessing that she *is* the person whom her (presumably) malicious parent sees. Julia's complicated response has three features: she experiences her mother as furiously rejecting of her; she believes that her mother condemns her motives for visiting the sick bed; and finally she feels that both this rejection and condemnation are deserved, for she is "known" to the maternal object that can see her for the wretch that she is. She is guiltily identified (by herself, by her mother as repository of her projections) as the bad daughter of the paranoid-schizoid position who wished to devour the object into bits—rather than as the daughter struggling courageously for a difficult, depressive balance of hate and love.

Here Julia expresses a condition afflicting the infant when, as Klein claims, her own aggressive parts are disavowed and projected onto another: guilt is carried in the baby's unconscious in the form of an anxiety over the object that is now holding the split-off, hated parts of the self ("Notes" 305–06). Although Klein describes this particular species of guilt as characteristic of the paranoid-schizoid position, insofar as it involves deflection of a sense of responsibility for oneself onto the other who acts as container for one's hostility, it also suggests some preliminary realization, removed from conscious access, of the otherness of the object as a whole being. This otherness must be experienced, as noted above, to allow for the mourning associated with loss of that object, as well as the deeper guilt arising from phantasized attacks upon it, to occur as one begins movement into the depressive position. In the depressive position proper, the individual experiences an intensification of feelings embryonic in the paranoid-schizoid phase, with the outcome "an *increased* fear of loss, states akin to mourning and a *strong* feeling of guilt, because the aggressive impulses are felt to be directed against the loved object" (308; emphasis added). Rhys places Julia's recognition of her own culpability at this cusp of depressive awareness while she struggles to find an intact, whole object at her mother's bedside. However, the narrative then shows Julia in retreat, back to the paranoid-schizoid state in which others are no more than containers for persecutorial and terrifying parts of herself. In contrast to the peaceful atmosphere that reigned in her first glance at her mother's prone body, after the death of her parent Julia recoils, for "her mother's sunken face, bound with white linen, looked frightening—horribly frightening, like a mask. Always masks had frightened and fascinated her" (124).

Rhys identifies in Julia's simultaneous fear of and gravitation to the mother's mask what happens when an infant who is consumed by dread and the need for reparation is actually confronted, as is Julia, with maternal abandonment. She also suggests that Julia may have learned how to respond to abandonment from the same masked woman who deserted her, and thus Rhys builds on the treatment of masquerade already presented in *Voyage in the Dark*. Most recurrently electing action over voice, Julia compulsively powders her face and thereby dons her own symbolic mask. In this way she attempts a False Self defense, as Winnicott has termed this, analogous to that adopted by the infant who learns that he must encapsulate his "real" being. The False Self operates to defend the True Self from harm in a situation in which the mother fails to respond with attunement to the infant's needs. She establishes within the mother–baby dyad an imperative that the infant comply with her desires. The child becomes overly responsive to her wishes, and eventually those of all others in his world, as he learns that he must eschew spontaneity as the price of self-protection ("Ego" 145–47). At this stage, Winnicott argues, "The individual then *exists by not being found*" ("Aggression" 212). The False Self deceives society but may seem in some way incomplete, and, paradoxically, the individual with a False Self defense apparently must perpetuate a state of unsatisfaction. This wounded person actually needs "to collect impingements from external reality so that the living-time of the individual can be filled by reactions to these impingements" ("Ego" 150).

This behavior is the antithesis of what Winnicott terms "creative living," for it is predicated on compulsions and results in a feeling of emptiness. To live in a creative way would entail having the strength not to comply at all moments or seek out impingements; rather, every experience would be a new one filled with the potential for growth ("Living" 41). Nevertheless, most individuals find it necessary to develop some degree of False Selfhood to function in the world.[5] As difficult as it may seem, the ability to put on and take off the False Self at will characterizes an emotionally flexible personality. For the more damaged individual, the processes of arming and disarming are fraught with anxiety as well as conflict.

As Julia, like her mother before her, learns to apply a mask of survival even at the cost of genuine living, Rhys's narrative is explicit about how habituated and essential this behavior is: "She made herself up elaborately and carefully; yet it was clear that what she was doing had long ceased to be a labour of love and had become partly a mechanical process, partly a substitute for the mask she would have liked to wear" (14). Horsfield observes that Julia's face-powdering is accompanied by "a furtive and calculating expression" (40), suggestive of the link between her making-up and her attempt to conceal her true motivations. In her Uncle Griffiths's house, where Julia feels especially threatened for reasons that will be discussed below, "She felt as though her real self had taken cover [. . .]" (82), demonstrating the gulf between the being she presents to the world and the core, such as it is, that she carries inside.

As aesthetic emblem for Julia's disenfranchised emotional state is a painting she remembers by Modigliani that presents a nude woman with body fully displayed but face heavily made-up and stylized. It offers the illusion of truth but is actually false: " 'The eyes were blank, like a mask, but when you looked at it a bit *it was as if* you were looking at a real woman, a live woman,' " Julia recalls (52; emphasis added). Her identification with the body on display and the face hidden behind a façade is further elaborated as she recollects her reactions to the painting: " 'I felt as if the woman in the picture were laughing at me and saying: "I am more real than you. But at the same time I *am* you. I'm all that matters of you" ' " (53). The paradox of the False Self defensive armor is that eventually and inexorably it becomes the self with which the wounded individual most clearly identifies and the self that she most assuredly knows. For the severely impinged-upon person, the True Self becomes buried under its own armament. This self within, layered over by conventional responses and accommodating behavior, remains largely out of sight in a state of internal self-alienation.

The death of the mother signals the failure of Julia's False Self defense. Despite all of the deliberation with which she has hidden her interior from the world and attempted compliance to others' desires, death is the final abandonment and demonstrates the futility of her gestures of appeasement. From this moment, as she begins her downward slide into despair, Julia's habitual, defensive maneuvers are ineffectual—for instance, removing her powder from her purse and then putting it back again "obviously under the impression that she had used it" (137–38). Rather than suggesting affirmation of a True (and accepted) Self, this misperception of her own gesture puts readers on notice of Julia's increased distance from reality, which is now irrevocably obscured.

Following the funeral, Julia is fixed in the paranoid-schizoid position, from which she will not move for the rest of the narrative. The failure to make reparation with her mother results in a static view of external reality that she confirms in a conversation with her sister, in which she corrects

Norah's impression that she has been feeling remorseful by insisting that what she has experienced at her mother's funeral is " 'rage.' " When Norah asks for clarification, Julia explains: " 'Animals are better than we are, aren't they? They're not all the time pretending and lying and sneering, like loathsome human beings.' " Norah's response expresses her capacity for sadism: " 'You're an extraordinary creature.' [. . .] She enjoyed seeing her sister grow red and angry, and began to talk in an incoherent voice" (134–35).

The passage evidences Julia's view that all external objects are persecutory and exploitative. She also projects onto the world her own tendency to mask, to "[pretend] and [lie]." Norah confirms that external reality is hostile as she revels in Julia's unhappiness, taking pleasure in watching her lose control. Her own eyes become animal-like: they gleam with "yellow" malice as she listens to Julia (135). Both she and Julia directly reference animals. Norah calls Julia " 'an extraordinary creature,' " a phrase she has already used once, in her first meeting with Julia upon her return to London and a label by which Julia is again placed and fixed when the nurse Wyatt, who is Norah's intimate, thinks of Julia as a "creature" as well (75; 107). Julia will proceed to refer to people as " 'beasts, such mean beasts' " (135) even though she has also determined that animals are superior to humans, a contradiction best explained by her understanding that humans are more predatory and calculatingly bloodthirsty than other animals, who, in their natural and instinctive responses, express a kind of pure, unpremeditated living.

The source for all of these comments, by both sisters, traces back to their perception of their mother as she is dying: "And yet the strange thing was that she was still beautiful, as an animal would be in old age," and both Julia and Norah follow with comments on her beauty and attractiveness (97). This is in sharp contrast with a preceding narrative description in which the compelling residue of their mother's beauty is debauched by illness: her delicate, almost aristocratic features ravaged by the loss of muscular control; her breath coming grotesquely as she heaves from the side of her mouth. The daughters' insistence on their mother's beauty confirms that they are both at least momentarily caught in the web of infantile desire, perceiving only parts of the maternal presence rather than the object as whole, and coloring these fragments with the idealization that attends all longed-for things (see Meltzer 8–9). Therefore, after this desired mother fails her children, and they recognize the abandonment, the animal imagery is maintained and complicated. When Julia's mother is described as a beautiful animal, when Julia then reviles people for bestial avarice, the text bears witness to the ways in which the adored can be replaced by the menacing, the idealized by the damned. In effect, what is described is the loss of the good object to the bad. The deep needs of the babies were ignored as this bad object simply and inexplicably turned away.

That Norah herself is in need of acceptance and caregiving by a woman is suggested in her relationship with Wyatt, who is described in an unflattering way by the narrative as a mannish, stereotypic lesbian; her avaricious and repellent proprietorship of Norah signals her role as parody of the real thing, the nurturing mother. With Norah's abandonment of any hope of direct access to maternal love has come a compensatory substitution having, at its base, a belief in the ameliorative effects of relationships. Unlike Julia, Norah does not seek out in men stand-ins for the earliest love, her mother; yet the martyred pose she adopts as sole responsible caretaker for her dying parent, and the anger she levels at Julia, suggest the limits of her own strategy of self-sustainment. Nevertheless, she has found companionship with Wyatt; Julia is unable to make even a tenuously loving connection with another.

Her inability to achieve union with the mother, and hence attain self-acceptance and the full capacity for loving others, is reinscribed after the death of her parent as the novel descends into increasingly malign and surreal imagery of death spaces, *danse macabres*, and proliferating skeletons, ghouls, and automatons that reflect Julia's distorted vision. In a restaurant that Julia and Horsfield enter, Rhys establishes the tone that will prevail for the rest of the narrative: a preoccupying hunger, with an accompanying rage. The space offers a parodically vaginal decor, described as "long and narrow. Red-shaded lamps stood on the tables, and the walls were decorated with paintings of dead lobsters and birds served up on plates ready to be eaten [. . .]." With its emblems of creatures that ironically *cannot* be devoured, the passage fashions, from the clichéd entryway back into the womb, an undertaking to the mother's body as dead site offering only the illusion of sustenance to the hungry. The responses of another patron reflect Julia's frustration:

> A row was going on. One of the customers was bawling at the waiter that the soup was muck, and the other diners were listening with shocked but rather smirking expressions, like good little boys who were going to hear the bad little boy told off. The complainant, who must have been sensitive and have felt the universal disapproval, put up his hand to shield a face that grew redder and redder. However, he bawled again: "Take it away. I won't eat it. It's not mulligatawny, it's muck." (144)

The ravenous, infantile figure who refuses to accept the inadequate food he is being served is surrounded by others whose conventional expressions—of dismay and self-satisfaction—express an expectation that those who voice their consuming need will, assuredly, be censured. Nevertheless, an atmosphere of need dominates. Two other occupants in the restaurant, including "a very thin woman, dressed in black" who speaks in "a thin, mincing voice," and a "fat Italian" who "pick[s] his teeth with a worried expression, shielding the toothpick with one hand," together suggest a state of actual or incipient deprivation. Julia herself, at the close of this episode, looks to Horsfield "thinner and somehow more youthful than when he had last seen her" (145), a comment on how the restaurant makes visible the starvation she has felt since childhood.

To suggest that all of Julia's difficulties stem from a fractured relationship with her mother is to minimize an emphasis the novel places on her strained and damaging relationships with the others who follow from that initial intimacy. Rhys thus demonstrates that successive relationships may function as reinforcements of the original maternal trauma, with the people who populate one's later life taking shape on the template of the unconscious as entities in collusion with early, internalized persecutors. Accordingly, the wound of the abandoned child is deepened. The sequencing of traumas in Julia's life may thereby be reconstructed: first the distance experienced from a mother who was herself subsumed by infantile needs; then the further gap attendant on her sister Norah's birth; the abandonment caused by her father's death a year later; and the suggestion of molestation by her paternal uncle sometime during Julia's latency stage (i.e., at around age ten or "probably younger," as the narrative cryptically notes, making a point of her innocent and vulnerable state [159]).

The loss of the beloved mother who is always somehow out of reach is poignantly evoked as Julia remembers, "when she was a very young child she had loved her mother. Her mother had been the warm centre of the world. You loved to watch her brushing her long hair; and when you missed the caresses and the warmth you groped for them . . . ." This is followed by a memory of further loss: "And then her mother—entirely wrapped up in the new baby—had said things like, 'Don't be a cry-baby. [. . .] You're a great big girl of six.' And from being the warm centre of the world her mother had gradually become a dark, austere, rather plump woman, who, because she was worried, slapped you for no reason that you knew" (106–07). The capriciousness of the parental behavior and her apparently sudden metamorphosis from the locus of light to darkness is tied to her role as bearer of new baby; not coincidentally, as she becomes darker she also becomes "plump," as if to suggest the chance of perennial gestation and thus the threat of a succession of babies who will take her ever further from Julia. This displacement by a sibling sets the stage for Julia's inability to achieve connection with Norah during the ordeal of her mother's dying and helps explain the animosity between the sisters throughout their conversations in Part II of the narrative.[6]

The father's death, mentioned and dismissed in a sentence to suggest his relatively fleeting trajectory in Julia's development, is followed by the appearance of her Uncle Griffiths. As brother to (and thus double for) the absent father, he serves as emblem for the damage that masculine behavior may inflict and for the ways in which this can underscore the trauma of the first, maternal abandonment. Julia remembers her uncle's compliments to her, as a child, which reinforce the sense that he fulfilled a particularly male function of dispensing sexual favors to the females within his domestic space. But her adult behavior with him reveals a dark undercurrent of feeling. After her mother's funeral, she faces Uncle Griffiths in the car and her posture is so awkward as to merit observation: she positions herself at an angle, keeping herself from leaning into his knees, while he casts at her "one disapproving, almost furtive look, then turn[s] his head away and look[s] out the window." The narrative additionally registers the atmosphere he tries to exude, one that is "spick and span, solemn and decorous." Julia's aversion to physical contact with him, followed immediately by her uncle's expression of distaste and subterfuge, imply a history of possibly illicit contact that is signaled in the narrative description of his "spick and span," that is, faultless, appearance. The implication that things are not as they seem is amplified in the uncle's internal monologue that follows:

> He thought how he disliked that woman and her expression, and her eyes, which said: "Oh, for God's sake, leave me alone. I'm not troubling you; you've no right to trouble me. I've as much right as you to live, haven't I?" But you were sure that, underneath that expression, people like her were preparing the filthy abuse they would use, the dirty tricks they would try to play, if they imagined you were not leaving them alone. (129)

As the narrative moves into the uncle's interior, the mechanism of denial is shown at work, enabling him to envision Julia as his persecutor. His anticipation that she will "[imagine]" he won't "[leave her] alone" suggests that in fact he has *not* left her alone, while his anxiety about "the filthy abuse" and "dirty tricks" she may level at him gains no support from her distancing behavior. The resulting implication is that it is he who has actually abused and tricked others, and presumably Julia, in the past.

All of these suggestions are given weight in Julia's extended reverie of childhood, beginning with a feeling of "The last time you were really happy" but turning swiftly to a grimmer note, to a memory of "the first time you were afraid" (158; 159). In Julia's recollection of catching a butterfly and putting it in a tin, fascinated by its sound as it beat its wings against the side in captivity, the sadism of her behavior marks a displacement of Julia's own feelings of entrapment. Further disavowal of her feelings is evident in her thought, when she removed the insect from its confinement, that "it was so battered that you lost all interest in it." Suggesting Julia's loss of interest in herself,[7] this memory is accompanied by an unattributed voice that in its harsh, scolding tone recalls her mother's accusing voice as Julia had imagined it when she stood by her parent's deathbed. The voice of this internalized mother rails at her for being " 'a cruel, horrid child [. . .] I'm surprised at you.' " Julia's disclaiming of responsibility for the vulnerable butterfly is suggested by a subtle shift in tone as the internal voice insists, "[. . .] if the idiot broke its own wings, that wasn't your fault, and the only thing to do was to chuck it away and try again." Here, the voice that would blame the victim rather than the aggressor precisely mimics the disapproving, fault-finding voice of Uncle Griffiths, another internalized source of contempt. That Julia, like the butterfly, has been preyed upon is further suggested when Julia remembers her first experience of fear, as she chased butterflies in the sun: "The sunlight was still, desolate, and arid. And you knew that something huge was just behind you. You ran. You fell and cut your knee. You got up and ran again, panting, your heart thumping, much too frightened to cry."

The terrifying sunlight forms a metaphoric reminder of the warm center of the world that had been Julia's mother: now the light has become harsh and menacing, as the mother's dominance has given way to the uncle's and the "huge" thing stalking young Julia is the predatory, sexually intent male. This suggestion of molestation is enforced by her reaction to the unnamed trauma she has experienced: "But when you got home you cried. You cried for a long time; and you never told anybody why" (160). The successive moments of this reverie—of brief and then spoiled happiness, displaced cruelty, internalized self-condemnation, terror in the presence of an implacable force, and, finally, silence and isolation within a world that must inexorably misunderstand—all serve as reinforcements of the bad, persecuting objects that Julia carries within and help to explain why movement out of the paranoid-schizoid position seems, despite her efforts, virtually impossible.

Julia's habitual silence—the phrase "you never told anybody why" that becomes the hollow mantra of her unvoiced responsiveness as an adult—defines her inability to manage the full force of her need by articulating what it is that she wants. It also has the secondary function of keeping others from gaining access to her psychic interior even, or especially, when physical penetration has occurred. In effect, Julia keeps intact her inner world, filled though it may be with bad objects. This may seem a perverse choice unless one understands that resistance is the handmaid to familiarity: that it is safer to retain what one knows than to allow the dangerous possibilities of the unknown to make entry into one's emotional constellation. Critiquing Klein's emphasis on the child herself as the source of instinctually motivated aggression, which is then directed at her caretakers, Fairbairn succinctly describes the phenomenon that occurs when a child is in fact the victim of inadequate caregivers and reacts by internalizing them into his object world. "If a child's parents are bad objects," Fairbairn argues, "he cannot reject them, even if they do not force themselves upon him; for he cannot do without them. Even if they neglect him, he cannot reject them; for, if they neglect him, his need for them is increased" ("Repression" 67). One way to control and maintain internalized bad objects is to use repression as a defense against the truth; to combat the new; and to keep, thereby, one's inner world intact ("On the Nature" 380).

Although the events of Rhys's novel are related primarily by a third-person voice, it is notably limited in its insights and also accedes to the second person to invoke the muddled depths of profound feeling. For example, when Julia recalls to herself the ending of her first love affair, with a Mr. James, the second person intones: "You felt as if your back was broken, as if you would never move again. But you did not make a scene" (109). This sleight of hand on the part of the narrator suggests intimacy with Julia's thoughts even while demonstrating the disassociated, split quality of her perception. Julia's use of the internal "you" offers up the strategy of a child whose responses have never been known as legitimate in their own right. If subjected, rather, to a mother–baby culture in which all states of being center in her object, the infant is suspended in a void of nonrecognition of her capacity to know. Thus the unaffirmed infant learns to credit the (m)other rather than herself as a source of knowledge (Socor 87–88). When that bearer of "truth" is gone, as Julia's mother actually is and metaphorically has been since early memory, what is perceived cannot be constituted except by internal references to a phantasized listener: the "you" whom Julia's mind repeatedly addresses.

In contrast to Julia, whose use of "you" has its source in her inability to legitimize her own feelings by locating them within herself, the male figures in the text—Mackenzie, Horsfield, and, as shown above, Uncle Griffiths—characteristically deploy the second person in a determined refusal of their own culpability. Lapsing into "you," they voice their internal defense against personal responsibility toward those whom they have hurt or are about to harm. The narrative satirizes Mackenzie for this tendency in its description of his "code," which precludes succumbing to impulsive behavior unless he can be sure that he will not be found out; very easily, he tells himself, "You didn't argue about these things. Simply, under certain circumstances you did this, and under other circumstances you did that" (24). This code of misconduct, as it were, which is designed to keep him free of scandal and trouble, comes to the fore when he dispenses with Julia as she becomes increasingly needy and he feels, in turn, that he is dangerously close to losing control. He therefore obeys his own rationalizing dictates: "He had lied; he had made her promises which he never intended to keep; and so on, and so on. All part of the insanity, for which he was not responsible" (25). Here the shift back into a third-person voice allows for narrative distance and irony, serving up moral judgment on Mackenzie as a complacent, bourgeois immoralist.

Horsfield, who is presented with greater tolerance and more dimension throughout the novel, occasionally reverts to the second person when he feels, like Julia, persecuted and alone; but more frequently he makes use of the "you" just as Mackenzie does, when situations become morally problematic. Thus his decision to cut free of Julia and her needs: "Undertaking a fresh responsibility was not the way to escape when you came to think of it. . . ." (169), he reflects, as he is on the brink of vanishing forever from her life. The second person functions for these male characters as a buffer against awareness, helping them to remain securely insensitive to the woman whom they have used to serve their own ends.

In Julia's choice of men who will replicate the abandonment that she has experienced in her earliest intimacies, she moves along a vicious cycle, enacting a repetition compulsion to ensure that external factors will confirm the "truth" of bad internal objects and work to exteriorize prevailing and dominating anxieties in the intrapsychic world (see S. Mitchell 74–75). This pattern is established in all of Julia's engagements with men, from the ex-lover, Mackenzie, who has already abandoned her before the narrative begins; to James, her first lover who palms her off with money during her visit to London; to Horsfield, who, despite kindly intentions, ultimately leaves her; and finally back to Mackenzie again, who runs into Julia at novel's close, offers her money, and then eagerly flees the scene.

The essentially dead-end quality of Julia's movements is graphically rendered in Part II. When she visits a dance hall with Horsfield, they are approached by a horrifyingly skeletal man who makes advances that she is powerless to resist. Her dance of death with him, as she lapses into a relenting pose of exhaustion, commences: "Mr Horsfield lowered his eyes moodily, so that as Julia and her partner passed his table he saw only her legs, appearing rather too plump in flesh-coloured stockings. She seemed to him to be moving stiffly and rather jerkily. It was like watching a clockwork toy that has nearly run down" (148). Julia's hapless posture here again draws attention to her powerlessness, and her mechanical, "clockwork" motion implies that she is ceasing to be a living organism and is descending into the realm of the dead. Even her legs, "in flesh-coloured stockings," offer the suggestion of the inhuman, with flesh coloring donned to cover what is not flesh. Their plumpness also recalls Julia's mother, aligning Julia with that which is lost and longed for in her continual circles backward into desire and despair. It is after this incident that Julia will sleep with Horsfield for the first and only time, as if to suggest her desperation to forge connection with the living—and her disappointment in failing to achieve it.

Rhys demonstrates that internalized persecutors can draw one ever further from life and deeper into the murderous realm of paranoid-schizoid space. On Horsfield's second visit to her London lodgings, as he follows her up the stairs in the dark Julia screams at his touch, believing it to be the touch of death gripping her. She has in effect been touched by death. By the time Part III begins, with Julia returning to Paris, no hope of movement into life-affirming, depressive empathy with others is likely, and death encloses her. Sulfurous smells emanate from the room next to hers in her hotel, and the hellish atmosphere increases as she wanders through Halles noting the menacingly decayed vegetation and "a thin man, so thin that he was like a clothed skeleton" (188). All around Julia reflect her own state of starvation and decline. The choice of Halles, with its reverberation of the English word "Hell" accompanied by its French location as "marketplace," offers Rhys the opportunity to stress the evil effects of Julia's commodification. As she sells herself to men in exchange for the promise, always unfulfilled, of union with a loved object, she sinks further and further into a state of demise.

Part III also reestablishes, forcibly, that it is impossible for Julia to retrieve a soothing maternal presence. She has a tantalizing vision of a woman at a café who represents the ideal of maternity, who is "slim" (she does not house rival babies as Julia's "plump" mother did) and yet has "full, soft breasts" (good breasts that are inviting and receptive). Aware of her own acute desire, Julia wishes that she could begin a conversation: " '[. . .] if only I could go up and tell her all about myself and why I am unhappy, everything would be different afterwards' " (184). This is precisely what she cannot do, but again the narrative becomes silent at this moment, a spatial break on the page directly following Julia's expression of longing and the action resuming with her walk out of the café, unaccompanied by any explanation of how she managed (or presumably was unable to manage) her desire. The failure to couple with a loved object is striking here, as in earlier instances of the text, iterating the impossibility of reparation and thus of movement out of a paranoid-schizoid arena. As Julia enters a shop to listen to the recording of a contemporary song, the female voice tells her, " *'Pars, sans te retourner, pars'* " (Leave, don't come back, leave) (185). The door is closed with finality on Julia's attempts at reclamation.

Rhys suggests further that the downward movement of Julia's story be contrasted with the more fluid possibilities of a male narrative; that her hopelessness is linked specifically to the fact that she is a woman in a world that is dominated by male constructions of power. For all that Mackenzie and Horsfield experience moments of identification with Julia, they are able to leave her and move on, as she cannot. Their prowess is signaled at the outset, in Part I, when she notices a picture in a Paris shop window with "a male figure encircled by what appeared to be a huge mauve corkscrew." The picture contains the legend, " *'La vie est un spiral, flottant dans l'espace, que les hommes grimpent et redescendent très, très, très sérieusement'* " (Life is a spiral, floating in space, that men scale and come down again very, very, very seriously) (17). Men can, at least hypothetically, traverse the space leading up to depressive modes and back into paranoid-schizoid realms, and then repeat the process to begin their ascent again—although Rhys shows little evidence of their willingness to loiter in depressively empathic stances. But women have, in contrast, a much more restricted range of choice. In the case of Julia, upward motion is blocked by the mother who will not acknowledge her or allow for compensation; she transmits, in fact, the heritage of her own thwarted effort and ultimate resignation. As a child, the narrative records, the mother had lived in South America but later, when married, had weakly allowed herself to be transported to England. Julia recalls the ineffectuality of her mother's subsequent complaint: " 'This is a cold, grey country. This isn't a country to be really happy in' " (105). She thereby communicated across generations a message that the feminine exists in an abject condition, always at an impasse.

To offer final proofs of this inevitable, female inaction, the third part of the novel stresses imagery of impassive women. As Julia considers applying for a job as a governess or lady's companion (but then remains inert), she looks out from her hotel and sees, in the houses that face her, "[. . .] at each window a woman sat staring mournfully, like a prisoner, straight into her bedroom" (179). The chapter in which this occurs is significantly titled "Île de la Cité," to call attention to Julia's isolated state and the inaccessibility of any who would offer her means of reparation. She is instead alone, islanded, surrounded by figures who simply mirror her state of internal imprisonment. The chapter that follows, "The Second Unknown," overtly refers to another self-serving stranger who begins to approach Julia on the street only to back away when he sees her ravaged condition. But, as before, the term "unknown" has larger implications: in this case, to evoke the once-known and since-reclaimed infant of the paranoid-schizoid realm, which is grimly rendered in the chapter that concludes both Part III and the novel itself. This chapter is entitled, in finality, "Last." With a relentless logic, the plot loops back upon itself as Julia once more encounters Mackenzie, who dutifully invites her for a drink, which she immediately transforms into an occasion to ask for money. But when he provides it, again dutifully, she puts the money away "without counting it" (191); her actions are automated, ritualistic, and unthinking. Whether or not Julia has actually decided to commit suicide—the text offers some suggestion that she considers drowning herself[8]—she has the appearance of someone whose feelings are split off from one another, and from her actions, as well.

To further darken the suggestiveness of its final moments, the last words of the narrative locate Julia at a moment of transition, in "the hour between dog and wolf" (191). Throughout the novel, dogs are associated with the subjugated, with those who bend to others' will and suffer for it (see, e.g., 11; 145); and also they are related to England itself, where Julia's mother lay helpless on a death bed. In her journey to London in "The First Unknown" Julia recalls the lines of a popular song that make explicit the connection between canine imagery and the country of her mother's demise: "England. . . . English. . . . Our doggy page. . . ." (61). With "dog" operating as trope for the feeble and domesticated, Julia's location at novel's close "between dog and wolf" suggests her renunciation of the craving for fusion with a beloved object, for to long to connect is to become, as experience repeatedly teaches, intolerably hurt. She appears poised to metamorphose into the emblematic and aggressive figure of the "wolf"—here, Rhys's symbolic evocation of the devouring, primitive aggressor. Notably, Rhys does not actually depict the transformation, thereby maintaining the elusive possibility that Julia may still work toward the depressive mode even while she is pulled toward the paranoid-schizoid position she knows best. The inevitable is forestalled; bleak as it may seem, in this Rhysian narrative an escape from fate is not impossible.[9] Yet hope, such as it is, is under erasure from the text's beginning to its end.

What Marianne DeKoven describes as Modernism's "*sous-rature,*" in which texts propose solutions for identified ills but often do so in an ambivalent, internally contradictory vein (20), is the aesthetic guiding Rhys as she constructs the life of her protagonist. To read any of her fictional characters solely as case studies rather than as structural elements that enforce thematic concerns is to elide the critique of the wasted conditions of postwar culture that profoundly informs this novel. This pushes against the limitations of a psychoanalytic critical approach and invites exploration of the text's broader implications. From the beginning, Rhys stresses Julia's typicality rather than singularity and thereby positions her as an Everywoman figure speaking to conditions of twentieth-century life. Her age is indeterminate, and she is without definable cultural or national identification; at one point she takes out a piece of blotting paper and illustrates it with "little flags," suggesting that she is a woman without a country (20). Thus rootless and adrift, she tells the story of all Europeans lost in the newly ravaged, postwar landscape. Her narrative bears the firm stamp of World War I. She tells Mackenzie that when the war ended she emigrated from England, gave birth to a baby, and then witnessed the baby's death, after which her marriage ended under circumstances that she allows to remain unclear—"Or perhaps she had never been married at all," as Mackenzie muses (25). That the death of the baby follows so closely on the armistice symbolically points to the death of the future for genera-tions born after the war to end all wars; the nonchalance with which Julia reports that the infant's death occurred "in Central Europe somewhere" implies the pervasiveness of destruction throughout the Western world. Further, that Julia's tenuous link with her husband, if he was even that, is broken after the war, suggests that any prescriptive form of domestic life has been severely undermined by the conditions of postwar culture.

In the chapter "It Might Have Been Anywhere," Rhys implies that the disaffection she is depicting between Horsfield and Julia, after their sexual encounter, is determined not only by individual history but also by national politics. As they enter Julia's room, a train whistle sounds and Horsfield comments that it " 'must be the Great Western' "; he is hearing the echoing sound of Western civilization itself (151). He notices the whistle again later. In this doubled moment, Rhys stresses that deprivation and discon-nection are a universal condition, for Europeans at least, as their civilization approaches a distant vanishing line. This sense of far-ranging damage is underscored when Horsfield tells Julia that he has suffered the effects of history, that his own psyche has been bruised by the war. His uncanny experience, as he leaves the next morning, confirms the extent of cultural malaise: "In the dimness of the hall a white face glimmered at him. He started, and braced himself for an encounter. Then, relieved, he saw it was a bust of the Duke of Wellington" (155). This confrontation with a fac-simile of the heroic acts both as a poignant longing to recover an idealized past and as indictment of the blasted legacy of imperial power. It challenges the notion of lingering heroism in any place in the world ("it might have been anywhere," as the chapter title underlines), suggesting that a mode of life has vanished forever, its chivalry and fanfare irretrievable.

However, Rhys also notes that the war has affected women and men in different ways. Julia's visit to James, her first lover, has at its center a telling moment when he informs her that he had once had contempt for those who could not take care of themselves; the war has changed all that. Now he is accustomed to friendships with the emotionally wounded, with the disoriented, with men as well as women disenfranchised by the war. Then he modifies his claim: " '[. . .] mind you, women are a different thing altogether. Because it's all nonsense; the life of a man and the life of a woman can't be compared. They're up against entirely different things the whole time' " (114–15).

As the novel demonstrates, the world is populated by the mad, the hungry, and the disavowed; but there is also a distinction, as James asserts, between what men and women have suffered since the war. The men in the text, wounded as they clearly are, nevertheless maintain positions of inflated hegemony and are able to prey upon those weaker than themselves in the attempt to satisfy their desires. The women, most concretely represented by Julia but also suggested by her sister Norah, are confined to lives of giving others what they want, in the slim hope of having their own needs met. In a postwar world, Rhys locates all of her characters in conditions of despair; yet some varieties of despair are more profound than others, and it is women who ache most acutely because of their powerlessness.

Although Rhys's thematics are deeply evocative of alienation and isolation, the narrative strategy of *After Leaving Mr. Mackenzie* maintains the possibility of connection between self and other—between the author who composes and reader who responds. The novel's instances of textual muteness, its unsaid moments of trauma and hunger, can be read not only as sites of repression but also as Modernist invitations to a textual collaboration. In this regard Rhys shares a narrative attitude with her contemporaries— Hemingway, for example—although she deploys her silences for different ends.[10] Still, as in works by other Modernists, the writerly gesture toward audience involvement presents the hope, framed as technique, that art of the early twentieth century can offer. And here a psychoanalytic approach may be wed, after all, to a Modernist consideration of the text, as Rhys models the positive enactment that projective identification may allow. The reader who inhabits elusive textual prompts and enigmatic cues with her own interpretive desire finds that the novel's pages offer an answering response—modifying, challenging, and enriching diverse gestures of explanation.

Of the works Rhys composed in the period between the wars, *After Leaving Mr. Mackenzie* may elicit the strongest interest in the current generation of readers. It offers a complex thematic treatment of the unconscious processes that serve to keep the self in pieces and tenaciously defend against ongoing trauma; and it skillfully engages narrative strategies of distancing as well as intimacy to evoke the flight from, and need for, others in an alienating, barren landscape. Its insistence on the centrality of the mother–daughter dyad also marks this most particularly as the work of a woman writer refusing to capitulate to conventional and male-inscribed claims about the appropriate contents for aesthetic discourse: traditionally masculinized renditions of Oedipal conflict, for example. And in its demand for reciprocity between the writer's text and the reader's, this novel reinscribes the tenets of Modernism to meet its own specific, and reverberating, aims.

4. *Quartet*: A Constellation of Desires ✍

[. . .] greed, envy, and persecutory anxiety, which are bound up with each other, inevitably increase each other.

—Melanie Klein, *Envy and Gratitude: A Study of Unconscious Sources*

Although *Quartet* was the first of Rhys's novels to be published, it offers a more sophisticated view of social masquerade than *Voyage in the Dark*, which had been drafted earlier, as it enacts masking behaviors across several major characterizations. Further, its interrogation of the fiercely vexed psychological states that characterize the beginning years of life position its psychology as intermediary between the dyadic, pre-Oedipal concerns of *After Leaving Mr. Mackenzie* and the triangulated, Oedipal dynamics of *Good Morning, Midnight*. At first glance *Quartet*'s focus of interest seems more single-minded than my language would suggest: it enlists a configuration familiar to readers of Western narratives of jealousy and betrayal, as the protagonist, Marya, becomes trapped in a web of desire for a surrogate father and rivalry with a maternal figure, both of whom solicit as well as repel her entry into their domestic melodrama. However, the erotics of the three participants screen another pain to which the text bears witness, that of Marya's infantile longing, as it is commingled with envy, toward a constructed vision of withholding motherhood. Complicating matters is the fact that the novel's maternal and paternal imagos are at times conflated, stressing Marya's state of isolation but also propelling Rhys's audience to share in the confusion about the locus of this protagonist's desires.

The autobiographical elements in *Quartet* derive from an entanglement that is similarly difficult to interpret, one that had arisen among Rhys, her early mentor Ford Madox Ford, his common-law wife Stella Bowen, and

Rhys's husband John Lenglet, whose imprisonment had left her stranded without him in Paris. As Paul Delany notes, there are at least six relevant accounts of this situation. In addition to Rhys's narrative, her husband also offered a fictionalized rendition of the events in his novel *Barred*, translated by Rhys from the French to include small emendations of material that she thought unjust to herself. Lenglet's original, untranslated version of his work was published some years later under the title *Sous Les Verrous*. Preceding all three of these works, Ford's novel *The Good Soldier* uncannily anticipated the affair that he had not yet had with Rhys, outlining the dynamics that would characterize the ensuing relationship as well as the responses of the other players in the action. Ford's later novel *The Wicked Man* paints a damning portrait of a thinly disguised Rhys as reconstructed to serve Ford's own self-justifying ends. Finally Stella Bowen's autobiography, *Drawn From Life*, presents the single version of events that purports to be a truthful record of the situation, although its hostility and sense of outrage, toward Rhys in particular, are marked.[1] The need of all four participants to revisit the terrain of the affair suggests that their texts performed the function of necessary fictions, creating spaces in which each author might shape and reshape otherwise oblique events.

Rhys's narrative rendition unfolds, accordingly, in a complex presentation of shifting relationships, as the initial plot structuring that encloses two married couples, Marya and Stephan Zelli and Lois and Hugh Heidler, is almost immediately destabilized when Marya's husband, Stephan, is arrested and thus effectively removed from the central force of the action. In the course of ensuing events, the triangle among Hugh, Lois, and Marya, with Lois tacitly promoting an affair between her husband and the young girl, acts as framing device for a presentation in which the tense involvement of Marya with a phantasized vision of Lois assumes increasing significance. The most enigmatic aspect of the narrative lies in its subtlety of approach to the difficult emotion of envy, a two-person dynamic that is as culturally ubiquitous as it is generally disavowed. The novel's more overtly figured presentation of jealousy, a condition predicated on the involvement, actual or imagined, among three people, records feeling-states that may not be precisely sanctioned by the general populace but that are usually understood and even forgiven; and this is the aspect of Rhys's text that has elicited the most critical response.[2]

To understand why envy might seem so much less acceptable an emotion than jealousy, and further to suggest why the treatment of envy in *Quartet* is indirect, in contrast with its incarnations of jealousy, which are overt, Melanie Klein's pioneering late study, *Envy and Gratitude*, offers salient insights. Klein notes,

> Envy is the angry feeling that another person possesses and enjoys something desirable—the envious impulse being to take it away or to spoil it. Moreover, envy implies the subject's relation to one person only and goes back to the earliest exclusive relation with the mother. Jealousy is based on envy, but involves a relation to at least two people; it is mainly concerned with love that the subject feels is his due and has been taken away, or is in danger of being taken away, from him by his rival. (6–7)

It is the dependence of envy on the very earliest relation, that of infant with maternal object, that sets it off from jealousy as the more ancient and thus more primal and terrifying of emotions. Further, envy's investment in the wish to destroy, as opposed to jealousy's posture of inherent mourning; envy's phantasy of rageful spoiling, as juxtaposed with jealousy's search for the management of grief, mark envy as an almost diabolical state. It is therefore an emotion that seems far more toxic than jealousy when viewed within the context of a Western, Judeo-Christian milieu in which imperatives to disclaim all signs of malice run deep.

A schematic summary of *Quartet* demonstrates how the plot entices readers to focus attention on the triangle of Hugh, Lois, and Marya to the exclusion of the dyadic relation between Marya and Lois. Following Stephan Zelli's imprisonment, the older and apparently very respectable Heidlers invite Marya to live with them under the guise of protecting her from harm. Immediately, therefore, Rhys positions them as self-elected parental figures to a needy, child-like, orphaned character; and the dynamics necessary for staging an Oedipal scene are put into play. Despite Marya's misgivings, Stephan from his prison cell urges her to accept their offer, and she weakly capitulates; thus her husband's complicity in allowing the triangulated situation to develop elaborates on a portrait of Marya as the innocent who is being thrust into a threatening and seductive adult world.

The Heidlers's motives seem obscure and are clarified only in the course of her time with them, as it becomes apparent that Marya's role is to serve as Heidler's mistress while remaining under the watchful eye of his wife. Again, within an Oedipal frame, Marya is located as the daughter sacrificed to the father's incestuous wishes, with the sanction of a mother whose primary concern is to maintain some form of control of the father's illicit sexuality. When this daughter figure has been effectively ravaged and corrupted, so much so, in fact, that she poses too much of a challenge to the mother's dominion, she is installed in unsavory hotel rooms where

Hugh's ascendancy over her, out of sight of the maternal Lois, may be even more assured. Having by this time sunk to the level of prostitution (he leaves her money after their sexual encounters), Marya illustrates the complete subjugation of youth to the machinations of a corrupt parent generation; and she has not far to travel from here to a situation of abject worthlessness in the father's eyes. His disregard of his own conduct and responsibility in besmirching her are the operatives when he has her relocated to the south of France, as if this superficial geographic prescription is all that it will take for her to "get well" after the abuses to which she has been subject; and he then dispenses with her, erasing the evidence of his sexual wrongdoings, as quickly as possible. However, like the incest victim indoctrinated into the father's will, when Marya returns to Paris and the newly released Stephan she is thoroughly invested in maintaining her allegiance to Heidler. Stephan's ensuing rage and assault on her after being told of the affair leave her on ambiguous view to readers as an inert heap, not distinguished by the narrative as either living or dead but rather in the limp, hapless, and child-like posture of one whose trust has been so battered that nothing of her volition remains. She is ultimately deemed unworthy of any attribution at all by those who have exploited and disregarded her, with the point underlined in the narrative's refusal to make a determination about Marya's final condition.

In a simpler form, Rhys had already written a sketch that described the sort of alliance between partners that could occur when engaging a third party for the ostensible purpose of serving the man's sexual needs. In her short story "Trio," published in *The Left Bank* about a year before *Quartet* appeared, the narrator observes dining at a Parisian restaurant a group comprising a man and woman from the Antilles and a very young girl with a charmingly coy manner whom he kisses at intervals, "long, lingering kisses," while the woman appreciatively looks on. The story offers the distinct suggestion that the girl derives exhibitionist pleasure from the attention she receives, as the narrative remarks on her "vulgar, impudent" face, "voluptuous" lips, and "cunning" eyes (*Collected* 34). The text also has a concern to locate all three characters racially: the man's blackness is stressed, the woman's coffee complexion is noted, and the girl is described as part-white, suggesting that her appeal and also pride of manner derive from the relative lightness of her skin. On the one hand, Rhys positions them as "other" for her European audience and thereby seems to keep them at a safe remove, rendering their behavior as exotics relatively unthreatening. On the other hand, and more subversively, the narrator's comment at story's end that he or she also comes from the Antilles acts to suggest correspondence between observer and observed, narrator as well as reader and the objects of their attention, and therefore implies that these foreigners are engaging in behavior that may be seen elsewhere, at any time, among any inhabitants of Montparnasse. The story thereby makes pointed notation of the prevalence of perverse triadic relations. The threesome it depicts appears decadent and repellent, with the two adult characters enjoying, together, the sexual use of the young girl, and the girl herself presented not as victim but as willing coconspirator.

By the time she composed *Quartet*, Rhys's perception of such trios was further complicated; while retaining the vision of a collusive partnership between husband and wife, she now paid greater attention both to the way the young girl in their midst was being exploited and also to the nuances of relationship between the girl and the more experienced woman. Thus, notwithstanding the apparently straightforward causality of its action, *Quartet* offers up a provocative portrait of Lois Heidler and a highly suggestive account of her effect on Marya. Despite the text's apparent concern with an Oedipal configuration, the narrative reveals another interest, one that draws upon a daughter's rageful feelings about a maternal figure by painting that mother as eminently desirable, as well as withholding and malign. The very insistence in *Quartet* on Lois's primacy in the Heidler marriage serves up its subtextual preoccupation. In spite of the tensions that Marya faces as she contends with her desire for a surrogate father, she has another and unquenchable longing, one that centers on her mother. Rhys uses her protagonist's state of insatiable need as nodal point for an examination of the interconnected and fraught conditions of deprivation, loss, greed, and envy as these relate to infant phantasies and, in particular, feminine experience.

In citing powerful, early longings for a bond with the maternal as these create the template upon which later desires will be erected, Rhys's insights parallel those under consideration among her psychoanalytic contemporaries. A discussion of their shifting sites of interest in examining erotic development might usefully begin by tracing the evolution of Freud's own thoughts on the subject. In his initial conception of the Oedipus complex, centered on male experience, Freud had described its "complete" form as expressive of the innate bisexuality of childhood. Specifying that a boy does not only desire his mother and feel conflicted about his father, Freud claimed that the child also experiences a "feminine attitude" toward his father suggestive of a close identification with his mother (*Ego* 33). This insight gave rise to an inevitable corollary, in Freud's subsequent claim that a girl's turn toward her father as a love object had been prepared for by an initial attachment to her mother ("Some Psychical" 254). Although his interest in Oedipal constructs was maintained, Freud now began to focus on another, distinct, and more preliminary stage of growth that was elaborated in his study "Female Sexuality" (1931) and the account, "Femininity," given in his *New Introductory Lectures on Psycho-Analysis* (1933). Here he proposed a stage of pre-Oedipal involvement that was particularly pertinent in the understanding of female psychology, as he rehearsed the thesis that a daughter's passionate attachment to her mother formed the first and actually most essential component of a girl's erotic life.

In "Female Sexuality," Freud proposed that a girl with a particularly strong attachment to her father probably would have been intensely involved with her mother in her earliest moments of experience; this passionate connection could dominate her for as much as the first four years, with the further suggestion of "the possibility that a number of women remain arrested in their original attachment to their mother and never achieve a true change-over towards men" (226). Even if the change to a new love object was effected, Freud presented it as modeled on the girl's first erotic phase and thereby having at its base her longing for her mother. Thus the significance of the early connection with the mother was stressed. As articulated in "Femininity," "Almost everything that we find later in her relation to her father was already present in this earlier attachment and has been transferred subsequently on to her father. In short, we get an impression that we cannot understand women unless we appreciate this phase of their pre-Oedipus attachment to their mother" (*New Introductory* 119). Freud's interest in the maternal foundations of female eroticism is provocative but notoriously incomplete;[3] however, in the location of desire at the earliest, oral stage of development, his work provides an explanatory frame for examining one of the first attributes of *Quartet* that makes symbolic impact: its insistent referencing of both eating and starvation.

The novel's recurrent imagery of feeders and fed-upon summons up states of satiation and potency, sufficiency and need, respectively. *Quartet* seems to offer a general commentary on the scanty resources and imbalance of privilege in European culture, post–World War I, as it locates individuals in their societal positions by the rhetoric of depletion and fullness. The disenfranchised are starving and parched: the Jewish artist Miss De Solla has eyes that betray a "hunger for the softness and warmth of life," while the hapless Stephan is "thin," "frail," and "shrunken" (9; 36; 133). By contrast, those in positions of societal power are almost bursting with satisfaction, as warders in Stephan's various sites of imprisonment, for example, have "fat" hands and "pear-shaped stomach[s]" (55; 35). But even more primitive conditions of repletion and desire are reflected in Rhys's presentation of her major characters. While the stuffed Heidler, as he appears in one of Marya's dreams, has connections with a patriarchal and particularly well-fed

God—" 'a pal of mine,' " the imaginary Heidler boasts, who " 'looks rather
like me, with cold eyes and fattish hands' " (161)—Marya herself
experiences an obsession that is primarily oral in character and that cannot
be satisfied: "arid, torturing, gigantic, possessing her as utterly as the longing for water possesses someone who is dying of thirst" (145).

The terrible need of the have-nots like Marya is rendered as that much
more desperate because of the utter inability of the haves to understand
their plight. Heidler expresses his annoyance with the stage of arrest that
Marya's orality suggests: " '[. . .] if I'm alone with you for five minutes,' "
he complains, " 'you smoke or you paint your mouth or you perform some
other monkey trick of the sort—instead of listening to me [. . .]' " (78). His
notation of Marya's compulsive involvement with her own mouth points to
her lack of success in concealing her primitive needs; as the narrative
comments, she is unable to keep her lips hidden from his view. The unsat-
ifiable quality of her hunger—her incapacity to attend to and digest that
which is proffered by those around her—is anticipated at novel's opening
in the song of a concertina outside playing "Yes, we have no bananas" (7).
The food, such as it is, that is offered to those in the text who hunger is not
the right food; they cannot find the satisfaction for which they long. The
song's lyric foreshadows, by sly allusion, the primal, monkey-like urges, the
urges of the uncivilized part of her psyche, that Heidler will notice in
Marya and find offensive. His reduction of her behavior to a "monkey
trick" additionally serves to diminish her human status, which is a conven-
ient line for him to adopt as he starts to bring their affair to a close. When
she notes the hostile turn that Hugh's feelings have taken, significantly
Marya's "lips trembled" (121). The uncontrollable movements of her
mouth are expressive of continuous and unsatisfied oral longing, as well as
helplessness; the trembling additionally substitutes for effectual speech on
her own behalf.

Her silence here as elsewhere in the text underscores the stunted nature
of Marya's development. Again Rhys invites an analysis of Marya that relies
on a model of primitive experience, with the work of Klein and Riviere,
whose investigations of early childhood return to but also emend the
insights of Freud, offering a protonarrative for the vision of infant longing
enacted within *Quartet*.[4] Like an intellectually unformed infant, Marya
expresses the frustration of the primal unconscious that does not yet have
access to verbalization; she is metaphorically the baby confronted by so
many confusing elements in her environment that she can hardly process
them, and the words she hears around her make no sense (see Klein, "Early"
188). The inarticulate quality of Marya's responses expresses her bewilder-
ment in the face of the complex machinations of other people, machinations

that she is powerless to oppose. Her pre-verbal condition is described by Klein's evocative phrase "memories in feelings" (*Envy* 5), stressing as it does a state in which one is held captive by ancient recollections within that are felt deeply, in painful states that often cannot find expression in words. Instead of verbalizing with Hugh, Marya reacts with a heavy, almost inert and primeval, posture, which he misreads as "savagery." Thus his vision of her in a moment of repose: "Her head had dropped backwards over the edge of the bed and from that angle her face seemed strange to him: the cheek-bones looked higher and more prominent, the nostrils wider, the lips thicker. [. . .] He whispered: 'Open your eyes, savage. Open your eyes, savage' " (131). In the attribution of Marya as "savage," Rhys registers a political comment on the relation of colonized foreigner to empowered colonizer. Her presentation of Heidler's condescension also locates the arrest that has occurred in Marya and its effect upon the outer world. She is positioned as a grotesque—disfigured, speechless, apparently ineffable— and as such she creates a revulsion in the "adult" or "civilized" for whom Hugh speaks, who do not and need not acknowledge their own primitive needs because these have receded as other forms of desire evolved.

That Marya's longing is not only infantile but also specifically contoured by conditions of feminine experience is apparent as her preoccupation with Lois melds into a vision of the tantalizing and frustrating maternal. Marya's conscious fantasies are expressive of the splitting process that Klein had discussed in theorizing that a baby imagines her mother (represented, as we have seen, by her breasts, the sources of connection with her) as divided up into good and bad objects. The baby who feels that the mother's "bad breast" is too depriving to meet her needs has a marked difficulty in building up a strong sense of a "good breast" as compensatory. This in turn gives rise to greed, which Klein described as "an impetuous and insatiable craving, exceeding what the subject needs and what the object is able and willing to give" (*Envy* 7); the frustrated infant develops the destructive wish to devour the entire contents of the mother's breast precisely because she has received too little of what she desired. In other words, the very enormity of the wish is testament to the degree of perceived deprivation that prompted it. As the baby envies that which she feels the breast is containing and yet withholding, she creates a phantasy of putting her own badness into the object; the breast in possession of what the baby needs arouses a rage for spoiling that which is possessed. Klein's argument also takes up the baby's response to a "good breast," the part of the mother that is experienced as nurturing, which may be held in the infant unconscious and aid in ego formation. But when the good breast is unseen or ineffectual, as it is for some infants and for Rhys's Marya, envy and the need for destruction reign supreme.

Marya's transformation of Lois into depriving maternal object, and the envy this object then arouses, is strongly figured in two passages remarkable for the aggressive hostility that they express. At her initial meeting with Lois, Marya produces a fantasy that suggests she has located a current object onto which she may transfer ancient feelings:

> A strong, dark woman, her body would be duskily solid like her face. There was something of the earth about her, something of the peasant. Her mouth was large and thick-lipped, but not insensitive, and she had an odd habit of wincing when Heidler spoke to her sharply. A tremor would screw up one side of her face so that for an instant she looked like a hurt animal. (12)

Marya perceives Lois's body as maternal, and not only maternal but historically so, as she evokes a mythic Mother Earth who serves as archetype for all mothers of all time. Also demonstrating her class snobbery in the suggestion of Lois's lowly, "peasant" status, Marya finds a way to debase or spoil this maternal figure. The focus on Lois's mouth suggests Marya's own obsession with orality, the thick lips troping a sensual connection for which Marya longs. The additional perception, almost as afterthought, of Lois as herself wounded and victimized bears witness to the fact that Marya has been projecting, making Lois over in the image that her deprivation requires. The other, more compassionate vision of Lois that peeks through at the end of the passage locates in her a fellow-sufferer, a woman also exploited, who might in some different context be someone for whom Marya could feel identification rather than disdain. Lois's own behavior in the course of the narrative, as she discourages comradeship and positions Marya as daughter-rival, destroys the possibility of any fruitful union between them; but Rhys establishes that the possibility does exist at the outset. Thus she is able to go onto show how envy, on the one hand, and competitiveness, on the other, thwart the development of loving bonds between women and stunt the psychic growth for the child, in this case Marya, that could ensue under better circumstances.

In a second telling passage, Marya speaks of Lois spitefully when recounting their relationship to Stephan: " 'She was always sneering. She has that sort of mouth. You don't know how often I've lain awake and longed . . . to smash her mouth so that she could never sneer again' " (180). The narrative itself relates Lois's actions in a somewhat cursory way that demonstrates her rivalrous feelings toward Marya but refrains from any thoroughgoing exploration of her motives.[5] Marya's obsession with Lois's mouth conveys much less about Lois than about herself, again underscoring her own oral preoccupations and linking the source of her desires with the compulsions that drive her, as evacuations of rage over an unsatisfactory "feed" at the bad breast.

Compounding Marya's deprivation is an incapacity to introject any goodness that may be available from outside and thereby enhance a sense of internal security. Unable to partake of goodness, in fear of losing inner security by falling apart, she develops excessive greed for the unattainable nurturance that would fill her up and assuage her terrors. As Klein's colleague Riviere noted, greed is a correlative of envy insofar as it typifies the person who believes that she has been robbed of her sources of safety by other people. If only she could reclaim what she feels those others have taken, the unimaginably much that has been stolen away, she feels she could be satiated as well as secure. Although the longing for more is doomed, by virtue of its impossibly huge proportions and also by the individual's incapacity to introject what she may in fact be offered, the elaborate belief structure at the heart of this all accomplishes a secondary aim. In such a person who cannot be satisfied, whose desires are unquenchable even as they are tied to dependent and loving emotions that feel imperiling, the keen disappointment she experiences also spurs aggression and the expression of hatred toward anyone who has let her down. As Riviere maintains, "[. . .] it throws the responsibility for feelings of poverty and worthlessness, especially for poverty in love and goodwill, on to other people; and it brings absolution of all guilt, greed or selfishness towards them, for *they* are the cause of one's being 'no good in the world' " ("Hate" 187).

Riviere's vision of strategies of denial reveals a tendency in this species of object relations theory that was discussed earlier in this study; that is, to place blame on the infant for an invariably heightened sense of deprivation that no one, even the most conscientious of objects, could heal. The withholding "bad breast" serves for both her and Klein primarily as a projection of the baby's own hatred that has been split off from its love, rather than as metaphor for an interplay between the infant's profound need and others' realistically limited capacities. I am unable to credit such a condemnatory view of infant phantasy. Nevertheless, the proposal that a baby experiencing its unsatisfiable desire would find a shadow of relief in viewing the other as selfish and denying does describe the circulatory of perception that is one of the more fascinating, and maddening, characteristics of all of Rhys's protagonists.

The link between one's own greed and fear of persecution from others is made apparent when, like other Rhys heroines, Marya projects her feelings onto numerous sites in the outer world. Expressive of the infant's preoccupation with biting into and devouring her first object, the novel's phantasies of introjection are, by virtue of their aggression, companioned by terror. A dread lest one's object exact revenge is an inevitable outcome of intense oral longings, as Rhys had persuasively documented in *Voyage in the Dark;* such dread follows inexorably in this narrative from Marya's voracious needs. In expelling destructive elements from within by projecting them outside herself, Marya is in turn terrified by other people. Like other Rhys novels, *Quartet* thus challenges any wish on the part of readers to distinguish between the protagonist's disfiguring perceptions of others and that which may be actually malevolent behavior by those in power, who routinely victimize the vulnerable. It is often impossible to determine where a heroine's victimization is depicted as "real" and where it functions as a disavowal of personal responsibility that the author fails to critique and even, at times, seems to excuse. But to read *Quartet* or almost any Rhys narrative is to come to know how the world takes the shape of one's own image; as one looks through the lenses of suspicion, those on the outside obligingly comply by producing deceitful and exploitative behavior. Life itself, within a Rhysian text, proves as hostile as the protagonist perceives it to be.

Marya experiences greed all around her; men on the boulevards make salacious advances and in fact men in general, as she thinks, stare with " 'hard, greedy eyes' " (72). Her conviction of persecution is highlighted in a thickly suggestive passage:

> She spent the foggy day in endless, aimless walking, for it seemed to her that if she moved quickly enough she would escape the fear that hunted her. It was a vague and shadowy fear of something cruel and stupid that had caught her and would never let her go. She had always known that it was there—hidden under the more or less pleasant surface of things. Always. Ever since she was a child.
>
> You could argue about hunger or cold or loneliness, but with that fear you couldn't argue. It went too deep. You were too mysteriously sure of its terror. You could only walk very fast and try to leave it behind you. (33)

Denying rage at those who have withheld from her, by displacing her anger onto others outside herself, Marya experiences a powerful terror that in turn has the effect of making her feel ever more distrustful of the malign forces that she believes to be everywhere. In the circular shape of this logic she cannot progress in her relationship with any others. Rhys offers the pointed insight that an infantile investment in a state of deprivation renders forward movement, and the development of more sophisticated modes of understanding, finally impossible.

The apparently triangulated nexus of conflict among Marya, Heidler, and Lois is necessarily bewildering to Marya, all the more so because of the very early stage of development at which she is stalled. To understand her responses to the mock-family romance in which she is enlisted, Klein's Oedipal model serves up a more apt description of Marya's plight with the Heidlers than does Freud's initial conception of the Oedipus complex. Unlike Freud, who had located the child's dawning awareness of the Oedipal configuration between the ages of four and six or thereabouts, Klein saw it as the final outcome of the oral stage; that is, as occurring during the early weaning period somewhere between the end of the first and the beginning of the baby's second year. Although this portrait of child development has not been congenial to later twentieth- and twenty-first-century psychology, and it does not serve well in understanding the version of Oedipal conflict that Rhys herself goes onto explore in *Good Morning, Midnight*, Klein's seemingly premature dating of Oedipal aware-ness provides a key to the particularities and peculiarities of Marya's perception of the Heidlers.

She is distinctly paranoid about their collusive behavior as a couple, failing at times to see them as distinct and viewing them as a conjoined and predatory authoritative figure. To one arrested at a moment of early devel-opment, Klein notes, it may indeed be possible to be blinded to the reality of the parents as separate beings and phantasize instead that they are com-bined into one monstrous and overpowering entity. In this rendition of infantile, Oedipal terror, the baby constructs "phantasies of the mother's breast and the mother containing the penis of the father, or the father con-taining the mother"—the two are one and the same (*Envy* 33). Klein here builds on Freud's claim that a girl directing her first love toward her mother is in fact directing it at a "*phallic* mother," that is, a mother believed to pos-sess the penis (*New Introductory* 126). If unable to resolve the ensuing tasks of the Oedipal period, a child may descend into an illness characterized in part by persecutory imagos of parent figures combined and conspiring against her.[6] Thus Marya experiences the Heidlers as "in some strange way a little alike," with Hugh beside Lois "like the same chord repeated in a lower key, sitting with his hands clasped in exactly the same posture as hers" (97–98). Their potency is contrasted with Marya's feeble sense of herself, and that this configuration seems inevitable further speaks to a perception of her dwarfed stature: they appear to her, "[o]f course," with the phrase indicating how her expectations have been fulfilled, as "inscrutable people, invulnerable people" whom she, as a "naïve sinner," cannot resist (101).

The ultimate demonstration of the Heidlers's combined parenthood comes when Marya writes to Hugh from the south of France to beg for enough money to return to Paris. After being informed by Lois's emissary, a Miss Nicholson who visits Marya in her exile, that Lois has read Marya's

" 'letter to them,' " Marya is acutely conscious of the invincibility of this husband–wife combination (159). Reflecting that Hugh has given her letter to Lois to read, she feels that she has been left naked, a subject of their joint mockery. She stands exposed, emotionally stripped bare, as her sexual usefulness comes to an end.

Marya's oxymoronic self-attribution "naïve sinner" suggests, in turn, the role she performs for the Heidlers in the game that they insist she play: she is to appear untouched even as she is already despoiled and ripe for further despoiling. Marya is often viewed as a child by all of those with whom she comes in contact, and most particularly and provocatively by the Heidlers once Stephan has left for prison and she is available to meet their needs. After Stephan has persuaded her to stay with them, she intuits the perverse ramifications that will ensue from her apparently child-like state as she comes upon a merry-go-round where she notes boys and girls "being hoisted on to the backs of the gaily painted wooden horses." They appear powerless, without volition, as they are placed in an arena that offers the enticements of play but will take them nowhere, just as Marya is about to be driven into a liaison with Heidler which, far from providing pleasure, will simply bring her round again to the point at which she began— forsaken and alone. The episode by the carousel continues with Marya observing a small child rush by "holding tightly on to the neck of her steed, her face tense and strained with delight" (57). The very apparent anxiety in her expression undercuts the exuberance that such a scene might be expected to arouse; the "delight" she seems to experience, like the "delight" Marya will be called upon to produce in Hugh's arms, is only to be had at the price of peace of mind and self-control. In responding to both Heidlers, Marya is often reminded of her own disempowered and child-like condition; in her state of exile in the south of France, her continuous drinking invokes hallucinations about the inescapable bind they have put her in: "She was trying to climb out of the blackness up an interminable ladder. She was very small, as small as a fly, yet so heavy, so weighted down that it was impossible to hoist herself to the next rung" (162). The perception that she cannot "hoist herself" recalls the merry-go-round children "being hoisted" by implacable forces larger than themselves.

Existing as a simulation of childhood to serve perverse needs in both Heidlers, Marya is exploited for her apparent innocence but it is important to both that this innocence be inauthentic. The imperative to mask sexual sophistication with the appearance of naïveté is communicated to Marya when they enlist her attentions in watching naked "girls" performing on a music-hall stage (86). After these dancers complete their number, a singer appears whose simplicity and genuinely child-like presence Marya finds enchanting. Lois, on the other hand, repeatedly announces her dissatisfaction, as if regretting the departure of the previous performers who, despite their youth, paraded an enticing decadence. It is important that Marya *seem* childish while actually proffering her body for others' use; the Heidlers are not accidentally selecting a married woman rather than a virgin for their manipulations. The very fact of Marya's already-experienced condition erotically combines with her innocence of manner to suggest for the Heidlers that the delights of being first to ravage an apparently unspoiled girl will deepen when there emerges, from beneath the surface, a sexually adept partner.

Marya colludes in the genital relations that are required of her, for the sake of self-preservation when at the mercy of powerful others and also as a means for redirecting unfulfilled oral needs. Her own genitality functions essentially as an escape from oral longings, and thus it is doomed to failure. As Klein posits, a premature turn toward genital satisfactions will be contaminated by unresolved oral urges, with the movement from an ungratifying mother to a father figure acting as a mode of avoidance and thus forestalling the possibility of a relationship with a man who is a peer. In those instances in which she is capable of seeing the Heidlers as distinct, Hugh appears to Marya not as a lover who can give her companionship and sexual satisfaction but rather in the guise of a father whose stature is overwhelming: "[. . .] he was very majestic and paternal in a dressing-gown, and it seemed natural that she should wait on him" at the outset of her stay at his flat (59), a description that at once establishes his authority and her subordinate positioning. He is always defined as large against her smallness, strong against her weakness. His ability to coerce her articulates the inequity of power between them, so much so that in his arms Marya becomes conscious of deep needs for a home and a safe resting place. At these moments her thoughts of him directly express a reversion back to the maternal sources of her longing, as her language feminizes and idealizes him: " 'How gentle he is. I was lost before I knew him. All my life before I knew him was like being lost on a cold, dark night' " (83). The life before she knew him, when she was chilled and alone, is the life of the infant seeking nurturance of the mother, and her ability to regress is precisely the aspect of Marya that makes her ripe for Heidler's manipulation of her. In the infantile posture of utmost vulnerability—sleep—Marya so appeals to Heidler that he cannot resist nocturnal visitations to her room to stare at and over her in her slumber. Marya's passivity and helplessness, which again reproduce the experiences of early childhood, are demonstrated when she awakens to a board creaking outside her room and notably cannot protect herself: "[. . .] during the few moments that passed from the time she heard the board creak to the time she saw Heidler and said, 'Oh, it's you then, it's you,' she was in a frenzy of senseless fright. Fright of a child shut up in a dark room. Fright of an animal caught in a trap" (89–90).

Heidler's ease with the dynamics of power is evident in the reassuring words he offers, with the tone and statement characteristic of parent to child: " 'What is it? What is it, then? [. . .] My darling! There, there, there!' " (90). Thus even as he violates her he claims, in his wooing, a paternal status. Rhys tips her hand to the familial interaction between them with a play on words: Marya's maiden name was Hughes, and Heidler's given name is Hugh (15; 9), an uncannily significant correspondence suggestive of their incestuous connection. She is, punningly, *Hugh's*. Here as elsewhere in her oeuvre Rhys demonstrates how a paternal figure may exploit the need of a young girl who is already suffering from maternal deprivation: stepping into the space that the missing mother has left behind, the surrogate father preys upon the child to service his own desires and so fortifies her experience of others in the world as betrayers and destroyers.

In responding to the abuses to which she is subjected, which in turn suggest the reproduction of much more ancient traumas in Marya's personal history, she becomes ever more unreadable both to other people and herself. Rhys illustrates thereby how internal states may be sealed-off but also preserved as a primitive strategy of self-containment. The phenomenon of sealing-off described by Frances Tustin in her recent study, "Autistic Encapsulation in Neurotic Patients," characterizes severely damaged individuals who must secure part of the personality. This part holds and hides some "original agony" of experience (118)—an early situation that felt so devastating that it must be simultaneously known and unknown. Tustin attributes the state of encapsulation to a premature awareness in the infant of its physical separateness from the nursing mother; the child is simply not yet prepared to experience the distinctness and integrity of her own body, and reacts defensively by creating a shell around a segment of her being. This thesis could usefully extend to any developmental history in which the infant was exposed to a non-nurturing environment at too early a stage to integrate the experience of isolation with experiences that had already been established, in a more positive way, between objects and self. The fundamental and intractable quality of Marya's grievance speaks to a preliminary sense of separation that has been kept islanded, unincorporated with and unmodified by later developments; as Tustin reasons, it is precisely because such trauma is islanded that an individual who has suffered as has Marya preserves the trauma intact. Since a damagingly early sense of separation precedes the baby's ability to verbalize, the experience is necessarily uncommunicable to others; but such individuals cannot even speak to themselves of this trauma, for, as Tustin puts it, "They are grieving about the loss of they know not what. They have an agonized sense of loss and brokenness that is unthinkable and inarticulate" (124). Marya's characteristically trembling lips shudder evidence of a trauma that happened to her in a time before words. Continually feeding this deeply buried, inner grievance about what has occurred, she demonstrates virtually unassailable sites of frustration in her incapacity to speak her experience.

Although her early life is never rendered explicitly, the narrative provides information that Marya's parents are dead and that her relatives are indifferent to her situation. The one instance Rhys provides of her contact with family, in the form of a letter from Marya's aunt, is marked by her aunt's reproaches that Marya has not written fully enough of her circumstances to warrant sympathy and by the repeated implication that she is not equipped to meet Marya's needs. The accusation that Marya has not adequately voiced her situation, and the summarily critical tone of the letter, are in direct and symbiotic relation to one another. Marya's inability to speak her deprivation corresponds to her sense of isolation from others, all others, who appear to her as unwilling to provide her with what she craves. The only name that Marya can give to her need is "love," which codes the unquenchable desire that she cannot understand. It speaks, rather, through her body, as

[. . .] this perpetual aching longing, this wound that bled persistently and very slowly. And the devouring hope. And the fear. That was the worst. The fear she lived with—that the little she had would be taken from her. Love was a terrible thing. You poisoned it and stabbed at it and knocked it down into the mud—well down—and it got up and staggered on, bleeding and muddy and awful. (122–23)

The image of a personified Love knocked "well down" suggests Marya's need to bury a part of her experience as far out of sight as possible; its power as a psychic presence is captured in the image of its enfeebled and bloodied but nevertheless insistent continuation.

As established throughout the text, Marya's perceptions both determine the world and are reinforced by the world's behavior toward her. The self-involvement of others provides the evidence that she unwittingly seeks of how little anyone will give her and how alone, ultimately, she must be. The narrative stresses ways in which Marya's needs are routinely unacknowledged as she serves as vehicle for the narcissism of each of the Heidlers as well as her own husband. None of them is capable of viewing her as autonomous; nor is she capable of asserting her many desires. Demonstrating how all three of the other major players in the action are devoid of empathy, most particularly with Marya, Rhys establishes varying patterns of narcissistic response. The range of Lois's thought, for instance, points to her impatience with emotions and her recourse—or retreat—to a kind of intellectual dilettantism: Lois "discussed Love, Childbirth (especially childbirth, for the subject fascinated her), Complexes, Paris, Men, Prostitution, and Sensitiveness, which she thought an unmitigated nuisance" (61). The randomness of her approach to issues of cardinal importance to Marya, with Men and Prostitution itemized as part of a laundry list of topics, suggests her inability to understand Marya's subjective experience and the depths of her distress. The reference to childbirth is particularly revealing, for where Marya occupies the site of infancy in her needs for maternal nurturing, Lois is simply "fascinated" with the issue, which implies a detached curiosity rather than any felt engagement.

Hugh is similarly unable to think through Marya's experience and relies on expressions of mawkish sentiment in the place of genuine concern. When her instincts alert her to the inherent dangers of the situation the Heidlers propose to her, when she deduces that they cannot grasp the extent of her dilemma over having been left alone by Stephan, her resistance encounters the force of an overbearing pseudo-concern. In attempting to express the plight of someone in a vulnerable position who is trying to ward off further pain, Marya is met by Hugh's reassurance that he does understand: " 'Oh, yes, I do, my dear. [. . .] Oh, yes, I do' " (83). The repetition of the statement points to its function as rhetoric of persuasion and the false note that it sounds. When their affair no longer suits him, he drops the avuncular façade and allows his self-centeredness to come to the fore, at which point he spits out hateful and demonizing words that implicitly disallow any feelings she may have. " 'I have a horror of you,' " he announces. " 'When I think of you I feel sick' "—this because Stephan has been released from jail and he refuses to "share" her with her husband; this despite his insistence that she share him with Lois during the course of their affair (148). His ensuing behavior demonstrates his need to remove her, as an inconvenience, from public view; and once he has cajoled her into leaving for the south of France, he is effectively done with her, as his silence in reaction to her pleading letters illustrates. Marya is from first to last the object of his desires; her own desires are never acknowledged and her welfare is irrelevant.[7]

Marya fares no better at the hands of her own husband. On first meeting Stephan, she is informed he sells pictures, art objects, " 'and other things' " (17), with the deliberate vagueness of the comment acting as statement about the duplicity that underlies his dealings. Stephan's exertions of power with Marya are all the more striking because he is presented elsewhere in the narrative as needy and child-like, enacting the desperate craving of early states of deprivation and actually quite vulnerable; he is in fact very much like his wife, helpless when held in the grip of forces larger than himself. Unable to tolerate his imprisonment, which he finds terrifying, he whines in a "little boy's voice" about his situation. This contrasts on the very next page with Lois's "masterful voice," as Marya thinks of it (44; 45). The juxtaposition of impotence and strength is recalled in the final moments of the novel, when Stephan's temporary companion, a prostitute, chooses to address him in a commanding tone as if he were her own small child. His life with Marya is characterized by their mutual child-likeness, a devil-may-care, live-for-today recklessness; when together they are continually drinking and eating delicacies, highlighting through their infantilism the ways in which they are unable to nourish themselves on substantial food. But his basic preoccupation with himself and only himself is figured in the image of Napoleon's sabre, an item he procured under surreptitious circumstances and with no apparent qualms. The sword also serves as phallic totem of Stephan's influence over Marya, as he places it "naked and astonishing on her bed" (20). Like a prop used in playacting adult maleness, it establishes that the oppressed imitate the strategies of their oppressors and that the hapless Stephan, who can wield power nowhere else, can at least masquerade in the presence of his wife. The trope is elaborated in the information provided in the sabre case that this was presented to Napoleon as " 'the hero of Aboukir—Mouhrad Bey' " and that its hilt is modeled "in the Oriental fashion" (21). These references to imperial conquest and the capitulation of the oppressed reinforce the portrait of Stephan as would-be colonizer; he has stolen the sword to mimic the role of a hero, rather than acting with any genuine heroism, and even his dominance of his wife is illusory, as it is vanquished by the much more powerful Heidler as soon as Stephan is out of reach in prison. It is in reclamation of an insecurely held ideal of masculinity that he lashes out against Marya in the final pages of the narrative, with an assertion of physical power followed by the spiteful comment of a bullying child: after hurling her aside, " '*Voilà pour toi*,' " he crows (185).

As elsewhere in Rhys's fiction, *Quartet* presents alternatives to the debasing varieties of heterosexual romance it offers, in visions of other kinds of erotic intimacy, but these alternatives appear, on closer inspection, as simply perverse variants of the dominating cultural ideology.[8] *Quartet* obsessively registers lesbian figures on the horizon of Marya's awareness, but the masculinity of the lesbians points repeatedly to their function as emissaries of the patriarchy. Miss Nicholson is parodically represented as "long-bodied, short-legged, neat, full of common sense, grit, pep and all the rest," and she has a stereotypically male look, with "very hairy legs through her thin silk stockings" (158). That she appears as ambassador for Lois merits further comment, since Lois herself is repeatedly described as having mannish characteristics: for instance, in her first meeting with Marya she speaks with "the voice of a well-educated young male" (10). Thus, like the enfeebled Stephan mimicking models of male prowess with a wife who is even weaker than he, these women who occupy positions of less power than the men in their world reproduce male strategies of oppression when confronting the hapless Marya.

In suggesting that the bond between Lois and Miss Nicholson is somehow antifeminine, Rhys symbolically figures one alternative to heterosexuality as not really an alternative at all, insofar as it imitates in repellent forms the moves of those who hold cultural power. She further indicts this variety of lesbian behavior by ascribing to it the qualities of voyeurism in her presentation of artists like Miss De Solla, who has a mannishly imposing physique and collects drawings of "Groups of women. Masses of flesh arranged to form intricate and absorbing patterns" (6). Her apparent detachment from sites of erotic interest and the posture of watching from afar contrast with Marya's painful, intimate involvements. Miss De Solla's reduction of women to "masses of flesh" acts to align lesbianism with a masculine ideology that objectifies women and must therefore be condemned, as part of Rhys's indictment of a phallocentric culture that preys upon the feminine. Marya is indeterminate regarding overtures from women, as evidenced when Lois "put out her hand caressingly. Marya thought how odd it was that she could never make up her mind whether she liked or intensely disliked Mrs Heidler's touch" (48). The seductiveness of masculinized lesbianism is suggested, but also its dangers: it is presented as one more form of erotic engagement in which the weak may be exploited to serve the needs of those with power.

In the final pages of the text, Rhys registers criticism of the persecutory machinations of a patriarchal system by returning to imagery of family life to reveal the ways in which intimate social organizations may serve larger societal aims. When Marya and Stephan take refuge from Parisian authorities in the flat of acquaintances, they find themselves in a macabre, dust-covered room in which enlarged photographs surround them—"mostly family groups"—that menacingly hang above them, looking down (173). The gigantic stature of the pictures points to both Marya's and Stephan's diminutive, child-like status, a condition that had once bound them to one another. Following her revelation of infidelity and his enraged response, however, she is suddenly confronted with the specter of an impending isolation; she is gripped by fear over the prospect of finding herself without him "in that sinister, dusty-smelling room with the enlarged photographs of young men in their Sunday-best smirking down at her" (185). The photos, which have notably changed from family groups to complacent young men, reinforce the correspondences among all of those who have been persecutory presences in Marya's life. The triangulated dynamics of the Heidler "family" in which she has been enlisted and then disavowed dissolve into a vision of masculine superiority and prowess; patriarchy dictates the terms of the triadic configuration that has made Marya its victim. In *Quartet* the family group acts as agent of masculine desire, placing women like Marya in debased positions and casting women like Lois in its own male image. Lois's own state of victimhood, which peeped through in Marya's earliest perceptions of her, comes to the fore when Marya is finally able to acknowledge Lois's misery and "her eyes of a well-trained domestic animal" and, in a surprisingly empathic gesture, entreats Hugh to be kind to his wife (107). His response—that there is no need to have concern over Lois—speaks to his characteristic moral insensitivity but also to his awareness that Lois is complicit in the arrangement that their marriage, predicated on his terms, demands.

Therefore the interest of this narrative moves outward, from suggesting the most primary and nuanced interactions between infant and her first objects to exposing the organized yet insidious social structures that support masculine power. In a surreally pastoral moment that acts as ironic comment on the inescapability of male oppression, Marya observes a man passing her hotel window herding a flock of goats. The melodies he plays on his pipe function "to keep his flock in order. They were wonderful goats, five of them, all black and white, and they crossed the street calmly, avoiding trams with dignity and skill. One behind the other and no jostling, like the perfect ladies that they were" (111). The evocation of Pan leading his group of feminine creatures with seductively alluring sounds, and their orderly procession behind him, suggests the triumph of the male and the compliance of the female. Even the goats' coloring, "all black and white," points up the ineradicable nature of the power structure: there are no grays here, no places where control may shift between the sexes. In this text it is always, predictably, men who lead and women who follow.

The novel's enactment of heterosexual dynamics underscores another, related concern with critiquing the powerful fantasies embedded in male narrative models. *Quartet* invites an intertextual reading that reveals the ideological chasm that had opened up between Rhys, as author gaining confidence in her own perceptions, and Ford, as her creative mentor. By the time that she wrote *Quartet* she had learned valuable lessons from this literary father but was poised to reexamine, from a differing vantage point, the amoral coding of such relationships as those Ford had described years earlier in *The Good Soldier*. Judith Kegan Gardiner documents that *Quartet* and *The Good Soldier* share both characterizations and plot, with a wife betraying her foreign-born husband by sleeping with an Englishman who seeks consolation from other women because his own wife's responses to him are frigid. But despite these parallels, Rhys's text operates as ironic comment on its predecessor, noting the selfish and predatory behavior of English "gentlemen" of the kind Ford intimately understood and implicitly defended ("Rhys Recalls" 69).[9] *Quartet* offers a discourse on the hegemony of social constructions of the self as these are inflected by gender inequities. In this regard it differs from *The Good Soldier*, which has a thematic preoccupation with the subterranean bonds and homoerotic identifications between men. In contrast, the exploration in *Quartet* of why and how a woman would allow herself to be inscribed within an exploitative, patriarchal code works back to expose primitive states of consciousness and locate the springs of a profound longing—a condition of eternal grievance—that places emphasis elsewhere, outside the boundaries of conventional concern as determined by a literary patriarchy.

In the successive titles given to this novel, Rhys offered tacit comment on the strategies adopted by the four participants involved in the tangle of relationships that the narrative records. The erotic passion is a ruse, as her initial choice, *Masquerade*, suggests: something is at stake here beyond the apparently familiar tale of cuckoldry and vengeance. Although she dropped *Masquerade* in favor of *Quartet*, Rhys was persuaded by her publisher to use the title *Postures* for the British edition of the novel (Emery 108; *Letters* 138). This was a decision she came to regret, and she reverted to *Quartet* for her publication in America; it is now published everywhere with this title. The intermediary *Postures*, however, does reflect the sense that the participants in the events Rhys describes are all posing in one way or another: the women adopting, initially, a falsely pragmatic attitude, the men disingenuously manufacturing, in their varying modes, displays of sentiment. The feelings that are masked, on the one hand, and imitated, on the other, speak to the ways in which the social structure, as Rhys observes it in this narrative, cannot support a candid demonstration of emotion and the articulation of anyone's genuine subjectivity.

Quartet seeks to explain why and how true selfhood cannot be expressed in the social engagements with which individuals are enmeshed from birth into adulthood. In its representation of those who oppose Marya's well-being, Rhys exposes the damage inflicted by a deficient maternal object, the horror aroused by conjoined parental imagos, the exploitation effected when women comply in adopting masculinized roles, and ultimately, the inexorable power wielded by a cultural insistence that the masculine be positioned as central, the feminine as marginal. The thematics that resonate through Rhys's novels are established here, in an extended narrative that marks the emergence of a distinctive and compelling psychological understanding. For the urgency that drives *Quartet* is an urgency to understand the elemental, conflictual, and overlapping determinants at work in the construction of the self, as well as the world that the self must inhabit.

5. *Good Morning, Midnight*: A Story of Soul Murder ⌇

The unconscious is that chapter of my history that is marked by a blank or occupied by a falsehood: it is the censored chapter. But the truth can be rediscovered; usually it has already been written down elsewhere.

—Jacques Lacan, "The Function and Field of Speech and Language in Psychoanalysis"

O f the four novels Rhys composed in the period between the wars, the last in the sequence, *Good Morning, Midnight* (1939), poses the most strenuous challenges to those who crave in an aesthetic encounter some form of epistemological certainty. Recurring confrontations with the disjointed, the symbolic, and the elliptical work to structure the reading experience of this novel. Rhys thereby exhorts her audience to share in the overdetermined chaos, and the attempts to exert control, of the protagonist Sasha Jensen's life. Inviting a close attentiveness to echoes of the unsaid, the narrative loops through time to place central importance on Oedipal dynamics even as multiple, related sites of trauma are located throughout the text.

The reader who recalls the close of *After Leaving Mr. Mackenzie*, with its suggestion of Julia's contemplated suicide by drowning, may well consider that the Sasha who has emerged from the river at the opening of *Good Morning, Midnight* is the same protagonist reinscribed: older here, and apparently more helpless and despairing. Her psychic difficulties show a shift in Rhys's focus from the dyadic motifs of the former narrative into a more distinctly triangulated series of conflicts and irresolutions. Thus Julia, the chronologically younger character, serves to delineate the complexities of infancy; Sasha, in turn, demonstrates that the triadic "family romance" with which an older child becomes involved may have effects that continue to resonate through middle age. Rhys's vision of Oedipal desire, guilt, and betrayal is linked to her perceptive understanding of the mother–daughter relation; as such it has a distinctively feminized cast, elaborating but also modifying male constructions of psychological development.

Unlike Rhys's previous heroines, Sasha has an apparent haplessness and weakness that are belied by the narrating strategy Rhys accords her. On the surface of the text, the reader "listens" as Sasha relates what appears to be a simple and depressingly familiar story: she is in her forties, down and out, and apparently without familial background; she now finds herself living in a seedy boarding house in Paris, and she cryptically remarks that she has been saved from drowning by someone, somehow, but no elucidation follows. Insofar as Sasha's livelihood has generally depended on her attractiveness to men, she now confronts the terrifying specter of aging and the possibility of a life of chronic destitution and aimlessness. Wandering through the streets of the city, she locates herself at bars just long enough to get herself drunk and then invariably returns to her room, where she doses herself with the barbiturate luminal and sleeps. Thus, as narrating voice, she recurrently offers herself to the reader in states of dreaming, drunkenness, or narcotized unconsciousness; and accordingly the novel produces hallucinatory and surreal, disorienting effects.

A reliance on the activities of the illogical unconscious accounts for some of the specific problems that the narrative poses for its audience. Many of the visions, dreams, and substance-induced passages are considerably more vivid than the sections of the text that chronicle events in Sasha's waking life. The primary process thinking that characterizes those moments revealing elements in her unconscious defeats conventional sense-making activities, and recalls Freud's assertion: "Dreams, as everyone knows, may be confused, unintelligible or positively nonsensical, what they say may contradict all that we know of reality, and we behave in them like insane people, since, so long as we are dreaming, we attribute objective reality to the contents of the dream" (*Outline* 165). The bizarre quality of Sasha's perceptions has the flavor of dream-work, as Freud defined this, in which elements of latent dream-thoughts are manipulated by the ego to surface in the manifest content of the dream, as it is subsequently remembered or reported.[1] Incongruities and distortions are the residue of this process of transformation.

In particular, Sasha as narrator deploys mechanisms that Freud frequently identified when discussing how features of the unconscious are recollected from a dream. She relies, specifically, on the techniques of condensation and displacement. Condensation, which Freud describes as a tendency to join apparent opposites into a single image (167), characterizes many of the grotesquely linked contraries that Sasha perceives.

Displacement, in which phenomena that have only the slightest resemblance to one another in waking life are used as substitutions for each other (Freud, *Outline* 168), operates in many of Sasha's fantastic visions. Thus, as in a dream, when a single event, person, or thing may act as figure for many different and often contradictory dream-thoughts, so too Sasha's dream-like narrative does not keep elements separated and distinct but often places them in close proximity to one another or allows them to stand in for each other even though they are usually opposed. "A dream, then," as Freud asserts, "is a psychosis [. . .]" (172); and the reader of *Good Morning, Midnight* who is unwilling or unable to tolerate this psychosis—who is intent on transforming the material into a linear sequence of coherent elements—will be unable to move through the labyrinths of this text.

The second half of the novel is increasingly surreal, for example in its introduction of the gigolo character, René, with whom Sasha forms a temporary bond. He seems to mirror Sasha, in his self-conscious deployment of sexuality to serve narcissistic and parasitic ends; and in her internal interpretations of him, the commentary blurs into a set of statements about herself. However, in its final chapters the narrative swings into a violent encounter between them that works to reestablish their difference; when he turns upon Sasha and attempts to rape her in her lodging-house room, the gigolo is abruptly transformed from someone who seems the same into a very distinct, and dangerous, other. The closing pages of the novel become even darker and more enigmatic although she successfully wards him off and sends him away. Rather than gathering herself together at this sign of her own strength, Sasha simply lies on her bed, waiting as if in a sequela for a second visitation. She ultimately presents the reader with a vision of herself in a corpse-like pose, prone and stiffening, as she prepares for an inevitable terror. In short order, with the relentless force of events within a nightmare, the inevitable does appear.

Because Sasha's narrative is incongruous and disjointed, it requires of its audience the suspension of disbelief and open willingness that (ideally) characterize an analyst's stance in relation to the free associations and dream reportage of her analysand. In working subtextually to identify the sources of Sasha Jensen's difficulties, the reader of *Good Morning, Midnight* must also listen closely, like an analyst, to the reverberations of its silence. I stress the analogy between reading and analysis because this novel, more than any other fiction that Rhys wrote, relies for its effects on interchanges between the narrator's and the reader's states of unconscious awareness. Despite the well-documented fallaciousness of relying on any concept of a "universal reader,"[2] Sasha's audience must have the capacity to adapt to this narrative in a mode that complements Sasha's style. Her insistence on what she does not know, as this chapter argues, urges the reader to experience rumblings from below the surface of her own consciousness if she is to find a way "in" to an alogical text. Thus the reader must refine her skills of empathy and attunement; like a skilled analyst, she must be receptive to traces, in this narration, of what Christopher Bollas, in his study *The Shadow of the Object*, lyrically terms "the unthought known" (4).

A striking feature of Rhys's narrative is its apparent dedication to broken phrases and lacunae, and the effects these aporia produce. *Good Morning, Midnight*, which frustrates at every turn any readerly desire for reasoned, intellectual understanding, concurrently heightens the reader's compulsion *to read* through teasing—and thereby provoking an engagement. This engagement, in turn, tests the reader's ability to locate, in the interstices of a discourse, the truths that must be heard.

To say this is also to make the claim that speech, when it is offered, always falls short. It is used as much to evade as it is to tell, a paradox that is stressed in Rhys's manipulation of the language of her text. If speech, as Jacques Lacan has asserted, is always predicated upon reply, it is as inauthentic as it is necessary. In his essay "The Function and Field of Speech and Language in Psychoanalysis," Lacan demonstrates the complications that beset all speakers who use language to fulfill a need for the other who is listening. Because Lacan sees any pre-verbal experience of fusion with another as being impossible, by virtue of our ontological status as creatures who are cast alone into a world, it is a poignant feature of our human lives that we quest, always, to experience connection. This becomes the *raison d'etre* for attempts to communicate in language. "Even if it communicates nothing," Lacan avers, "the discourse represents the existence of communication; even if it denies the evidence, it affirms that speech constitutes truth; even if it is intended to deceive, the discourse speculates on faith in testimony" (43). The communicative act, in effect, relies on the belief that it will achieve its goal against all odds.

And so with *Good Morning, Midnight* the reader/analyst is brought in to the narrator/analysand's stuttering attempts at communication. Words are the guarantors of an absence that is manifestly also present, and they trace a "nothingness" by seeking in the other, the auditor, an answering validation as a remedy for the speaker's sense of emptiness and need. Yet this immediately catches the speaker in a double-bind, for in constructing speech to be heard by that other, the speaker creates it to be *like* the other's; and thus it is an alienating form that is not a fulfillment of her own past or present subjectivity but (at best) a mere gesture toward what she may come to be. "I identify myself in language, but only by losing myself in it like an object," Lacan argues. "What is realized in my history is not the past definite of what was, since it is no more, or even the present perfect of what has been in what I am, but the future anterior of what I shall have been for what I am in the process of becoming" (86). Even as the speaker enters the world of language, her discourse is determined by the need for another. Ironically, however, the speaker simultaneously obliterates the auditor as an actual other who might fill her need because that listener is used only as a projection for her own wishes, rather than experienced in his own right. This underscores the inadequacy of human enterprises to communicate—and understand—through either oral or written discourse.

Sasha's narration speaks the preeminent dilemma of expression; the reader, like the analyst attuned to her analysand's verbal difficulty, is presented with multiple vaguenesses and insufficiencies in Sasha's language. As she narrates, Sasha demonstrates the tension that inheres in constructing the words to be read by another that thereby mark one's self-alienation. Sasha attempts to be like that other whose validation she seeks but is thus trapped because she is not genuinely voicing herself. Nevertheless, and paradoxically, it is in her apparent failures of communication that the potential triumphs lie. In the spaces between the words may emerge the Other of the text—Lacan's term for the personal unconscious, as opposed to that other person who is listening to one's articulations (Benvenuto and Kennedy 86–87). Where Sasha's discursive style seems marred by gaps in information, often at central moments in the unfolding of the narrative action, her audience is confronted with the same necessity that urges an analyst to listen closely to an analysand's silences, assuming ears "*in order not to hear*, in other words, in order to pick up what is to be heard" (Lacan, "Function" 45). Only then is it possible for Sasha's reader/analyst to begin feeling the pulsations of an unconscious that "speaks" of forces that have been repressed and yet fervently seek expression.

In the enigmas of Sasha's text, therefore, a hidden story leaves a trail; and that story is one of soul murder.[3] The exploiter of young Sasha, as the narrative obliquely suggests, was her father, who molested her and abused her trust. This story is complicated, however, by the fact that Sasha's elusive comments also imply her own guilt-laden, Oedipal desire for the father,[4] as well as a complex, conflicted relationship with her mother. Thus she has multiple reasons for attempting to suppress the trauma that has occurred; and yet the wounding does not disappear but instead manifests itself, repeatedly, through Rhys's use of grotesque and eerily unfamiliar, but also familiar, elements.

This aesthetic choice may invoke a *frisson* in the reader. The unique quality of the terror that Rhys summons is best described by turning to Freud's persuasive work "The Uncanny," in which he defines the specific feature of that horror that overcomes an individual who is confronted with the fragments of his life that he has attempted to forget. Positing that what has once been repressed is always, in some psychic space, remembered, Freud reinforces the point through a painstaking etymological investigation of the German terms for that which is concealed out of some necessity (*unheimlich*) and that which is pleasantly familiar (*heimlich*). The similarity of the words leads him to an account of the multiple meanings that they carry in popular speech as well as written discourse, as he discovers that the apparent opposites combine to describe the same sensation. This is the shivering awareness that one may feel when what was once known and then covered over nevertheless comes, unbidden yet relentless, to partial consciousness. In literature, the sense of the uncanny is most particularly exploited in the *doppelgänger* figure, as Freud notes in a detailed reading of E. T. A. Hoffman's story "The Sandman." This "double" character reinforces the notion of an eternal, inevitable return—he is not, like other figures in a narrative, the bearer of new experiences and possibilities—and thus he symbolically functions within a text as the emissary as stasis, of non-vitality; in short, of death. The *doppelgänger* serves as trope for the general tendency of the psyche toward "the constant recurrence of the same thing—the repetition of the same features or character-traits or vicissitudes, of the same crimes [. . .]" (Freud, "Uncanny" 234). As such, the "double" is frightening and inevitable.[5]

That Sasha is trying to escape unbidden specters from the past is evident in her insistent attempts to mute all of her perceptions through alcohol, drugs, and mindless wandering. At times, this struggle takes the form of a very deliberate suppression of material housed in the preconscious, as for instance when she enjoins herself to forget: she tells herself that she has "had enough of thinking, enough of remembering" (43), and thereby she illustrates that she is aware of a need to obliterate psychic phenomena. Because elements from the past continually threaten to emerge in full consciousness, many of her thoughts and statements are colored by her resistance to the something, somethings, someone, and someones that seem always ready to appear, spectrally, before her. The motive for her most strident denials slips out in the ellipses that suggest that she remembers, as one of perhaps many traumas, some violating sexual contact. When she comments that the gigolo who is her sometime-companion "laughs and puts his hand on my knee under my dress. I hate that. It reminds me of—Never mind. . . ." (179), Sasha is pushing hard to bury that which is already partially unearthed. And she is plagued by the unbidden that she cannot fully resist, so much so that she distrusts the language she must use to speak and reflect: "Every word I say has chains round its ankles; every thought I think is weighted with heavy weights. Since I was born, hasn't every word I've said, every thought I've thought, everything I've done, been tied up, weighted, chained?" she asks (106). The note of futility proves Freud's thesis—in the kingdom of the psyche, all is coextant; nothing is ever banished.

Sasha's continuous but only partially successful attempts at suppression leave her reader working hard to understand what Sasha is *willing* that she will not know. In a bar with a friend, as she begins to cry, she says, elusively, that her tears were caused by " 'something I remembered' "—with the "something" left dangling, unexplained either to her companion or to her reader. As she proceeds into the bathroom to observe herself in the mirror, her internal monologue continues in the same unclear vein. Thus Sasha's thought: "Saved, rescued, fished-up, half-drowned, out of the deep, dark river, dry clothes, hair shampooed and set. Nobody would know I had ever been in it. Except, of course, that there always remains something. Yes, there always remains something. . . ." (10). Again, the "something" is unexplored, although its force to remain at the edges of Sasha's consciousness is a conspicuous feature of this passage.

Sasha's resistances to the half-remembered warp her account of working as a salesgirl in Paris. In this narrative she recalls that she was given unintelligible instructions, by her English manager, to deliver a message to some other person in the building. Not knowing where she is to go, this younger Sasha of memory wanders through corridors that lead nowhere: "up stairs, past doors, along passages—all different, all exactly alike." Feeling that she must perform this "very urgent" action, she persists alone and finds before her only closed doors (26). The feeling of necessity that compels her from without is also a voice echoing within, urging her to confront in conscious, waking life the trauma she has suffered. All roads, however, lead to impasse, because she is committed to erecting walls and remaining outside the realm of full knowledge.

It is no coincidence that the manager who sends Sasha on the hopeless expedition is named "Mr. Blank," as the emptiness she encounters at every turn is created by the force of her suppressions that have almost, but not altogether, wiped clean the slate of her conscious memory. Her head is, as she says, "a blank"; she claims, with the strenuousness of one who must prove a point at all costs, that it is "vacant, neutral" (20; 19). For Sasha, time loses its function as process and is instead figured spatially, as a wasteland that can serve her in her attempts not to remember: "You fall into blackness," she muses, that may be "the past—or perhaps the future." Yet, on the other hand, "you know that there is no past, no future, there is only this blackness, changing faintly, slowly, but always the same" (172). And again: "[. . .] when I think 'tomorrow' there is a gap in my head, a blank—as if I were falling through emptiness. Tomorrow never comes" (159). The insistence on blankness—within her own mind, through the tunnels of the past and any prospect of days to come—signals the urgency of Sasha's need to suppress.

Sasha's spatializing of the temporal also informs the technical choice that Rhys makes in presenting a narrating protagonist who moves with apparent indiscrimination between past and present tenses. The effect is to provide the reader with the experience of blurred time; with a negation of time-as-process. Among the numerous examples of this fluid use of temporality, Sasha's following "recollection" of an episode with her husband Enno offers perhaps the most obvious instance. "What *happened* then? . . . Well, what *happens*?" she asks herself. The memory proceeds: "The room in the Brussels hotel—very hot. The bell of the cinema next door *ringing*. A long, narrow room with a long, narrow window and the bell of the cinema next door, sharp and meaningless." She concludes the reverie with the comment, "The bell of the cinema *kept* on *ringing* and every time it *rang* I *could feel* him *start*" (118; emphases added). The passage, enlisting at its beginning the past tense, moves immediately to the present. The sentence that follows omits any verb, to locate the scene without reference to its time of occurrence; and then the "ringing" cinema bell signals an unspecified temporal continuity. In the last statement cited here (for the sake of brevity, an intervening section is omitted), the past tense appears again, referencing in this way the past tense of Sasha's opening sentence. Thus a circular rather than linear patterning of time is inscribed in the text, a pattern that resists any forward movement for Sasha, who is kept safe from a progression toward understanding.

As distinct from her suppressions that appear, by virtue of the careful wording in which they are couched, to be intentional, Sasha engages in compulsions that seem undeliberated and reflexive, as if deriving from factors that have been repressed without her conscious knowledge. She is propelled by some need that she cannot explicate to repeat destructive experiences with men who are the eerie doubles of her father, and the father himself irresistibly appears when Sasha's consciousness is not on the alert; in other words, when she dreams. The illicit atmosphere that surrounds this father is a key feature of the dream she records at an early stage of the narrative, a dream that merits extended consideration because of the clues that it offers an alert reader.

As the dreaming Sasha finds herself in the tunnel of a London Underground, she sees that she is surrounded by placards printed in blood-red. Although this color and the tunnel could associate to the conventional metaphor of a birth canal, she seems instead to be subliminally producing a symbolic death route for herself. It is the repetitious quality of the interior that suggests that this locus is opposed to both movement and vitality. For example, the placards read "This Way to the Exhibition, This Way to the Exhibition," the reiteration of phrasing here stressing that something in her mind repeats and that she cannot in fact move beyond it into life. Although Sasha seeks to find her way out of the tunnel, she cannot; she is aggressively ushered further in by a man who points with a hand "made of steel." The dream culminates in violence:

> Now a little man, bearded, with a snub nose, dressed in a long white nightshirt, is talking earnestly to me. "I am your father," he says. "Remember that I am your father." But blood is streaming from a wound in his forehead. "Murder," he shouts, "murder, murder." Helplessly I watch the blood streaming. At last my voice tears itself loose from my chest. I too shout: "Murder, murder, help, help," and the sound fills the room. I wake up and a man in the street outside is singing the waltz from *Les Saltimbanques.* "C'est l'amour que flotte dans l'air à la ronde," he sings. (13)

Because the novel provides no clear biographical details about its protagonist's childhood, this dream is particularly salient. It may operate, like the dream of an analysand, as an oblique citation of an individual's most primitive experiences of aggression and sexuality; as contemporary analyst Leon Altman puts it, this "may constitute our sole means of reconstructing the past" (209). Sasha's dream calls for a careful interpretive reconstruction, with a primary focus on the figure who occupies a central position: the father in a night-shirt. The night-shirt conjures up the idea of the father of the night, the father of the bedroom; and his cry of murder, repeated by Sasha, echoes on several registers of meaning. Most explicitly, it demonstrates that he has been the victim of a homicide, which immediately begs the question: why? Because Sasha is present in the scene, and because she reproduces his cry, the narrative implicates her in his death; she may be the murderer of her father. Again, this leads to a query—to the "why?"—that can be answered in considering the placement of his wound as in fact a *dis*placement. As a substitution of damage in the lower body to damage up above, the gash in the father's head tropes a castration that is, in this case, fatal. At the same time, the cry of murder that is voiced by Sasha, as well, blurs the subject/object division between herself and her father and leads to the possibility that she is describing her own displaced wound. In this sense, the gushing blood from the forehead references her own genitals, violated and torn so brutally as to have killed her.

Thus, the loaded cry of "Murder" resounds with the horror experienced by an abused child whose trust has been destroyed by her father, even as it reverberates with the agony of a father who has been vengefully murdered, at least in phantasy, by his traumatized child. This dream, with its detailed and evocative presentation, contrasts starkly with Sasha's foggy experiences of everyday events. In this narrating choice, she resembles the analytic client who, as John Steiner notes, may feel that her own phantasied attacks on a bad object are more "real" than elements in her actual life. She may imagine that this hatred and desire for revenge that can be conjured up so powerfully are in effect strong enough to destroy the entire world (436), a phenomenon that is enacted in *Good Morning, Midnight* by Sasha's figurative destruction of "true" events when she renders them so hazily.

As the dream ends and Sasha hears music from "The Acrobats," Rhys punningly alludes to the mental gymnastics that have occurred in Sasha's unconscious as she has transformatively knotted elements of trauma into her manifest dream content. The singer's lyrics, "It's love that floats in the air all around," act as ironic comment on how love and trust may be abused, and also how a victim may become possessed by hatred because of the wounding she has suffered. Along these lines, the very title of the novel, *Good Morning, Midnight,* borrowed from a poem by Emily Dickinson, takes on a particular resonance. It refers darkly to the child awakened in the middle of the night—as if it were morning—to provide satisfaction of a parent's incestuous desire.

Such trauma, even as it is repressed from consciousness, nevertheless shapes all of Sasha's behavior in a pattern that Freud discusses in his late study, "The Return of the Repressed." Building on his treatment of the repetitive nature of the uncanny, he argues that experiences etched upon an individual in early childhood may not be consciously recollected but will invariably appear later, in the form of obsessive behaviors that rule the damaging choices one may make, in particular the selection of impossible loves. He locates the sources of these behaviors in powerful instinctual needs, libidinal and/or aggressive, that are so strong as to feel either overwhelming or destructive. In reaction, the ego attempts to ward off danger through its repressive activities, which damn up the instincts and allow for forgetting. Despite its reliance on a nineteenth-century thermodynamic model that is rarely employed by modern psychoanalysts, Freud's account does offer evidence that what is repressed is never gone. It will return and will again come knocking, as it were, insisting on expression. We observe this phenomenon when we discover the sources of symptoms, which offer modifications and distortions of that which has been repressed.

Sasha's most pronounced symptom is apparent in her penchant for viewing, and presenting, the men who populate her narrative as reincarnations of a predatory father. As such, they are products of her injured love as well as her rage, which is directed at multiple targets. They also serve to reinforce her victimized sense of herself as "an instrument, something to be made use of. . . ." by them all (58). In recollecting her marriage to the charming but vacillating Enno, she focuses on the many ways in which he betrayed her trust: in his dishonesty about money, in his promises and then failures to provide for her, in his dalliances with other women, in his verbal abusiveness, and, finally, in his unilateral decision to leave her. Enno's compelling ability to keep Sasha in a state of almost exquisite insecurity—wooing her one moment, ridiculing her the next—is figured in a scene that highlights his sadism. It begins as he pours her a glass of wine that he has sheltered " 'away from the sun.' " The passage continues with his casual comment that her " 'hands are so cold' " followed with an attribution, " 'My girl . . . .,' " that claims the primacy of his possession while reducing her to the status of a child. He then "draws the curtains" and finally, as Sasha recalls, "When he kissed my eyelids to wake me it was dark" (129). Intent on not providing any warmth, with his cooled wine and his closed drapes, this man who disrupts her sleep in the night with his kisses completes the portrait of Enno as a reflection of Sasha's father, whose love served his self-interest at the price of his daughter's welfare. Again the slippage of tense ("He *draws* . . . "; "he *kissed*") points up the irrelevance of time: in the irrationality of the unconscious, temporal sequence is erased. The man whom Sasha experiences in the scene with Enno is the same man she has experienced before, in an eternal pattern of return.

Both major and minor male characters appear to her as duplications of the one, most significant, man. As Sasha walks through the park, she sees someone "strutting like a cock" and wrapped up tightly in his clothes, the image of masculine propriety. Pushing a pram, he is the signifier of fatherhood. Then a second man appears, one who is almost identical to the first; he is accompanied by a little girl whom he teases and pursues until the two "disappear into the trees" (54). If the fathers are one and the same man, at different stages of corruption (with the suspiciously and pompously "correct" father devolving into the pursuer chasing his young daughter into darkness), it follows that the two children stand in for one child at different ages, first in infancy and then in toddlerhood. In this way the scene offers a reenactment of Sasha's early life experience, that of an utterly dependent baby who grew into a still-dependent and trusting daughter marked for victimization.

In a much more specific and vivid mode than she employs in her descriptions of these men, Sasha continually comments on the stranger who lives in a room next door to her. Once more, what she fantasizes has more presence for both her and her reader than any reality. She speculatively decides that he is a *commis voyageur*, a commercial traveler, although they have never spoken and she knows nothing about him. Her shorthand term for him, *commis*, bears the literal meaning of "the appointed, the entrusted." He is thereby positioned in her narration as a man to whom one gives one's trust. Sasha sees him, or elects to see him, as always wearing a dressing-gown, which is usually white. The night-shirted father of dark midnight encounters is invoked once more, with the whiteness of his gown combined with his status as "the entrusted" offering a bitterly ironic comment on his moral impurity and his betrayal of her. In rare instances that are, by virtue of their infrequency, all the more noteworthy, Sasha describes the *commis* in a blue dressing-gown dotted with black; the black-and-blue here suggests the father's bruising of Sasha's emotions and her body, as well as his own morally damaged condition. Sasha muses that he may be "a traveller in dressing-gowns" (32). In some sense, indeed, he is, for this *commis voyageur* carries the father of long ago into the present, his travels through time serving in the same way that time references serve the entire narrative: to muddle all distinctions between past and present.

The familiar and eerie quality of the man is suggested as Sasha uses death imagery to describe him; she sees him alternately as either ghostly or skeletal. Further, Sasha believes that he understands her in some mysterious way, for his sinister eyes reflect a look of "cringing, ingratiating, knowing," as if there is a special and terrible bond between them (14). Sasha elaborates on the sinister implications by fantasizing that he is "the priest of some obscene, half-understood religion" (35). In her allusion to religion, Sasha also invokes ritual, in this case ritual gone awry; the obscenity of the rite to which she refers points to some form of unclean, unholy action. Her phrasing works to suggest the repeated trauma of rape performed in a ritualistic manner by a father who seductively presents his behavior to the child as "special," as the expression of an almost magical tie between them. Sasha's demonizing of this *commis* reinforces Freud's thesis that the uncanny is often given the attributes of evil and other-worldly prowess, as this visitor from the distant past is transformed into a figure who seems malevolently omnipotent ("Uncanny" 243). In every instance in which Sasha refers to him, she depicts the *commis* as gravely threatening and, most notably, unavoidable.

His inevitable appearances throughout the plot presage the novel's fatalistic ending, for despite Sasha's successful resistance to the gigolo's would-be rape, in the final chapter of the text it seems that she has become suddenly helpless, lying stiffly and "as if [. . .] dead," waiting for a presence to enter the room (190). This posture characterizes incest victims, who often dissociate by rigidifying their bodies both in anticipation of and response to sexual violation (Weintraub). Here Sasha is certain even before opening her eyes that the presence in her room is to be the diabolic *commis*—and so it is, whether in reality or in a fantasy, as he appears before her dressed in his white dressing-gown and poised to take action. Sasha narrates: "I look straight into his eyes and despise another poor devil of a human being for the last time. For the last time. . . . " The novel concludes with the cryptic statement, "Then I put my arms round him and pull him down on to the bed, saying: 'Yes—yes—yes . . . .' " (190).

The passage suggests a resolution for Sasha, even as her communication to the reader breaks into stammering ellipses. The repetitive diction may sound, as it has elsewhere in this text, as the echo of an event that was repeated in the past as well as in the depth of Sasha's unconscious. Her open arms that are ready to embrace offer two mutually incompatible possibilities. In one interpretive frame, Sasha is here embracing the macabre visitor to plunge into the relief of death—a space devoid of pain. In an alternative reading, Sasha is accepting into consciousness, at last, the trauma that she has repressed; and perhaps she is even ready to forgive the abusive father, as her language modifies him from demon into "poor devil." To forgive him would be to forgive herself for any supposed complicity, and the three final words would then resound with the affirmation, finally, of a new life for her. But neither reading stands alone, and the tension between them is maintained after the covers of the novel are closed. In the last act of her discourse, Sasha as narrating voice provides her reader with the enticing frustration of an irresolvable "resolution"—in effect no resolution at all. The text thereby underscores Lacan's dictum: "[. . .] the function of language is not to inform but to evoke" ("Function" 86). For the reader of *Good Morning, Midnight*, Sasha's final words punctuate the entire experience of reading this novel: it is enigmatic, it is multilayered, and the narrator will not assist in providing any clear and singular "meaning."

As the preceding argument suggests, one factor that complicates resolution here is the conflicted, ambivalent attitude that a victim like Sasha may hold both to her attacker and herself. Deepening the profound trauma of child abuse is the accompanying but by no means less devastating trauma formed by the conviction, on the part of the victim, that she has in some way been complicit in the event or events; that she has in effect courted her molestation. This dynamic is starkly illustrated in Sasha's relationship with the gigolo whom she has gradually allowed to charm her and who then turns on her as a sexual attacker. As she resists, he becomes increasingly dangerous and at the same time increasingly accusatory: as he tells her, " 'Je te ferai mal [. . .] It's your fault' " (182). The fact that she has viewed this man as similar to herself from the time of their first meeting—both display themselves for others, in a calculating use of sexuality—suggests that she feels that they act and therefore are the same; if he can be "bad," this means that she can be "bad," as well. Her success in fending him off and even finding a way to expel him from her room could offer the optimistic possibility that Sasha is able to shed guilt in herself as she rejects the idea of her complicity.

Characteristically, the novel does not allow for such a simple and positive reading of this interaction. Shortly after René has gone, Sasha pleads aloud, into the empty room: " 'You must come back, you shall come back. I'll force you to come back. No, that's wrong . . . . I mean, please come back, I beg you to come back' " (188). She appears to be reestablishing her guilt, even insisting that it return to her. When the gigolo for whom she yearns dissolves into the *commis* entering her room through the door that she's left ajar, the time sequence becomes completely unhinged and Sasha's commentary on herself splits: "I am walking up and down the room. She has gone. I am alone." She follows with a second-person directive: "Put your coat on and go after him. It isn't too late, it isn't too late. For the last time, for the last time. . . ." (187). Even as she insists on her isolation, she produces two "Sashas" in an enactment of her confusion, while the repetition of phrasing suggests that this is not the final such experience but is rather a phenomenon that will occur again and again, that in fact she commands to happen again and again, forever.[6] Once more, all men blur into the same figure; and it is the father for whom this daughter pleads.

The novel points up the tragedy that may come of Oedipal desire. The wish for a loving intimacy with her father that is typically present in a young daughter's psychic inventory becomes a weapon that abusers can deploy against their victims: in effect, the father (or father-figure) says to the vulnerable female under his influence, "You were bad. It's your fault," which serves to halt her resistance and ward off the possibility of disclosure. The victim, in turn, complies with an image of herself as provocative conspirator in the crime (Rutter 78). She will accede to his vision of her, berating herself for engaging in the illicit behavior, if it is the only way that she can achieve closeness to the father she desires. Sasha summons her own Oedipal wishes in a memory that she leaves unclarified:

> I am in a little whitewashed room. The sun is hot outside. A man is standing with his back to me, whistling that tune and cleaning his shoes. I am wearing a black dress, very short, and heel-less slippers. My legs are bare. I am watching for the expression on the man's face when he turns around. Now he ill-treats me, now he betrays me. He often brings home other women and I have to wait on them, and I don't like that. But as long as he is alive and near me I am not unhappy. If he were to die I should kill myself. (176)

The short-skirted, bare-legged girl is a young, naïve Sasha; the possibility that the man will die suggests that he is an older, fatherly figure whose love she desperately craves.[7] His parading of other women before her heightens her jealousy and her resentment over sharing him with anyone else. This obscurely recollected scene traces a daughter's subordinate position to the parent she adores; and this is the precise emotion for which she will be held accountable and condemned as she is being exploited by her victimizer.

Although I have drawn on Freud's model to define the contours of a young daughter's love and her positioning in relation to her father, the Victorian milieu that informed Freud's investigation of the Oedipus complex in women led him to a theory of female psychosexual development that was sketchy at best and derived from male paradigms,[8] a limitation alluded to in Chapter 4 of this study and one that has been exhaustively criticized, for decades, by Freud's detractors of diverse camps. Because the Freudian framework is limiting, it benefits from both amplification and modification in light of subsequent studies of feminine identity. Most particularly, Freud's preliminary but unsustained investigation of the role of the mother, the third participant in the family triangle, is patently inadequate in any current study of the complexities of a girl's growth; and it falls short in any reading of *Good Morning, Midnight*, which presents the vicissitudes of mother–daughter relationships all the way through Sasha's narrative.

Maternal figures surface throughout the novel, usually coupled with daughters who are, as Sasha observes, disturbingly cruel and rejecting. Although Sasha offers no information about her own mother (who does not appear even in her dreams, unlike the father who has been repressed but nonetheless surfaces symbolically), her addiction to substances, and most notably alcohol, demonstrates her need to seek oral fulfillment and thereby gratify deep longings for maternal nurturance.[9] Further, her obsessive notation of mother–daughter pairs, and her revulsion at the daughters' treatment of the parents, suggests that her feelings toward her own mother are complicated by guilt and shame. While patriarchal renditions of how a daughter responds to her mother rely on assumptions that women relate to one another solely as competitors over male figures (thus the daughter vies with the mother for the father's affections), recent analyses, informed by feminist insight, have offered another model for understanding the specific Oedipal dilemmas faced by a girl as they are transversed by her relation with her mother. The new paradigm offers, in turn, an alternative to the Kleinian view that the Oedipus conflict appears as early as the first and second years of life; placing the developmental stage later, contemporary reconceptions of Oedipal life produce a portrait of the vexed conditions that the maturing young girl must face.[10]

Deanna Holtzman and Nancy Kulish, for example, persuasively demarcate how the intimate bonding of the maternal–child pair and the entry into adult sexuality operate as competing, coextant experiences in feminine development. This situation is better likened to the story of Persephone than to that of Oedipus if one recalls Persephone's deep attachment to her mother, Demeter; and that a lustful Hades stole her away and took her with him to another (under)world, with all the suggestions this carries of deep intimacies of the "lower," sexual variety. Demeter's success in ensuring that her daughter would return to live with her in the upper realm was curtailed by the proviso that Persephone spend only six months of the year in the sole care of her mother and forfeit the other six months to living with the sexually potent Hades. Thus, in contrast to the Freudian scenario of Oedipal rejection of the mother as the girl turns toward her father, the Persephone myth provides "a sexual triangle in which the girl creates a compromise solution by separating in time and space her relationship with a woman/mother and a man/father. She oscillates between two worlds [. . .]." The girl continually moves between the sphere of the close mother–daughter dyad and that of an enticingly dangerous sexuality with a man (initially represented by her father). The result is that the daughter may be caught on the horns of a dilemma, ambivalent about her connection with her mother and the need to separate from her to form an adult sexual life (Holtzman and Kulish 1416–20). In some instances, the pull in both directions is so strong as to be paralyzing, a situation that prevails for Rhys's Sasha as her life fails to progress in any direction.

The novel continually elicits mother–daughter twosomes as projections of Sasha's hostility and conflict. Her repeated citations of daughters who abuse their mothers reflect her own tortured wish to injure a maternal figure who may be registered, in the recesses of the unconscious, as one who keeps her from sexual satisfaction. The ambivalence of connection with and separation from the mother is highlighted in numerous scenes, some demonstrating the ways mother–daughter couples may be symbiotically intertwined. Sasha remembers, for instance, working as a guide for a mother and daughter who seemed to share a deep melancholy and an inability to conceive of any sort of joy or experience pleasure for more than the most fleeting moments. These moments occurred, significantly, when they ate together, stressing the symbolic nature of their need to feed each other and thus maintain interdependence. The pains of separation are evoked in another episode that Sasha recollects of watching an elderly Englishwoman and her daughter together in the shop where Sasha worked,

the balding mother defiantly and rather comically in quest of a hair ornament, the daughter utterly mortified by her behavior. As they left, this
daughter spit out a stream of rage about her mother's foolishness in exposing herself to the ridicule of everyone else in the shop, and patently refused
to accompany her mother again on any similar expeditions. The vehement
verbal attack points up the difficulty for this daughter of any identification
with, and attempt to detach from, her mother.

For the observer Sasha, the daughter's abuse of the mother presented
itself as a form of prolonged torture that she characterizes as "the slow
death, the bloodless killing that leaves no stain on your conscience. . . . "
(23). The very mention of a stained conscience bespeaks her own guilty
stain, as does the second-person singular pronoun that functions here, as
elsewhere in Rhys's fiction, to generalize an experience. Sasha's horror but
also comprehension of the daughter's motives demonstrates that they resonate with her own feelings. The mother is depicted as a ridiculous, aging
figure who was trying to maintain her physical allure at any cost, while the
daughter mocked the mother's efforts—in an attempt to clear the field,
possibly, for her own sexual display, but more tellingly in the sheer, wrenching effort to dissolve a connection.

Sasha notes that not only daughters but mothers, as well, may be abusive. She recalls an acquaintance who was terrified of the mother who had
physically assaulted her for any minor infraction, and even without the
excuse of an infraction. In the relationship as it has continued into the
daughter's adulthood, " '[. . .] all the time she says bad things to me,' "
Sasha's acquaintance reports. " 'She likes to make me cry. She hates me, my
mother. I have no one' " (134). The final statement most clearly articulates
the problem: a daughter who maintains dependency on her mother is
trapped because this is an enclosed state admitting of no other relation,
even when the closeness itself is damaging and sadistic to the daughter. The
need for a daughter to find her way to detachment is thus rendered all the
more forcibly.

The daughter's double-bind of relying on the mother who opposes her
nascent sexuality is brought closer to home in Sasha's memory of giving birth
to her own child at a lying-in house populated with other needy woman like
herself looked after by a brusque, authoritarian matron. The older woman
whom Sasha reinvokes is most significantly non-nurturing: as other women
cry out in pain, " 'Jesus, Jesus,' " or " 'Mother, Mother,' " the matron's
response is to refuse these women in labor even the relief of chloroform. The
implicit equation (via verbal proximity) of the mother with Christ suggests
her god-like power to give salvation, but here all help is offered with a clini-
cal coldness. Nevertheless, Sasha has a peculiar connection with this woman

and the words she speaks; she hears them as "a language that is no language. But I understand it. [. . .] her old, old language of words that are not words" (58). She suggests the possibility that a link between individuals can be located behind the linguistic barrier; the "language" to which she alludes is not Lacan's "language," defined as symbolic verbalization, but a connecting mode of a different order. Simultaneously, Sasha demonstrates the disappointing aspects of such a connection as she depicts the remoteness and emotional unavailability of the matron. Because the episode chiefly stresses how little a maternal figure will give to the vulnerable daughter (or daughters) in her care, any girl's exclusive reliance on the mother, or hope to return to the mother for sustenance, is again demonstrably self-defeating.

Sasha's experience of dependency after the birth of her own child proves even more destructive. The matron binds her in bandages to erase from her body all traces of the birthing process. With the suggestion that this matron/mother is invested in removing any marks of the woman/daughter's sexual life, Sasha creates a polarity. The mother and daughter may exist in one realm, together, but the adult woman with a sexual presence must live without her mother's sanction in another. The matron also binds Sasha's baby, who is, not incidentally, a boy; and he dies of unexplained causes shortly after this. The fact that it is a male child who perishes is highly significant, emphasizing that the daughter's sexuality and reproductive ability may only be had at a price and that the sheer will of a vengeful mother may serve to obliterate the masculine. In other words, a space of feminine connection is only available with the negation of the male.

For Sasha, this either/or situation, in which she must pledge absolute and singular fidelity to the mother's world or to the realm of a sexuality that is linked to men, presents irresolvable problems. The place of the mother is deeply compelling, for reasons that bring this argument full circle to Rhys's concern with language in this novel. Lacan's theoretical premises, as developed over several decades in his writing, provide useful if incomplete grounds for explicating Rhys's process. Proffering the thesis that the earliest infantile experiences occur in the realm of the Imaginary, Lacan envisions a pre-Oedipal baby who lives in a world of "images, conscious or unconscious, perceived or imagined" (Sheridan ix); and such images can take diverse forms, both terrifying and marvelous. Lacan's Imaginary (a place of mother and child) exists before language, with its own multifaceted complications, develops.

At this point Lacan reworks Freud's Oedipal material, with emphasis on the significant entry of the masculine into the child's awareness. When the child becomes aware of the presence of the father, he begins on the journey toward differentiation and self-identity. This is predicated, mournfully, on loss of the connection to the maternal and the nonlinguistic. The child learns that because he is separate from rather than symbiotically linked to others, he must come to rely on signals to attempt connection with them. Thus he enters Lacan's realm of the Symbolic, where language is at his disposal and yet is always, poignantly, a substitution for what is felt to be irrevocably absent ("Function" 65).

In grappling with the complex permutations of language use, Rhys offers a feminized rendition of development that both substantiates and qualifies Lacanian theory. In *Good Morning, Midnight*, she illustrates that for a daughter the maternal–infant connection may be firmly retained, not lost, and keep the developing girl's sexuality frozen. Yet if the adult daughter rejects the mother, this daughter will catch herself on the prongs of guilt, a guilt that will in its turn make movement into a more autonomously functioning mode difficult, if not impossible. Rhys's vision of the possibilities that are available to a young woman is uncompromising, with no possibility of some gray area between complete dedication to the maternal figure and absolute independence from her. This is because, in the world of *Good Morning, Midnight*, no mother is to be relied upon: she will find a way to keep the girl bound tightly to her and thereby forestall her daughter's full emergence into adulthood. The girl then confronts an apparently impossible choice between extreme states of being; a choice that cannot, as Rhys illustrates, be resolved.

Because Sasha perceives that any movement toward autonomy and sexual engagement is blocked by an oppressive mother, the narrative's implication that she suffered sexual abuse at the hands of her father takes on an even darker cast. Again, rather than being able to move between the worlds of the pre-Oedipal/maternal and the Oedipal/paternal by concurrently managing both paradigms of intimacy, Sasha is haunted by the uncanny vision of the father who abused her. Thus, she is unable to enlist any positive model of parental availability. Her hallucinatory narration brings together all of the elements of Sasha's dilemma in a phantasm that appears during one of her drunken stupors and sets the stage for the nightmare of events that will conclude the novel. The surreal vision offers a grotesque parody of monstrously commingled male and female elements:

All that is left in the world is an enormous machine, made of white steel. It has innumerable flexible arms, made of steel. Long, thin arms. At the end of each arm is an eye, the eyelashes stiff with mascara. When I look more closely I see that only some of the arms have these eyes—others have lights. The arms that carry the eyes and the arms that carry the lights are all extraordinarily flexible and very beautiful. But the grey sky, which is the background,

terrifies me. . . . And the arms wave to an accompaniment of music and of
song. Like this: "Hotcha—hotcha—hotcha. . . ." And I know the music; I
can sing the song. . . . (187)

Notably, the passage begins with an observation that nothing but this
overwhelming machine inhabits the world, pointing to how limited Sasha's
possibilities seem and, at the same time, how powerful they are. The steel
arm carries a reminder of the steel finger that reached into the tunnel of the
London Underground in Sasha's earlier nightmare of the murdered father;
now the finger of that dream-vision operates as a synecdoche foreshadow-
ing the steel arm of this later, drunken fantasy. In a Lacanian reading, the
arm would in turn be suggestive of the phallic presence of the father, his
authority, and the entry into the Symbolic realm: "The phallus," Lacan
asserts "is the privileged signifier of that mark in which the role of the logos
is joined with the advent of desire" ("Signification" 287)—the boy's desire,
that is, for an Imaginary that has been lost. Rhys, however, does not rely on
a phallocentric vision of all human experience; she complicates the scenario
as she places mascara-stiffened eyes at the ends of some of these arms. In
her condensation, several seemingly disparate possibilities are conflated in
a single image. The elongated, phallic arms are male, yet they are tipped
with feminine eyes; the made-up eyelashes are female, yet their stiffened
lashes evoke the phallic. The intertwining of these associations presents the
complications faced by a female protagonist, complications that are colored
by her relations to the feminine as well as the masculine.

Sasha is drawn to both worlds, but she can perceive only a stark contrast
between possibilities, as signified by her notation of how the beautiful
lights on some of these arms are backgrounded by a sinister, dark sky. That
she is torn between them is implicit in the suggestive, auditory imagery
with which the fantasy concludes. The nonverbal, nonsense noise of
" 'Hotcha—hotcha—hotcha' " that Sasha "knows" and can reproduce herself evokes the nonlinguistic space of the Imaginary, the realm of the maternal; it also, however, suggests the panting breath of sexual engagement
(figured throughout this narrative as heterosexual, as enacted between
woman and man). Taken as a whole, the passage tropes the central dilemmas that have been elaborated throughout the text while reminding readers of the inescapability of the repressed.

The situation is not altogether as bleak as it may seem. Although in
Sasha's actions and interactions no progress is effected, movement is evident
in her narrative art. Throughout her story, Sasha journeys between the world
of words (she writes/speaks her tale to an audience) and the spaces of silence
(her statements are disrupted by ellipses and a variety of other strategies of

omission). She thereby expresses both the realm of the father and the Symbolic, and the world of the mother and the Imaginary. Language, as has been established throughout my argument, functions in this novel as Sasha's medium for communicating with the reader/listener; the desire for an audience is born out of the sense of existential aloneness. Yet communication via language betrays one's authenticity: it is shaped in the figure of the other to enlist that other's attentiveness, and as such it confirms that one is never fully present as an autonomous self who can be held in full acceptance by another. That holding would take place in a nonlinguistic space of the maternal Imaginary, if and only if that space were idealized by the phantasizing infant. Sasha's narrative pauses and stammerings utter the phantasy: that communication can and will occur in some blissful, nonverbal mode. However, there is nothing ideal about the maternal place that the action in the novel conjures; it is, like the paternal realm, corrupt and destructive. Thus Sasha moves in narrative modes between language and nonlanguage; as narrator she negotiates both the Imaginary and the Symbolic in refusing to align herself with either realm.

Sasha Jensen is one of only two female characters in Rhys's oeuvre who has actually been a creative writer.[11] It is worth lingering here to explain why my account of the novel has insisted on some self-consciousness in her narration, in addition to the unconscious processes that are in play. Sasha knows what it feels like to make one's keep by one's art, and she has a solid sense of the compromises that must be effected in managing competing aesthetic and pragmatic demands. Retrospectively, she describes a period of working as ghost-writer of tales of the fabulous and exotic that were commissioned by a wealthy married couple. Sasha was to take each clichéd and highly romanticized plot envisioned by her patroness (" 'an allegory,' " the woman would add [166], without clarifying the allegorical purpose), and she was to write it up in the professional-author's style that neither employer could or would attain. Thus Sasha demonstrates how writers must sometimes submit themselves to prostitution, and yet her own example shows her attempts to maintain integrity despite the obvious constraints of producing art at the bidding of others. Her prose style remained her own, insofar as her patrons eventually registered complaints: the husband, in particular, as his wife reported to Sasha, " 'thinks it strange that you should write [. . .] in words of one syllable' " (167). As it is precisely such brevity that marks Sasha's technique throughout *Good Morning, Midnight*, this memory points to Sasha's self-awareness as an artist, both earlier in the commissioned stories and here in her later narrative. She also stresses the pangs accompanying her attempts to modify her talent to meet employers' demands; when the husband insisted that she produce a more florid style,

Sasha sardonically reflected: "Long words. Chiaroscuro? Translucent? . . . I bet he'd like cataclysmal action and centrifugal flux, but the point is how can I get them into a Persian garden?" (167). With this commentary on the absurdity of a Sybaritic narrative that is as overwrought as the sentiments it expresses, Sasha tacitly invites her reader to note the effective silences and restraint of *Good Morning, Midnight.*

When she encounters another artist in the Paris of her later years, Sasha is immediately drawn to his work. His paintings "curl up" and "don't want to go into the frames" when a friend attempts to display them for her perusal and possible purchase, stressing the artist's own resistance to proffering his work for money (99). Although it seems that he would have Sasha buy at least one painting, he reverses his position and wishes to give it to her for nothing when he finds that she cannot immediately produce cash. Even when she insists that they arrange to meet later that evening, when she will be able to pay him, he does not appear—although, notably, he does send his friend as emissary to collect the fee. The struggle between necessity and dignity that is illustrated in this episode underlines Sasha's own struggle. Revealingly, the painting that she does eventually purchase is of "an old Jew with a red nose, playing the banjo." Because she initially described the painter himself as a "Jew," as well (100; 91), artists are grouped together as wounded outsiders to the dominant culture. The exile who produces his art (here, the music of the banjo) no matter what the emotional toll (the red nose signifying weeping, or inebriation, or both) is the socially outcast artist: Sasha herself.

To return, then, to the ending of the text, her " 'Yes—yes—yes,' " may resonate as Rhys's ironic comment on the non-affirmation that artists who also are women will suffer. Echoing another writer's work, Sasha's words reproduce the ending of Joyce's *Ulysses*, as a number of readers have observed.[12] But Sasha's ambiguous cry sounds in juxtaposition with the lusty affirmations of Molly Bloom, the archetypal earthy woman as imagined by a male Modernist. It was Joyce, not Rhys, whose work was championed in the predominantly masculine intellectual circles of the day; he could imagine an unconflicted, satiated feminine experience, whereas she could not. And yet it is a testimony to the power of Rhys's narrative that the text of *Good Morning, Midnight*, in all of the demands it places on its reader, can evoke the sublime.

This sublimity is integral to a definition of art itself. As Christopher Bollas postulates, art makes its claim on us because its notes reverberate within a scale that deeply pleases. These notes echo "a pre-verbal ego memory," eliciting in the audience a feeling of "uncanny fusion with the object"; in effect, the blissful side of the state of merger phantasied in earliest infancy (*Shadow* 16). The aesthetic production is experienced as a means, not an end, for its respondent: at its most efficacious, it offers the tools for self-development. Art is necessary to its audience because it subliminally conjures up primitive phantasies of complete union as well as transformation; the quest for self-transcendence propels one's search for meaning in response to aesthetic experience. Although it remains unclear in this novel whether or not art carries the same freight for its creator—Sasha Jensen's narrative tirelessly records the complications that beset those attempting to communicate in any mode—Rhys will go on to affirm, in *Wide Sargasso Sea*, the transformative power of art for the artist herself.

As she stood behind the author whom she had authored, Rhys produced a particularly noteworthy achievement in concluding *Good Morning, Midnight*. When she completed this text, she did not publish another novel for almost three decades. Her silence, like Sasha's silence, reverberates with possibilities; her personal problems in this period have been well documented,[13] but not the fact that she had finally interwoven the issues of parental betrayal, sexual abuse, and infantile guilt on the pages as well as in the spaces of a single narrative. Having comprehensively tackled the obsessions with which she had grappled, but only in part, in her three preceding novels, Rhys as developing writer had ended one stage of creative effort. Thus, in time, she could direct her energies toward a central problematic of art: that is, whether or not it is finally possible to achieve an authentic and original aesthetic.

6. *Wide Sargasso Sea*: The Transforming Vision ⤳

In [. . .] highly specialized conditions the individual can come together and exist as a unit, not as a defence against anxiety but as an expression of I AM, I am alive, I am myself. [. . .] From this position everything is creative.

—D. W. Winnicott, *Playing and Reality*

W*ide Sargasso Sea*, over which Rhys labored for many years, demonstrates her complex management of sometimes competing demands. In responding to Charlotte Brontë's 1847 novel *Jane Eyre*, Rhys found that she must make her way to a delicate balance of homage and critique as she revisited the work of her literary foremother and thereby traversed once again the realm of pre-Oedipal relations. The developmental journey of Rhys's protagonist Antoinette speaks to the multiple challenges that this novel addresses: offering ambiguous and mutually incompatible interpretive possibilities, Antoinette's story suggests her abject state of enthrallment to a maternal presence or, alternatively, her capacity for an empowered self-assertion. On the other hand, the discerning reconfiguration of elements of Brontë's text proves, for Rhys as author, to be ultimately affirmative, evidencing her agile negotiations on the terrain of both connection and difference.

Brontë had sensitively understood the plight of disenfranchised women and yet, as a Victorian English citizen, she had been unable to see her own Creole character, the first Mrs. Rochester, as fully human. Rhys, in contrast, created interconnected but increasingly complicating perspectives on the story of Bertha Mason. Because she opened up space for exploring the overdetermining strands of her protagonist's subjectivity, readers following the first-person narrative of Part One of *Wide Sargasso Sea* move within the Creole's mind and come to understand the elements that drive her to her apparent madness. Rhys additionally recalibrated the voice of Brontë's hero, Rochester, working from his representation in the original narrative by having him display himself as both self-pitying and self-deluding, but withholding much of the sympathy with which his story is presented in the earlier text. He appears within Rhys's novel as a man invested in a colonizing role that demands he renounce his own frailty to assert moral superiority and physical prowess over his foreign-born wife, which enacts the most chilling aspects of Brontë's characterization and then subjects these to a harsh interrogation. Rhys's choice of how to embody Rochester assured her triumph within an Oedipal arena over the oppressive paternity that he speaks, even if her heroine Antoinette is betrayed by the inexorability of his law.

Although she never found the process of composition easy, Rhys had a particularly difficult time working on the manuscript of *Wide Sargasso Sea*. Letters dating as far back as 1946, to her friend Peggy Kirkaldy, show that she was already struggling with something that she felt compelled to do and yet also felt she could not manage. In an account to Kirkaldy from 1946, she lamented her latest book of stories, which she felt were no good, and then added, "It's all right of course—if anyone believed the truth, that the novel I have half finished is a very different matter. [. . .] I debate the ethics of the thing very seriously. *Must* I finish the novel? 'not for fear of hell or hope of heaven but for love' as the Catholics say." Somewhat ruefully, she answered her own question: "Yes—obviously. [. . .] I'll try some tomorrow or other—" The quality of the love that Rhys was trying to express had, as yet, no name and was, at this stage, unclear about its source. In another letter, this written three years later, she cried out, "Oh *God* if I could finish it before I peg out or really turn into some fungus or other!" She added, "I think of calling it '*The first Mrs Rochester*' with profound apologies to Charlotte Brontë and a deep curtsey too. [. . .] It really haunts me that I can't finish it though" (*Letters* 44; 50). Her agitated response to Brontë's work as it comes, at this stage, into view, underscores the deep affiliation that was preventing her from finding her own voice. Her wry vision of herself as "some fungus" reveals her sense of herself as diminished to the level of mere parasite feeding from a mother-host.

Letters written over a decade later, as Rhys continued to work on revising the manuscript, point to her ongoing difficulty mediating between Brontë's vision and her own. She worried that her novel would join the ranks of "just another adaptation of 'Jane Eyre.' There have been umpteen thousand and sixty already"; and she suspected that her feeling of being "too anxious" as well as her tendency to "panic" were inhibiting her work (*Letters* 159; 160; 163). Her process of composition, over so many years, suggests that she was, at times, wrenchingly passionate about this particular manuscript. Her feelings were compounded of reverence for and intimidation by Brontë and unease over new technical problems she had set herself in dividing the narrative among several first-person voices. Even as late as 1959, after thirteen years of documenting her work on the book, her letters reveal that she was unable to see what she had achieved or that its specificity of milieu and her own personal obsessions would find reception by an audience and deeply resonate, in a way her earlier novels had not, in the culture at large.

The problems that Rhys initially faced were daunting, but it is clear why she would be drawn to a figure like Bertha Mason. She conceived of Brontë's marginalized character as belonging in a line of succession from her own earlier protagonists, positioning the figure she renamed Antoinette as last in an inevitable sequence. By placing her heroine within the frame of sensibility that enclosed her own earlier narratives, she thereby took a first important step in proclaiming her own vision and challenging Brontë's privilege as literary ancestor. The protagonist of *Wide Sargasso Sea*, like Anna Morgan, Julia Martin, Marya Zelli, and Sasha Jansen, is a subject colonized by others' desires; and what she resists, as do they, is the life-denying hypocrisy of social forms. Like Rhys's earlier protagonists, Antoinette also lives within a paranoid-schizoid awareness: her objects are either good or bad and ambivalence is unthinkable, either toward others or herself.

There are several ways in which Rhys went on to free herself more fully by making alterations to the text of *Jane Eyre*. She revised Brontë's time frame, changing it to a year following the slaves' Emancipation as opposed to the decade of 1798–1808 as described in *Jane Eyre* (Raiskin 31). This allowed Rhys to place emphasis on the chaos that followed Emancipation, a chaos that leaves her protagonist even more isolated than she might have been because her family is now without money and hated by those who were former slaves to plantation owners like Cosway. Further, as Peter Hulme notes in his chronicling of Rhys's revision of the data in Brontë's text, her re-dating of events enabled her to bring her own family history into the story, with 1825, the birthday of one of Rhys's aunts, paralleling the probable birthday of Antoinette. Her own personal investment in the story is very clear, underscoring the urgency of her need to address the problematics of the task she had set herself in this final novel. Rhys reworked Bertha's family structure as given in *Jane Eyre*, so that Antoinette of *Wide Sargasso Sea* is not related by blood to Mason, and her actual father is the morally suspect Cosway. This paved the way for creating in Cosway a vehicle for identifying problems of the slave-owning class, allowing Rhys to conceive of other relatives or assumed relatives whose "color" underscores issues of interracial relations within the West Indies and who thus complicate Brontë's easy description of "Creole" culture (Hulme 25–26). Most particularly, it was the invention of the character Daniel, himself a

However, in the split-apart world that this novel conjures, cold hatred always mediates against warm affection; and the other, frigid, mother, Annette, inhibits the course of Antoinette's growth. In one representative incident that Antoinette's narrative will recollect, the tantalizing and ultimately chilling quality of this bad mother is evoked: grasping Antoinette and briefly stimulating the hope that the mother who had always been so withdrawn would give her the gift of a sustained embrace, Annette then pushed her out of her arms as she searched for her other, favored, child, Pierre—the child who had already died. Rhys thereby establishes, as she has in earlier narratives, that her protagonist's relationship with her primary caregiver is determined not only by the daughter's projections but by actually rejecting behavior to which she is subjected.

From the outset Antoinette is under the sway of threatening, unloving objects, with many early experiences foretelling, with heavy inevitability, the life that is to come. In an initial, revealing episode, she faces betrayal by her friend Tia at the bathing pool, when she steals Antoinette's dress and leaves her own dirty one that Antoinette must wear for her return home. After she is then shamed by her mother for her slovenly appearance and retreats to bed, Antoinette has a terrifying nightmare of being with someone who despises her: "I dreamed that I was walking in the forest. Not alone. Someone who hated me was with me, out of sight. I could hear heavy footsteps coming closer and though I struggled and screamed I could not move. I woke crying. The covering sheet was on the floor and my mother was looking down at me" (15–16).[2] While the nightmare predicts her victimization by her husband, Rochester, the day-residue that seeds it is the distaste felt toward her by her mother, Annette, the presence who stands above her as the powerful, archetypal object.

Rhys creates a mother in Annette who is genuinely incapable of offering love to her daughter, who repeatedly fails to mirror Antoinette's attitudes and behavior, and who thereby demonstrates how a child's sense of her own reality may be steadily eroded. Antoinette's life is filled with malign possibilities that she cannot manage because this mother gives her nothing that would support her in the face of danger. In the cold domestic scene that Annette generates, Antoinette's spontaneous and needy articulations are all but negated by a narcissistically preoccupied parent who cannot see past herself into the eyes of her daughter (Scharfman 100). Christopher Bollas describes the child who exists within such a cold familial milieu, who, like Antoinette, must learn to abandon

> belief in love and in loving. Instead, ordinary hate establishes itself as the fundamental truth of life. The child experiences the parents' refusal of love

and their constant aloofness or harshness as hate, and he or she in turn finds his or her most intense private cathexis of the parents to be imbued with hate. [. . .] To be cathected by a parent, even to the point of becoming a reliable negative self-object for him or her, is a primary aim for children, as their true dread is that of being unnoticed and left for dead. (*Shadow* 129–30)

Because Annette as actual person disappears from Antoinette's world at a fairly early point in the narrative and then dies of unexplained causes, never spoken of by the relatives who remain, the hatred that the daughter might be expected to level at the abandoning parent is held within, as a paradigmatic way of object relating. In time, it will be the paradigm to which Antoinette returns when her attempts at loving gestures toward her husband are met with the same coldness as her mother's. Antoinette will choose the demonstration of hate, and the inspiring of hate, as her only avenue for being acknowledged by the husband/parent to whom she is emotionally bound.

She has many models for the presentation of hate. She registers the envy of those on the island from whom her family is separated due to color and class: the Jamaican women who disdain her mother for her beauty; the negroes who insist that the Cosways are unwanted "white cockroaches" (13). Although Mason accuses Annette of conjuring a hostility that has no reality base in the black population, she is accurately reporting on the atmosphere in which they are perilously living, as is apparent when Coulibri is burned down. Synecdochally figuring the attitude of the mob, Antoinette's young friend Tia hurls a rock at her as the crowd's hysteria mounts. Tia and the others' enraged responses to the indifference with which they are treated by the remaining colonial families anticipates the fury that Antoinette, in turn, will level at those who turn away from her as if she is not there: first her mother as held within her internal object world, and later her husband as externally persecuting figure. In Tia and Antoinette's mirrored responses to the fire, Rhys creates a portrait of what her heroine will be. Antoinette reports, "I looked at her and I saw her face crumple up as she began to cry. We stared at each other, blood on my face, tears on hers. It was as if I saw myself. Like in a looking-glass" (27). The text thus throws into relief the state of the wounded child who has become an assailant in reaction to repeated experiences of neglect and loss.

The alternative to the powerful phenomenon of rage, which is, in its intensity, life-affirming, is a condition of torpor and near-death. It is to this that members of the black population offer resistance and to which the former slaveowners succumb, for colonial Jamaica is in ruins, the garden at Coulibri "overgrown" and smelling "of dead flowers" (11). As Antoinette observes, people may be sapped of their vitality; literal, physical expiration is not the only death one can endure. Although her brother Pierre, for instance, died following the fire, she believes that he actually perished much earlier. Later she will tell Rochester, " '[t]here are always two deaths, the real one and the one people know about' "; and he will confirm this in his narrative, when he describes his perception of their lovemaking as a sort of dying, playing on the conventional association between orgasm and death and claiming it as "my way [of dying], not [. . .] hers" (77; 55). To die is to accept lies rather than truth—holding onto the past (as do the former slaveowners), renouncing agency (as Pierre was compelled to do), pretending feelings one does not have (as does Rochester in his conquest of Antoinette).

The novel insists on the widespread tendency toward suppression that will doom the person intent on feeling her own truth—someone like Antoinette—to a life outside the socially sanctioned codes of behavior. Her mother is the first to instruct her not to ask questions, and thereby she reveals her own strategies of evasion: " 'Why do you pester and bother me about all these things that happened long ago?' " she complains. " 'Christophine stayed with me because she wanted to stay. She had her own very good reasons you may be sure. I dare say we would have died if she'd turned against us and that would have been a better fate. To die and be forgotten and at peace. Not to know that one is abandoned, lied about, helpless' " (12). Annette moves, here, from a dismissive and then vague response to a self-pitying wish for death in the face of a reality she cannot bear. Ironically, in cutting off access to full knowledge, for her daughter and presumably also for herself, she already ensures a form of death: a death of the spirit, of spontaneity, of genuine responsiveness to the events of one's life.

As against such counsels of insincerity, Antoinette unharnesses deep aspects of herself in the early days of her marriage. Her sexual expression affirms her liveliness—this in spite of the unloving maternal object she carries within and in the face of an increasingly hostile object in her husband. When she finds that her passion for Rochester will become the excuse for his detachment from her rather than his emotional commitment, the wound cuts deep because of her experience of a mother who withheld love and drew further and further away from her. Correspondingly, Antoinette's expression of rage will be all the more dramatic because it speaks of her deepest need and disappointment, as well as the determination to be heard rather than negated, even if heard only by someone who hates rather than loves her. The novel asserts that not all experiences of aggression need be negative, despite cultural edicts that they be seen in such a light. As Bollas elaborates on notions of aggression within infants, noting the forms of "loving hate" in which the individual who is terrified of the other(s)' indifference gives up on the quest for love but determines to express and receive hatred, he identifies a substitutive emotion that has the virtue of being fully engaged rather than tepid or nonexistent (*Shadow* 118) and that describes the tenor of Antoinette's response to her chilly husband. It is the hot, vivid quality of Antoinette's rage that Rochester cannot face and tries to contain by labeling it as madness. His confinement of her in the attic of Thornfield Hall, in Part Three of the text, thus becomes a metaphor for his attempt to confine her ego-expressive mood so that he will never have to encounter a genuine aspect of who she is.

The warmth of Antoinette's anger countermands not only her husband's coldness but the cold that threatens her within. Demonstrating how the failures of early existence are recreated in the internal world, Antoinette must contend with a loveless environment inside her in which Annette's icy mode of response to her child is redramatized.[3] The experience of this environment is so fundamental that Antoinette senses it somatically, reflecting Bollas's contention that at a basic level we do not cogitate about who we are but rather *feel* an awareness of some state of our being. After her abandonment at the bathing pool by Tia, which replicates her more pervasive sense of abandonment by Annette, Antoinette is "shivering cold" and "the sun couldn't warm me" (14). The coldness inside her reproduces the chill of her others, a chill she both resists and tries to alleviate in her instances of hot aggression and a corresponding attraction to fire; she fights against pressures within that are as cold as death. The frigid "unthought known" that she experiences is one aspect of her primitively experiencing self (see *Shadow* 72), contrasting with a more proactive expression of her subjectivity that shapes itself around moments of heat and flame.

Rather than articulating any coherently elaborated idea of what drives her, Antoinette exists most genuinely through the cadences of her moods, which are, as Bollas argues, the most telling traces of the unthought known. The moods that we think of as representing someone's character most characteristically (as it were) are reflections of a retention process in which an experience that may literally be over is nevertheless still preserved, generally because a developmental process met with interference and thus the child's relation with his inadequate other(s) is being stored inside. This interior relationship may constitute an individual's most profoundly experienced state of being; if the person has been subject to trauma, as has Antoinette, that being may be fixed at an early stage of interaction with the other(s), who are kept alive, in all their inadequacy, while the individual's development is stalled.

Such an arrest may occur, as Bollas claims, because caretakers simply cannot or will not mirror and respond to a child's experience as it is presented to them: "[. . .] this aspect of the child's self may be left in isolation: apparently unnoticed, uncommented upon and with no facilitative resolution" (114). The child's seemingly perverse attachment to her unsustaining parenting is a function of the will to retain that little that she unknowingly felt; that object relation, however barren, that is her way of experiencing other people. If we recall Fairbairn's assertion that bad objects are better than no objects at all ("Repression" 67), this retention of a withholding experience of other(s) has its own clear logic, for it provides the child with an inner world of somebodies rather than a stark landscape of utter loneliness. Of course, such an inner world would severely interfere with an ability to perceive the "real," outer world, with its complexities and contradictions as well as richness, and the relationships in which the adult self must function would be gravely compromised.

As Antoinette, seeking her mother in her husband, looking to find a warmth that was withheld from her, is met by the same coldness with which her mother responded, she finds an object that seems simply to reenact the role of the detesting other who does not want her and who pushes her from sight. When she is incarcerated in Rochester's attic, the fact that she feels entirely at the mercy of bad maternal objects and their emanations is figured symbolically in the tapestry that hangs there, in which she has a vision of her "mother dressed in an evening gown but with bare feet. She looked away from me, over my head just as she used to do" (106). Her eerie presence without shoes marks her as the mad mother who lost all sense of social convention after her house was burned down by the angry mob and her weak and helpless son died. This is the mother who was then locked away from the outer world by her uncomprehending British husband, the mother whose fate foretold Antoinette's. The figure hanging in Rochester's tapestry, who seems willfully to ignore her daughter, is also the mother who, after the death of Pierre, offered Antoinette a tantalizing possibility only to withhold her love. It is appropriate that Annette should hang emblematically in the attic that Rochester owns, for this registers Antoinette's perception of how powerful the bad mother of the paranoid-schizoid phase really is; the good mother is nowhere in sight, and she has no grounding for movement toward an empathically depressive stance that would allow for ambivalence toward a mother who could be both bad and good, and would respond to a child's reparative gestures in a healing way.

Although Antoinette's history determines that she will remain at a pre-Oedipal state of longing that is reactivated in her marriage, her husband passes from inarticulate pre-Oedipal states toward a (temporary) Oedipal victory. Despite his will to disaffiliate himself from his wife, he shares with her the tendency to operate, always, from the basis of powerful moods. His behavior in Part Two, from his courtship through early marriage to Antoinette, is determined by the irrationality of infancy rather than by any sustained and mature deliberation. He is generally possessed by a fear of being overwhelmed—by the lushness of the island, by the customs of the people, by the obeah expressed in Christophine's rituals—and his responses to the terror of engulfment are impulsive and overbearing. He refuses to release Antoinette from her engagement to him despite her reservations; he seduces the servant Amélie within Antoinette's hearing; and he transports Antoinette to the prison-house of England, where he will claim possession of her as his "mad girl" (99) even though he will then abandon her to the caretaking of others. None of these behaviors expresses the rationality that Rochester has been conditioned to adopt as an English gentleman; rather, as the effects of mood, his actions belie his most primitive level of experiencing.

Characteristically, Rochester also deposits his own malignancy inside Antoinette and thus finds a way to disavow it. In a projective process, he sees her as the embodiment of everything that is to be feared: the devouringly lustful, the violently uncontrollable, and the murderously destructive. The animal that she becomes to him is an expression of his own responses that have been ejected from his sense of himself so as to be more safely lodged within a perceived other. His description of her sexual awakening stresses, paradoxically, how fatal it is to be for her because it allows him to put her completely at his disposal, serving as the repository for his "uncivilized" feelings: "Very soon she was as eager for what's called loving as I was—more lost and drowned afterwards" (55). Antoinette succumbs to the embrace of his infantile need and, insofar as he will never view her as fully human, she drowns; she is enmeshed in the murky growths of his lust, in the entangled Sargasso Sea of his feelings. His cultural code cannot allow him to love her, for her otherness of nationality and class is compounded when she proves sexually responsive and thus very much unlike a properly trained and restrained Victorian woman. More fundamentally, his own unthought being cannot allow her to exist, for she speaks for all that wants, that is vulnerable, that seeks solace from another—and it is this that he must deny.

Rochester's strategies of denial stage his narrative scene. He sees Granbois, the honeymoon house in Dominica, as having windows shut against the light and doors leading into "silence and dimness," both apt descriptions of his entry into marriage for spurious reasons that he will fail to acknowledge in himself (39). He sings to his new wife a song that stresses his own will not to allow the light of truth and understanding into himself: " 'Hail to the queen of the silent night / Shine bright, shine bright Robin as you *die'*" (49). On one level these lines refer to the death of his Creole wife's spirit, which is his aim. He is like the British Mason before him, who allowed Annette's parrot, symbolic of her own culture on the island, to be burned alive in the fire at Coulibri. Rochester is similarly capable of and committed to wielding imperial force against his wife. But on another level his song suggests his need to eclipse brightness and renounce speech in favor of the sanctuary of non-understanding: of the perceived other, Antoinette; of the lush island; and, most significantly, of himself.

Rochester perceives "blanks" within him of which he cannot and will not make sense (45), and yet he has counter-impulses to find that which is hidden, hidden in the island he does not understand. In this sense his long-ing for Antoinette, while it lasts, represents the possibility that Rochester may accept an infantile aspect of himself, adopting a mode of experiencing that acknowledges rather than denies. The West Indies, he thinks, keeps secrets; and he wants "what it *hides*—that is not nothing" (52).

The very truth within the island culture (and the island equates with his wife) is what he hopes to expose; his hatred of the place is a hatred of the true, but the true is what he also so desperately craves. When he quashes his longing for Antoinette, he kills the possibility of his own psychic aware-ness and expresses a primary characteristic of envy, as Rhys had addressed this with perspicacity in the pages of her earlier novels: that is, he demon-strates the will of the envious to spoil, paradoxically, the very thing for which he yearns. "For she belonged," he reflects, "to the magic and the love-liness. She had left me thirsty and all my life would be thirst and longing for what I had lost before I found it." Together they leave "the hidden place," and the quest for that truth that it hides. What he imagines for her next is an image of what he has already become:

> Very soon she'll join all the others who know the secret and will not tell it. Or cannot. Or try and fail because they do not know enough. They can be recognized. White faces, dazed eyes, aimless gestures, high-pitched laughter. The way they walk and talk and scream or try to kill (themselves or you) if you laugh back at them. Yes, they've got to be watched. For the time comes when they try to kill, then disappear. But others are waiting to take their places, it's a long, long line. She's one of them. I too can wait—for the day when she is only a memory to be avoided, locked away, and like all memories a legend. Or a lie. . . . (103)

The murderous undead, the zombies that he envisions, are those whose souls are robbed because they have been denied the truth. The form "a long, long line" of culturally imposed silence, of avoided memories, of suppres-sion of the real in favor of the lie that is not life. He wills Antoinette to become this because the truth she represents is both compelling and unbearable to him.

The novel's latticed references to light and dark reinforce the tension between truth and fiction, knowledge and denial. When he sits on the veranda of their honeymoon house with Antoinette, Rochester sees a large moth careen into a candle, snuff it out, and fall. Picking up the insect, he expresses a wish that the " 'gay gentleman' " will survive (48), with the attribution of "gentleman" pointing up his identification with the blundering presence that would put out the light at its own peril: he too will stumble into a world he does not understand and, rather than achieve knowledge of it, attempt to pull darkness over this that he does not know. In a walk through the forest he again expresses this will to blindness. Encountering a road that he believes to be paved, Rochester notices the air becoming colder and senses the approach of darkness; he is then passed by a girl who screams at the sight of him, and he sees the servant Baptiste approaching with light, a menacing light, along "the razor-sharp blue-white edge" of a machete he carries (63). The darkness that is coming points to his own desire to remain ignorant; and although Rochester thinks that the girl has screamed because she has seen a ghost or zombie, subtextually a suggestion is given that she has perceived Rochester himself as one of the undead, an uncanny and unseeing haunter of the forest. The light Baptiste carries associates, for Rochester, with danger, for it heralds the unfamiliar and as such can only threaten him. Baptiste insists that there was no paved road here, signaling this Englishman's inability to read the landscape clearly because he is so intent on imposing his own false realities on what he sees.[4] Not surprisingly, when Rochester returns to the cottage he finds that Antoinette's door is closed against him and no light is emerging; he then picks up a book and immerses himself in its accounts of the island rituals of obeah and the belief in zombies. Altogether, this sequence points to Rochester's inability and unwillingness to know what is actually before him; his appeals to successive, incorrect theories—of civilizing pavements, of exotic religious systems—fashion the West Indies as either reassuringly tamed or wildly malign and, in either case, keep the multilayered reality of his wife locked away from his view, residing in a darkness.

Again and again Rochester reveals his distrust of light; he feels that the light plays "a trick" in making his wife seem unblemished as she sleeps, and he puts out Antoinette's candles (83). When he dreams that he is "buried alive," he attributes this horrifying state to her malign magic rather than to his own desire not to see (82). The words he imagines speaking to her, as Part Two concludes and the megalomania of his own madness comes to the fore, speak of his desire; he beseeches her to "hide": "Hide your face. Hide yourself but in my arms"; and then, "Here's a cloudy day to help you. No brazen sun. [. . .] The weather's changed" (99–100). It is not she who must escape the sun, with its light and warmth, but he; and his injunction to her is in fact a reflection of his own need to hide. When he buries her up in the attic, he is trying to make of her the undead that he has already become. Ironically, in the attic Antoinette will narrate the light; from the opening of her section in Part Three she describes Grace Poole making a fire in the grate, causing beautiful flames to arise. Antoinette continues to seek the truth of herself and the power that the fire represents; her story is one of more ambition, however vexed, than his attempts simply to snuff her out will allow.

Rochester's narrative interrogates the reasons that the truth may seem too terrible to bear. He reports that he has learned to hide his feelings of vulnerability—learned this so long ago, presumably, that he cannot even remember it having happened. As a result his life is impoverished. This is signified when he looks at books in the honeymoon house and finds on the last shelf "*Life and Letters of . . .* " with the rest of the title obliterated by decay (44). His own diminishment, in life and letters, is apparent as he writes to his father that the arranged marriage has gone according to plan, that he is now at Granbois with Antoinette and is physically recovering from an illness, that he will write more soon—and then proceeds to put the letter into a desk drawer. Not only will it not be sent; his strongest feelings, his "confused impressions," will, by his own admission, "never be written" (45). Rochester's inner world cannot be said, either to others or himself.

In fact, the inner world terrifies him; and the landscape of the island becomes an external marker of that terror. He walks among its frightening undergrowth, which seems to pull at him even as the trees above close him in. The place is his "enemy," and he is "lost and afraid" within it (62). What frightens him is the tangle of wild unconscious impulses that he cannot face; and these, which are his truth, are defined as that from which he must run and hide, as if his life depended on it.

Daniel Cosway acts as foil for Rochester, underscoring the pathology of the more central figure in significant ways. Feeling, like Rochester, that he has been deprived of filial entitlement, this self-proclaimed son of the plantation owner Cosway complains to Antoinette's English husband that to keep bitter feelings locked away is too difficult to bear. In his inability to do so he unleashes a stream of venom about the motives of his rival, the legitimate child Antoinette, as well as her mad family, and thus provides Rochester the excuse he needs for hiding her out of sight forever. Rhys uses Daniel to serve notice, without editorializing, on what becomes of those who try to suppress what they cannot tolerate and then colonize the passionate aspects of themselves. The feelings emerge anyway, in destructive and grotesque forms, and by novel's end Rochester's himself is very much like Daniel—embittered, deceitful, exploitative of not only "Bertha," the wife he has renamed and imprisoned, but by implication also a manipulator of the Jane of Brontë's text, the fiancée to whom he will lie as he tries to claim her. What he will do to Jane he has already done to Antoinette—in Christophine's words, " 'make her think you can't see the sun for looking at her' " (92). If to see the sun is to see the truth, then Christophine's metaphor is apt; he pulls the blinds down over reality: his own, his wife's, and his wife's-to-be.

Thus it is fitting that as he wishes never to have come to the West Indies he absently says he would " 'give [his] eyes never to have seen' " it. Christophine's response—" 'You choose what you give, eh?' "—promises that his wish will come true (96). As we know from *Jane Eyre*, Rochester will temporarily lose his sight after the fire at Thornfield Hall. The loss of sight literalizes the inevitable; it is the outcome of the blindness he has willed upon himself in refusing to recognize his own truths and also in trying to deny the truths of others' realities.

His pain derives from Oedipal conflicts as these are layered over a template of pre-Oedipal longings. Rochester nurtures a grievance that his father preferred his brother to him and placed him in this impossible position of marriage to an unsuitable wife. He imagines yet another letter that he will never send to his father, reproaching him for his lack of love and for exploiting his youthful trust. "But I am not young now," he thinks, as he drinks Christophine's rum, which is "mild as mother's milk or father's blessing" (97). By implication these phrases speak to what he has never had—maternal nurturance, paternal approval—and his drinking, to forget, is just one more strategy of denial among the many that he exploits. His marriage to a mad Creole offers the occasion for a victory over the father who held so tightly to English inheritance law; Rochester in effect becomes his own law, placing Antoinette in a subordinated position and demonstrating, through his mastery of her, his filial triumph. The novel's richly contrasting narrative strategies serve to demonstrate, however, that this is a triumph he will not sustain.

In the first section of the text, Antoinette chronicles, as after a nightmare, the experiences of her early childhood. Her narration has the quality of a dream remembered, in which the reporter, who has journeyed, as Bollas puts this, "to foetal postures and to the hallucinatory thought of the infant," is still held in the ambiance of the mother (*Ideas* 73). In Antoinette's case, with her link to the bad mother of infancy unsevered, this atmosphere is dark and filled with dangers; reproducing phantasies she cannot yet understand and speaking a text that has as yet no translation, Antoinette produces a discourse that is solemnly oracular, as are the accounts of dreams. In a process of narration that may be likened to the phenomenon of dream reportage within the analytic setting, "the maternal oracle that held the dreamer inside it, spoke in the dreamer's ear, brought visionary events before the dreamer's very eyes" is summoned (*Ideas* 74). Antoinette's speech is characterized by an urgency to recollect terrible moments that must not be lost. "Quickly, while I can, I must remember the hot classroom," she narrates and then recalls the canvas she was embroidering: "Underneath, I will write my name in fire red, Antoinette Mason, née Cosway [. . .]" (31). The fire-red name is a dream-condensation of the fire at Coulibri that traumatized her and the fire at Thornfield that is to come. In reinvoking the image of fire and using the future tense ("I will write my name [. . .]"), Antoinette reports on the ongoingness-of-being for this memory: that it happened not once but many times, and that it will inevitably happen once more. Antoinette's vision is colored by her victimization, her name the identity of one who is always perishing, and she predicts the inescapable repetition of losses and pain. When she writes her name, she at once mimics the strategies of control, via naming, of those who hold the power and also creates a bold, fire-red marker of her life that very much contrasts with the attempts at erasure on the part of those who surround her—first her mother; then her aunt, stepfather, and teachers; and finally her husband.

The "madness" that others will condemn in Antoinette is that of the person who refuses the choice of self-deception, and in this respect she demonstrates some potential agency and is more sane than those others of her narrative. St. Innocenzia, the fourteen-year-old whose skeleton lay under the chapel of her convent school, fittingly carries in metaphor the fate to which Antoinette will be assigned: "We do not know her story, she is not in the book. The saints we hear about were all very beautiful and wealthy. All were loved by rich and handsome young men," Antoinette comments (32). The true innocent, whose life presumably did not take on the idealized colors of the storybook saints that the nuns like to talk about, is buried under the altar. She lies as an image of the suppressed self and a comment on how the innocent are damned by a culture that insists on material good above all, on marriage as a form of property exchange, and on a whitewashing of difficult truths.[5]

As Antoinette's narrative proceeds, it continues to voice, as from a dream recollected, an inevitable succession of events and uncanny visions that elliptically carry the truth of her past into her future. When her stepfather Mason insisted, as she reports, that she not remain secluded in the convent but rather accept his gifts, one of which was an inappropriately decorative dress, and prepare to venture out, she knew that what he was urging her to enter was the marital marketplace in which she would be displayed as a commodity to be consumed by the most promising bidder. Resisting this as a false sort of emergence into a false kind of living, Antoinette tells of her ultimately futile efforts as one tells of the episodes in a nightmare in which one is caught up in powerful forces against which all struggle is hopeless. Mason and the culture that he represents are predominant, as Antoinette narrates an actual dream of leaving Coulibri to follow a slyly smiling man: "We are no longer in the forest but in an enclosed garden surrounded by a stone wall and the trees are different trees. I do not know them. There are steps leading upwards. It is too dark to see the wall or the steps, but I know they are there and I think, 'It will be when I go up these steps. At the top' " (36). The tone of fatality that characterizes Antoinette's dream-thought— "It will be when I go up these steps. At the top"—signifies that this journey upward represents a journey that is forced upon her. What "it" will be that awaits her or happens next remains unspecified, suggesting an event or presence that Antoinette as narrator assumes her audience will already recognize. In chronicling this dream, Antoinette is completely contained by the oracle: she is within the undifferentiated space in which any active aspect of her selfhood cannot find expression, her movements have no meaning, her autonomy is denied. Further, she is merged with the listening audience, who will see all, she assumes, just as she sees it. Throughout the first section of Rhys's text, Antoinette, like an analysand, tells of her primitive longings and terrors through an account of events that hold her captive, from which she believes there is no escape.

In Part Two, the bulk of the narrative is managed by Rochester as he vacillates among violent emotions that he finally masters by willing himself into the patriarchy. Here Rhys enacts the Law of the Father, showing how the symbolic system may be wielded as infantile feeling-states are disowned and the mother's traces are all but eradicated. Rochester brandishes pictures and barks words to obliterate the maternal–infant dyad that he sees surviving in his wife and to pave the way for a suppression of all of his own emotions in the cold, rational attic of England. He resists the amorphous and unknown, the pungent smells and brilliant colors of the island, which represent that which he does not control. He renounces the features of his wife that frighten him and turns her into an image of her mother's inhuman madness; Antoinette appears to him as "this red-eyed wild-haired stranger who was my wife shouting obscenities at me" (89). Everything on the island becomes a danger: "That green menace. I had felt it ever since I saw this place. There was nothing I knew [. . .]" (90). Finally he finds his way to an image of

entranced by the voice that whispers in her ear. Although it is possible to read her ultimate act—setting fire to Thornfield, the master's house—as a positive seizure of her own agency, the fact that this fire has already happened within the text of her dream suggests that it is an event to which she moves without volition because it is fated to occur. As in the inconclusive endings of all of her novels, Rhys offers several powerfully contradictory suggestions and thus mimics the illogical logic of a dream-state. The fire that Antoinette carries both does and does not serve as her assertion of power, for it leads to the light of freedom but also guarantees that she will face the annihilation that she has always feared, outlining in fire-red, once more, her identity as victim.[7]

By Part Three of the novel, Rochester's voice has been reduced to quotations in others' narratives. He exists, first, as a line from a letter to Mrs. Fairfax directing her to increase Grace Poole's wages to ensure that she will remain at Thornfield and spare him any further decisions about his wife's welfare. His written statement is enclosed within quotations in Mrs. Fairfax's unpunctuated discourse to Grace, as recounted by an anonymous third person, and thus he is bracketed within layers of narrative apparatus and accordingly put at a far remove from the action, and diminished. During two of the dramatic incidents that Antoinette describes in the ensuing pages—the attempt to break through the ship's porthole and the attack on her stepbrother—Rochester is unmentioned, as if to suggest his ineffectuality and inconsequence in the face of overt aggression. All further references to him are within Antoinette's narrative as lines of quotation: his accusation of her intemperance in the red dress as " 'Infamous daughter of an infamous mother,' " and his cries of "Bertha! Bertha!" as she leaps within her dream to the stones below (110; 112). In both instances his cited discourse is notable for expressing his inability to see Antoinette as more than what he has made of her, the stick figure of his drawing whom he has sought to control and has converted into a focal point for his sanctimonious moral outrage. His name for her, Bertha, expressive of the Father's Law that uses words in place of what has been lost, speaks to his denial of Antoinette, whom he has put behind him, and his attempt to claim control in the face of what his denial has cost him—the magic and the loveliness that she promised.

The urge to name is parodied in Antoinette's final dream-vision of all of the elements of her life jumbled together:

> I saw the grandfather clock and Aunt Cora's patchwork, all colours, I saw the orchids and the stephanotis and the jasmine and the tree of life in flames. I saw the chandelier and the red carpet downstairs and the bamboos and the tree ferns, the gold ferns and the silver, and the soft green velvet of the moss

on the garden wall. I saw my doll's house and the books and the picture of
the Miller's Daughter. (112)

In this mélange of elements from indoors and those that flourish outside,
the detritus of civilization and the lush expressions of nature, the colors
both vivid and soothing, Antoinette serves up a discourse that mocks the
clear distinctions among things and the hierarchical assignment of every
one of those things to its place. Rochester himself, as he has been kept
unnamed throughout the entire text of *Wide Sargasso Sea*, is now referred
to by Antoinette in these final pages simply as "[t]hat man" and "the man
who hated me" (110; 112). The ludicrousness of naming, as against a more
primitive and genuine emotional response, is thereby underlined. Rhys
demonstrates that the authority that Rochester wields, to push what is
unwanted out of his sight, has the most tenuous of effects. Not only are his
own words bracketed and ridiculed within the final pages of the novel; but
also his prisoner will bring the entire edifice of his power, the house of his
denial, down about them—at whatever cost to herself this may entail.

The ambiguity of Antoinette's achievement points to the multifaceted
nature of Rhys's accomplishment in this last novel. *Wide Sargasso Sea* gives
evidence of complexly differing paradigms of development: within the text,
Antoinette's attempts to move into a fully autonomous being are fraught
with peril and lead to an uncertain outcome, in which her seizure of agency
both is and is not suggested; but in the creative effort Rhys herself makes a
shift from the disassociated experience of the world that characterized her
earlier novels into a connection with, and passage beyond, a literary maternal figure whose work enables her to come into full presence as a writer.

A contrast between Rhys's tormented protagonist and her author may be
highlighted in examining how each makes use of another entity as a "transitional object," to cite D. W. Winnicott's pioneering concept. Such an
object occupies, in early childhood, a realm intermediate between inner
and outer reality: it facilitates a process by which one learns to mediate
between sameness and difference, the me and the not-me, laying the foundation for connection, autonomy, and ambivalence. A child's successful use
of an object as transitional is contingent on an initial experience of her caregiver, the mother, as adapting as closely as possible to her requirements and
only gradually modifying these adaptations as the infant's capacity to
endure frustration develops. The child's awareness accordingly evolves,
from a preliminary sense of her own omnipotence as someone who can
control her object world completely, to a gradual recognition of objects as
external and to some extent beyond her ability to manage (*Playing* 10–11).
Carrying the prototypical security blanket, for example, she can, under

favorable conditions, assure herself of power over it, can hold and use it for her own pleasure and growth; and yet she can experience it as something beyond herself that has its own life, thus modifying her grandiosity. The child thereby moves from the enjoyment of illusion to a tolerance of disillusion, using the transitional object to facilitate her passage. Because such a device occupies the liminal space between subjective and objective experiencing, it is neither an internal object subject to the infant's phantasies of complete domination nor is it an external object that autonomously responds to the infant's being. It is an intermediary possession that promotes a child's idiosyncratic modes of expression, surviving her hating, aggressive treatment as well as withstanding her often overbearing love (5).

Wide Sargasso Sea suggests the kind of mothering that a journey toward healthy maturation and the capacity to enter transitional experience would entail; the course of Antoinette's development, if blighted, speaks of what she could have been as it models one kind of childhood experience as shaped by the effects of good-enough nurturance. By virtue of Christophine's sensitive registration of and responses to her deepest needs and fears, Antoinette demonstrates the ability to begin using an object in a transitional way. She turns to a stick of wood as a marvelously adaptive item; it is for use on her own behalf but, as transitional object, it is neither fully under her control nor quite alive in its own right. "[. . .] I believed in my stick," she recalls, and then offers a modifying statement that speaks to her uncertain definition of it, of what it was and what it could do: "It was not a stick, but a long narrow piece of wood, with two nails sticking out at the end, a shingle, perhaps. [. . .] Christophine knocked the nails out, but she let me keep the shingle and I grew very fond of it, I believed that no one could harm me when it was near me, to lose it would be a great misfortune" (22). Endowed with the atmosphere of the loving mother, made safe for Antoinette when Christophine knocks out its nails, the stick also provides the child with the possibility of imagining her own power and agency. Holding tightly to her stick, Antoinette, like the toddler who carries her blanket everywhere, attempts control of it; experiences it as having its own enigmatic properties to which she may turn for solace; yet feels that how it is managed and what it gives are the by-products of her own actions, as these reflect, in turn, her ability to imagine possibilities (Winnicott, *Playing* 5).

Although Christophine provides Antoinette with the experience of good-enough mothering that could offer the promise of a healthy psychological trajectory, her influence is countered by the power and oppressiveness of the other, malign maternal presence in Antoinette's life. In accordance with the split characterizations that the novel enlists, Annette's interactions with Antoinette determine the outcome that may be expected when a mother who is *not* good-enough consistently fails her child. In such instances, the child is not sufficiently equipped to make full use of an object for transitional purposes; it will not remain meaningful but will gradually become as inadequate as her initial parenting was (Winnicott, *Playing* 10). By the time of the mob attack on Coulibri, Antoinette's stick has mysteriously but notably vanished; its failure as means of transition to a state of independence is signaled by the fact that it has not survived. Having abandoned the "babyish" conviction that things around her may come to life (*Wide* 22), Antoinette cannot move into a sense of her own full agency; at this point she sees herself as being at the mercy of malevolent forces beyond her control, of persecutors external and internal with whom she will continuously do battle and against whom she cannot fully succeed. Although a good-enough mother would help a child respond to the impingements of life, which are inevitable, in a coping way, "Maternal failures produce phases of reaction to impingement and these reactions interrupt the 'going on being' of the infant. An excess of this reacting produces not frustration but a *threat of annihilation*" (Winnicott, "Primary" 303). Antoinette lives in terror, having never learned to sustain the act of creative and constructive living, and thus her action at novel's end cannot be translated, singlemindedly, into a victory achieved. The ambiguous readings that her final action invites, however, reflect the two threads of possibility that the narrative has enlisted. Following one line of potential, the Antoinette who was nurtured by a good-enough Christophine might be a heroine capable of seizing some agency and speaking her selfhood in her ultimate decision to burn down Thornfield Hall. Following the other possible meanings that her story suggests, the Antoinette who has been failed by *not* good-enough Annette is a daughter enmeshed in a coldly hating maternal realm, dictated to by an overpowering, destructive presence, and doomed, finally, to suicide by virtue of persistent internal pressures.

As against the undecidability that Antoinette's ending elicits, an interpretation of Rhys's own achievement with *Wide Sargasso Sea* reveals her ability, over many years, to process, successfully, the text that had so strongly claimed her interest. Her own creative journey illustrates, as Winnicott argues, that a transitional object may come to assume increasingly complex and enriching significance. Lending credence to his claim that in adult life the experience of aesthetic and other cultural expressions may give one the hope that a self that feels that it is in pieces will find, through a deeply felt experience of a work of art, the way to one's own separate coherence (*Playing* 14), Rhys approached Brontë's text as one seeking a transitional object that would set her free. She ultimately found that *Jane Eyre* provided an experience of closeness and distance that enabled the expression of her own creative vision.[8] This is not to minimize, however, the difficulty of the task in which she was engaged, for like all powerful forebears, Brontë as author of *Jane Eyre* was at first an almost overwhelming presence, as the self-denigrating references in Rhys's early letters make clear. The reverent attitude toward Brontë begins to explain, as well, why she was stalled in her first attempts to lay claim to the mother's work, to make use of *Jane Eyre* as a text for her own purposes that could serve her own transitional needs. Through her successive returns to the earlier narrative, however, her own emergence became possible, and this, I would argue, because of repeated encounters with the other text's differences from as well as similarities to the novel she needed to write. Having engaged in a dynamic rather than passive way with *Jane Eyre* as transitional object, Rhys could go onto conceive *Wide Sargasso Sea*.

This dynamism took the form of an increasingly clear sense of the need to provide a corrective for the embodiment of the cultural other in *Jane Eyre*. Troping the course of her own journey in bringing her vision to the pages of *Wide Sargasso Sea* is the episode in which Rhys portrays young Antoinette walking book-in-hand to her convent school. Speaking to Rhys's sense of having a smirched history to record that will in turn smirch the purity of another narrative, muddying its clear distinctions between self and other, us and them, English and Creole, Antoinette notes that her perspiration leaves "a mark on the palm of [her] hand and a stain on the cover of the book" (29). The complicated reality of who she is imprints itself in these insistently visible traces, while the ensuing action illustrates that her story cannot be held complacently in another's pages. Antoinette is confronted by two children: a boy of indeterminate racial background, and his black companion. Her taunt that Antoinette is as crazy as her mother, with her mother's zombie eyes, accompanied by both a push and the accusation, " 'You don't want to look at me, eh, I make you look at me,' " causes Antoinette to drop her books (30). The girl's words speak to the black West Indian's indignation at having been denied full humanity by the whites whom Antoinette's family represents, the decadent colonizers who nonetheless still maintain what is perceived to be an overbearing presence in the islands. But, in ironic and reverberating juxtaposition, the girl's statement also insists on the significance of Antoinette's experience, that it is *her* life that *Wide Sargasso Sea* will "make [readers] look at."

Retrieving one of the dropped books that Antoinette has almost abandoned in her attempt to run from the other children, and simultaneously promising to shelter her from future harassment, her cousin Sandi, a colored relation, delineates a locus that speaks of difference. The episode in its entirety points to the inadequacy of books like *Jane Eyre* to tell the lives of the colonized: of the girl, of her companion, of Sandi, and most pointedly of Antoinette, all the victims of misunderstanding and persecution. It demonstrates through Sandi's empathic gesture how a cultural other, that is, Rhys herself, can write another kind of narrative, one that reveals a complex understanding of relations among the islanders as well as the colonized and colonizers and thereby provides a nuanced account of the forces with which Antoinette must contend. The episode of the dropped books could be read as a purely destructive moment, in which all other narrative renditions are vanquished; but the books are picked up again—most tellingly, for emphasis, the one book that is nearly left behind is retrieved—as Rhys finds the place from which to speak another truth. The book that can be reclaimed functions symbolically in the in-between: establishing the significance of the work that informs her outlook, Rhys also corrects its limitations. She holds the book and she notices the stain. She mediates against the honoring of the English and the vilification as well as homogenization of West Indians; she protests Victorian pandering to an audience of loyal Britons and the further diminishment of those already subject to colonial misperception and ill-treatment, even as she continues to hold the powerful earlier narrative within the scope of her vision.[9]

Therefore *Jane Eyre* proved to be catalytic and liberating in the evolution of Rhys's art. In the use of this novel as transitional object, she demonstrates that aesthetic experience may make possible personal growth and autonomy and also a state of transcendence, with far-ranging implications for others as well as self. Rhys signals the acceptance of paradox in responding to the work of her forebear, an accomplishment that inscribes the end of her writing life as a territory of new beginning. For to accept paradox is also to lay the groundwork for conceptualizing in a depressive mode, in which the (m)others of the world are experienced as good and bad, nurturing as well as flawed. Rhys is able to paint *Wide Sargasso Sea* with the colors of both her understanding and her anger, acknowledging what is offered as well as what is lacking, accommodating another's achievement and protesting that which she has not been able to find. She is thus empowered to make a powerful statement to her readers. In this, her final novel, she widens the circles of her concern and demonstrates her growing understanding of issues that affect diversely configured social outcasts who are confronted by a mix of possibilities and limitations. And she ensures that Brontë's work survives in the pages of her narrative; *Jane Eyre* is not erased by *Wide Sargasso Sea*. In coming to and processing a transitional text, Rhys as literary child makes a claim that must be heard, that cannot be ignored, that directly addresses the mother herself and what she has made possible. In voicing her hatred, Rhys finds her love. She speaks, at last, with a sustained voice, of an original vision, to an audience of many.

Epilogue ✑

"There are a certain number of children, abandoned and unprotected, roaming the streets."

—Jean Rhys, "Fishy Waters"

In the story from which this epigraph derives, which was published in 1976, Rhys conveys with compression and understatement the preoccupations that were with her throughout her life. All of the elements are here in miniature: the displacement of people in a culture they do not understand; the hypocrisy of those in privileged social positions who disclaim their own responsibility; the duplicity of men in their dealings with women; the abuse of power between adult and child; and the psychological determinants of both action and reaction. The story is set in Rouseau, Dominica, Rhys's birthplace; and in the 1890s, the years of her earliest childhood. It contains the thematics that shaped her fiction from the first short sketches she composed as a young writer to the culminating achievement of *Wide Sargasso Sea*, completed in her old age.

In revealing the subterranean dynamics of a local scandal, "Fishy Waters" focuses attention on the deceptive strategies practiced by those who exploit others, insofar as they publicly misrepresent their own motives and also refuse to take personal stock of what they have done. The story opens with reports that an Englishman, one Jimmy Longa, who is a carpenter but also (to the general disfavor) an alcoholic and socialist, has just been accused of terrorizing and beating a vagrant child. As his trial gets underway, another Englishman, Matthew Penrice, who has recently moved to the island, is called to testify to the events he witnessed. He recalls that during a walk to his club he heard first the screams of a child, then their abrupt cessation; deciding to investigate, he proceeded into the garden of a nearby house just as Jimmy Longa declared, " 'Now I'm going to saw you in two, like they do in English music halls' " (302). According to Penrice, a young black girl was lying naked on a plank, with Longa over her, and when she rolled to the ground, unconscious, bruises all over her body were revealed. The witness took the child to a nearby house and called for the doctor. He then summoned police aid.

As the narrative proceeds with Penrice's testimony, his own positioning in relation to these events comes to seem increasingly suspicious. The defense emphasizes that he was acting in an irregular way: venturing out for his club early, finding a short cut despite the fact that he'd left so prematurely, and then taking the bruised child to the home of his own former servant rather than to the hospital, as might have been expected. The written declaration of Longa, who is apparently prostrate with illness, is brought into court; it paints a picture of his own sense of injustice as he claims that since his arrival on the island he has been harassed by vagabond children and simply thought to teach them a lesson by frightening one of them with what he describes as " 'a joke' " (307). The child herself, referred to by the diminutive Jojo, with her status accordingly reduced in the eyes of everyone present, is unable to testify because she cannot remember the incident. As the doctor in attendance comments, " 'I have known cases when, after a frightening and harmful experience, the mind has protected itself by forgetting' " (306).

Both Longa and Penrice reveal, through their own words about the incident, their potential as emotional terrorists; and what they have in common, despite the fact that they are positioned as adversaries in court, is a refusal to see any harm that they may have caused. The magistrate adds to the general disclaiming of responsibility by concluding that it is impossible to reach a clear decision about what actually occurred. The fishiness in "Fishy Waters" is the moral murkiness of the individuals who can find justifications for their actions through a process of displacing and disavowing their own feelings; and the correspondingly muddled behavior of those who support them. Their behavior is tacitly enabled by their intimates, by the community, and by a judicial system that does not hold them accountable. The narrative offers the strong suggestion that although Longa practiced a cruel species of "joke" upon the child, it is Penrice who is the perpetrator of the beating and possibly sexual assault. In his closing dialogue with his wife, Maggie, she reminds him that he characteristically sees " 'envy, malice, hatred everywhere' " and that this is something—either in himself or in the others he perceives (she fails to distinguish)—that he " 'can't escape' " (311). Her remark outlines a history for Penrice of trying to flee his own aggression as it has been projected outward; and that as someone who is envious, malicious, and filled with hate, he is capable of a terrible mistreatment of those over whom he can exert his power. His guilt is implicit as he sits in his armchair in the story's final moments, pretending to read a book but, as Maggie notes, not turning any of the pages. Once again the parallel between the apparently scurrilous Longa and the upright Penrice is stressed as he, like Longa, resolves to leave Dominica. Having found a woman on another island who is willing to take the victim in, Matthew responds to Maggie's concern that it appear he is trying to mask his culpability by insisting that he wants to move away. At this his wife has the sudden, alarming revelation—with all of the implications it carries—that she does not know her husband at all.

The plot depends for its impact on the correspondences it draws among the major characters, even as their deep sense of isolation is revealed. They deploy varying strategies for the management of their loneliness. For Longa, feeling adrift and besieged by the town's children, the antidote to his unhappiness comes in the form of vengeance upon a little girl. For Penrice, a dark isolation finds expression in his sinister actions and the self-pitying defensiveness he voices. For Maggie, who presumably turned a blind eye to her husband until this incident, the truth must be faced at story's end, when she is suffused with the sense of how terribly alone she is. Finally and most acutely, for the abandoned child who is at the mercy of circumstances over which she has no control, who is the object of others' malice and possibly their desire, there is nothing to be done on her own behalf except repress the memory of her abuse.

In presenting both victims and victimizers, the narrative offers the girl as trope for the condition of defensive self-enclosure that all of the other characters experience. But the situation into which she is placed, by the accident of her birth, clarifies that among those who are alone, she—as female, black, impoverished, and a child—is the least able to draw support from powerful institutional structures. She is also, as the story makes clear, one of many. Given the injustices perpetrated upon them, the world's victims are left with limited psychological options. They can hide from the horror of their experience; they can feel it and suffer.

It is with such a set of choices that all of Rhys's heroines must contend. The irony at the heart of the fiction is that these protagonists share with their victimizers the condition of having been assaulted by powerful emotions that shape all of their perceptions and subsequent behaviors and perpetuate the circumstances of their earliest deprivations. Sounding the chords that reverberate among us in spite of our feelings of isolation and the unsympathetic conventions of society, Rhys underscores the tragedy of our incapacity to connect with each other in any sustained and nurturing way. Instead, with a fineness of perception and a considered restraint, she registers the effects of projective processes on both the privileged and the disenfranchised and impels readers into their own evaluative stances. Her fiction documents the many ways in which people who are wounded attempt to manage their own isolation, protect themselves from further harm, and forge existences that can be at least endured in the landscapes that they traverse. She demonstrates that the haves often triumph within the cultures that express their desire, although the power they wield comes at the high price of self-alienation. The have-nots, given no support from prevailing institutions, face a bleaker set of prospects. But although they are shunned in the streets and bars, locked in dark attics and sent to other islands, the socially displaced lead lives that Rhys documents with an uncompromising specificity and understanding.

Her fiction attests to the nuances of psychic processes as people confront the inevitably traumatic circumstances of living. One can draw on an array of strategies to recover from full awareness, as does the child in "Fishy Waters" and as do many of the drunken, narcotized, and blank characters who populate Rhys's narratives. One can also attest to the suffering self and demand it achieve recognition—as do her heroines, at times briefly, but also at times triumphantly, and as does Rhys herself. Throughout her oeuvre, she insists that feeling, and feeling deeply, is the condition that makes us human. That the course of the soul's progress may be narrated through the life of the emotions is the truth to which her fiction profoundly, and resonantly, lays claim.

Notes

1 INTRODUCTORY: JEAN RHYS AND THE LANDSCAPE OF EMOTION

1. A recent review of listings in the *MLA Bibliography* (1992–2003) reveals a pronounced critical inclination to favor *Wide Sargasso Sea* over Rhys's other novels. The database includes one hundred and fifty-four entries on *Wide Sargasso Sea*, as contrasted with fourteen related to *Quartet*; thirty-nine to *Voyage in the Dark*; thirteen to *After Leaving Mr. Mackenzie*; and fourteen to *Good Morning, Midnight*, respectively.

Despite this inequity of critical treatment, there has been a general revival of interest in Rhys's work that can be attributed, in large part, to the groundbreaking efforts of feminist scholars reclaiming the contributions of forgotten or marginalized women writers. Accordingly, many studies of Rhys deploy feminist perspectives as they attempt to compensate for the earlier lack of critical discussion; complementing these is the growing body of assessments by postcolonial critics interested in the complicated permutations of nationhood and racial identity that her fiction enacts. Recent assessments tend to generalize the experience of Rhys's female subjects as illustrative of the ways in which women are victimized by a patriarchal milieu; or/and, to stress the multiple abuses of European colonialism as they inform the vision of this transplanted West Indian author. Those few full-length critical volumes on Rhys that directly acknowledge psychoanalytic premises, e.g., Mary Lou Emery's *Jean Rhys at "World's End": Novels of Colonial and Sexual Exile*; Deborah Kelly Kloepfer's *The Unspeakable Mother: Hidden Discourse in Jean Rhys and H. D.*; and Helen Nebeker's *Jean Rhys: Woman in Passage*, provide assessments of her considerable psychological acumen as framed variously by such theorists as Horney, Lacan, Kristeva, and Jung. Among journal articles, Elizabeth Abel's "Women and Schizophrenia: The Fiction of Jean Rhys," published in 1979, opened the door to a series of shorter studies that have emphasized the psychology of the individual, especially as she is socially disaffected, in Rhys's fiction. None of these treatments, however, demonstrates conversance with the exciting discoveries that are of cardinal interest to those within the psychoanalytic community today and that are clearly of relevance to scholars and students of modern literature, as I argue here.

2. Sheila Kineke offers a persuasive discussion of the colonizing aspects of Ford's patronage of Rhys, in which he attempted "literary possession" of her as Modernist protégée (288). Sanford Sternlicht addresses Rhys's adoption of a pseudonym as a possible bid for the approbation of select male figures and the literary patriarchy of her day (9).

3. For more on Rhys's sense of Paris, and her experiences of Hemingway and other notable Modernists, see Coral Ann Howells as well Louis James.

4. I am indebted to Howells for locating the passage from Rhys's unpublished Black Exercise Book that describes her search for and discovery of the psychoanalytic text at Sylvia Beach's shop in Paris. Howells offers a perceptive discussion of Rhys's opinion of the Freudian notion of female hysteria, as she was exposed to it (17).

5. Felman is among several scholars in recent years who have been instrumental in calling for a more sophisticated intertextual engagement of literary and psycho-analytic discourses. In addition to her anthology *Literature and Psychoanalysis: The Question of Reading: Otherwise*, which contains nuanced reconsiderations of such texts as *Hamlet* and *The Turn of the Screw*, Edith Kurzweil and William Phillips's volume *Literature and Psychoanalysis* presents an important historical perspective on approaches to literature from the early psychoanalysts through to the cultural commentators of the mid-twentieth century and contemporary French theorists. The emphasis in both anthologies is on the Freud/Lacan legacy, with scant attention given to the insights of other pioneering analytic figures. Several recent studies, however, argue for an incorporation of the work of other groundbreaking figures of psychoanalysis in the treatment of literary texts. Among these are Mary Jacobus's *First Things: The Maternal Imaginary in Literature, Art, and Psychoanalysis;* and Esther Sánchez-Pardo's *Cultures of the Death Drive: Melanie Klein and Modernist Melancholia*. These form significant, much-needed contributions to a growing critical awareness of the salience of Klein's thought in discussions of art in general and, by extension, in analyses of the shaping consciousness and self-identifications of Modernism.

6. The pioneers of analysis were on terms of familiarity with some of their patients that would shock even the most progressive in the analytic community of today. Freud's patient Irma was invited over for a birthday celebration with his family; Klein saw adult patients in the boarding house in Wales where she resided as London was being bombed during World War II (*Interpretation* 108; Grosskurth 266), to select just a few of many examples of the surprisingly loose, early notion of an analytic "frame."

7. For a chronological sequencing of first editions of Rhys's works, given with com-prehensive descriptions, see Melltown; for a listing of subsequent editions and publication dates through to the end of her life, see Jacobs.

2   *VOYAGE IN THE DARK*: PROPITIATING THE AVENGERS

1. I follow the lead of Kleinian analysts when using the spelling "phantasy" as dis-tinguished from "fantasy," the latter term describing conscious imaginings and the former the activities of the unconscious (see Mitchell, S. 68).

2. The degree to which Mrs. Adam shaped Rhys's notebooks into fiction is unclear. Rhys's biographer, Carole Angier, claims that Adam "cut and edited" them, and made divisions within the loosely assembled manuscript pages to create chapters and parts (131). Judith L. Raiskin suggests that the interpolations from Mrs. Adam were more considerable: that she took the diary-like material and "rewrote parts of it in the form of a novel" (133). Rhys's own account in *Smile Please* is unspecific; as she tells it, Mrs. Adam asked for permission to alter pieces of the manuscript because it was " 'perhaps a bit naïve here and there' " and also made some divisions within the text, but Rhys disliked these changes and when she used her material later as a basis for *Voyage* it was to the original notebooks, not Mrs. Adams's text, that she returned (155).

   As numerous readers have pointed out, the ending of *Voyage*, as Rhys was pressured to change it, offers some possibility of hope for Anna; but this hope is a muted one, and Rhys succeeded in remaining ambiguous in spite of her editor's wish for optimism (see Kleopfer 77; Morris 4; O'Connor 130).

3. Balint's work derives from the theories of Klein and other early object relations analysts—"the Londoners," as he refers to them, because many of them were working in England at mid-century—but he also voices reservations: "The Londoners studied only the vehement reactions after frustration, but the experience of the tranquil, quiet sense of well-being after proper satisfaction escaped their attention altogether or has not been appreciated according to its economic importance [i. e. in proportion to its significance]." He accordingly addresses, as neither Riviere nor Klein does, the "quiet sense of well-being" that may characterize the infant's first experience of object love ("Early" 102).

4. See Freud's claim in "Female Sexuality" (1931): "Childhood love is boundless; it demands exclusive possession, it is not content with less than all" (231).

5. When Rhys explained in a letter that her impetus for composing *Voyage* was "the West Indies [. . .] knocking at my heart" (171), she recognized, with characteristic attention to physical detail, the tangibility of heartache, which offers immediate, inescapable evidence of traumatic loss. Diana Athill notes that in old age Rhys suffered from a heart disorder (*Smile* 6; also Angier 503; 519), her body offering the inscription of pain borne by her young protagonist Anna. In documenting the interweaving of Rhys's art and life in this novel, Curtis (147–48); Harrison (69); Kleopfer (76); and O'Connor (89) offer perceptive insights.

6. For a similarly disturbing but more sympathetic portrait of a woman whose body has become a caricature of feminine display in a life that has relied on male attentions, see Rhys's story "La Grosse Fifi," in which an aging *femme fatale* tightly corsets her large figure, which nevertheless bulges out of its restraints, and wears rouge that "shriek[s]" and "bright blue" eyeshadow (*Collected* 80). She is eventually murdered by the gigolo she has supported, a pointed comment on the outcome that awaits the woman who has outlived her sexual appeal: in the eyes of men, she is utterly dispensable.

7. In an interview conducted in her old age, Rhys recalled her "fear of *obeah*. That's West Indian black magic. I remember we had this *obeah* woman as a cook once. She was rather a gaudy kind of woman, very tall and thin and always wore a red

7. A similar analogy between human and insect life is offered in Rhys's short story "The Insect World" (1976), in which the protagonist, who displays increasingly intense levels of claustrophobia and fear as the narrative progresses, comes to see the others in her world as insects—as termites swarming and building nests in persistent, mindless fashion, jiggers burrowing into bodies to plant their eggs out of sight, and all the other "minute crawling unseen things that got at you as you walked along harmlessly" (*Collected* 353). The story speaks to the heroine's terror of the overwhelming and predatory potential of everyone who surrounds her but also of her own unrecognized impulses and compulsive behaviors.

8. In the chapter "Île de la Cité," Julia stares into the river, mesmerized, until she is approached by a policeman. Her response to him—" 'I haven't the slightest intention of committing suicide, I assure you' " (183)—raises the possibility that suicide is in fact on her mind; as does her apparent indifference to Mackenzie's money at the close of the narrative, which may imply she has no use for it because she is not considering any future for herself.

9. Betsy Berry proposes that Rhys has reworked Naturalist conventions in this novel, a position that skirts the tantalizing ambiguities of the novel's conclusion.

10. See Harrison for a discussion of the ways in which Rhys's spare prose style acts as comment on the suppression of the feminine voice in a cultural discourse that is predominantly masculine (122). Note, also, Molly Hite's claim that Rhys's marginal protagonists speak outside the frame of male dialogue, which renders them "without a language, condemned to emit sounds that inside interlocuters will interpret as evidence of duplicity, infantilism, hypocrisy—or simply madness" (28). As I have argued here, "infantilism" is indeed character-istic of Julia Martin's speech as well as vision, but I do not subscribe to the tacit condemnation that usually attaches to the term, which I prefer to use as a neutral description of a condition of early life experience.

4 *QUARTET*: A CONSTELLATION OF DESIRES

1. Having suffered the affair between Ford and Rhys while it lasted but finding her trust in him irrevocably eroded as a result, Bowen felt that Rhys had first mistreated and then misrepresented her. She had experienced terrible disap-pointment in her relationship with Ford and resented what appeared to be Rhys's view of her as the preeminently controlling and masterful figure of the household. She felt that if anyone held power in the trio it was "Ford's girl," as she bitterly referred to Rhys, who had taught her how far one might fall from any moral responsibility if one were impoverished, desperate, and cynical. "To expect people who are destitute to be governed by any considerations whatever except money considerations is just hypocrisy," she commented. "I learnt what a powerful weapon lies in weakness and pathos and how strong is the position of the person who has nothing to lose [. . .]" (167). For other references to Bowen's portrait of Rhys, see Angier, Staley, and Gardner (143–44; 11–12; 71), in addition to Delany.

2. Note, e.g., Elaine Kraf's discussion of "[t]he unholy outrageousness of Heidler's ménage" (119); Coral Ann Howells's account of Marya as victim of the patronizing attitude of Hugh, the jealousy of Lois, and the disdain of both (46); Arnold Davidson's comments on how Lois treats Marya as, among other things, a "rival" for her husband (68); Thomas Staley's analysis of the growing tensions between the women as Lois comes to view Marya as a competitor (43); and Mary Lou Emery's examination of "the posturing trio [who] repeat among themselves actions of sadomasochistic torment" (110).

3. The insights of "Femininity," in particular, have been generative for numerous theorists investigating female development and early attachment to the mother. The investigation has also begged attack from diverse quarters for its assertion that a girl's Oedipal conflict is inaugurated when she notices the difference between her genitals and those of a boy; comes upon "[t]he discovery that she is castrated"; and develops penis envy (*New Introductory* 126). Freud argues for the claim that a girl must then demonstrate acceptance of her castrated condition by turning from her early, masculinized preoccupation with the clitoris, which he describes as a "small penis," in favor of "the truly feminine vagina" as the prime erogenous zone (118). She is able to overcome penis envy most fully when she can substitute a wish for a baby for her desire to possess a phallus in her own right. Freud avers, further, that because the castration complex inaugurates rather than demolishes the Oedipus complex in a girl, "[. . .] she enters the Oedipus situation as though into a haven of refuge" and thus remains in this phase much longer than a boy does (129). Oedipal needs are only partially overcome in the case of most women; and as a result the feminine superego does not form as fully as its male counterpart. The essay concludes with the astounding observation that women are bound to have "little sense of justice" in social concerns due to their incomplete superego formation (134).

It is not difficult to puncture each of these claims and locate much of Freud's argument within the confines of a severely restricted understanding of women. Yet his return to issues of feminine development and sexuality at repeated points in his career demonstrates the activities of someone in struggle to make sense of an unknown: the perceived "other" of woman. As he comments with some irony but also rueful admission at the opening of "Femininity," "Throughout history people have knocked their heads against the riddle of the nature of femininity. [. . .] Nor will *you* have escaped worrying over this problem—those of you who are men; to those of you who are women this will not apply—you are yourselves the problem" (113). While Freud here confirms a phallocentric view of woman as dark continent (see Cixous, "Laugh" 1,455), I would argue that he is also acknowledging the limits of his own capacity to understand feminine development.

4. In usefully clarifying the relationship between Oedipal and pre-Oedipal stages, the sites of development that captured Freud's attention and in turn led to the revisionary insights of Klein and her followers, Otto Fenichel notes that the Oedipal complex as Freud imagined it "belongs to the phallic stage"; however, "[. . .] it begins to develop earlier and so contains to a greater or lesser extent

elements of the 'incorporation' phase" (206), an idea that Klein would go onto elaborate and emphasize.

5. Lois does have brief moments of articulated spite, as in her comment to Hugh about "Mado" (i.e., Marya): " 'Let's go to Luna-park after dinner. [. . .] We'll put Mado on the joy wheel, and watch her being banged about a bit. Well, she ought to amuse us sometimes; she ought to sing for her supper; that's what she's here for, isn't it?' " (85). The overt hostility of the remark is notable for its atypicality, and she quickly moves onto other topics, with the narrative leaving the tenor of her feelings unexplored.

6. Robert Caper provides a cogent explanation of why parents may at times appear conjoined in the eyes of the infant as well as the undeveloped child. Discussing the part-object stage of early development as characterized by feelings that alternate between the loving and destructive, Caper notes, "[. . .] various parental imagos fluctuate with each other in the infant's mind, and each parent is experienced at various times as extremely good or bad, isolated or in various kinds of combination with the other. The prevailing imago depends on the type of emotion that has gripped the infant at the moment" (207). Marya is characteristically gripped by feelings of aloneness, and thus her perception of Lois and Hugh as combined serves the function of reinforcing her view of herself as victim, doomed to a state of eternal isolation.

7. Heidler's repulsion toward Marya, as it expresses the attempt of the sexual hypocrite to disavow both responsibility and shame, is a repulsion shared by men throughout Rhys's fiction as they renounce their former mistresses. As Vivian Gornick observes, the novels demonstrate a talent for detailing ways in which men who are afraid of their sensual impulses ultimately turn against the women who inflamed their lust and caused them to shed, even briefly, the shell of civilized behavior (60).

8. For presentations of homoerotic connection in Rhys's oeuvre, see, e.g., the lover-like bond between Marston and Julian in the story "Till September Petronella," in which the virulent misogyny Julian directs at the protagonist appears to derive from his jealousy over Marston's relation with her (*Collected* 125–50). In Rhys's story "Tigers Are Better-Looking," the protagonist, Mr. Severn, spends his day struggling to write and his evening trying to escape his feelings after having been left a glib note by the man who allowed Severn to take care of him for an interval but has now decided to move on. The implication of an erotic involvement that has been abruptly ended is offered in the effeminacy of the letter's prose style as well as Mr. Severn's condition of disequilibrium through much of the narrative (*Collected* 176–88). The lesbian attachment between Wyatt and Norah, the sister of Julia Martin in *After Leaving Mr. Mackenzie*, is discussed at length in Chapter 3 of this study. All of these portraits of homosexual erotics, the subtle and the more overt, are damning, as Rhys presents the relationships as merely imitative of the worst aspects of heterosexuality because of the inevitable inequities of power that they display.

One exception to this prevailing view occurs in *Good Morning, Midnight* when Sasha Jensen recounts the story of a girl she saw once in a bordello and to whom she felt deeply drawn because she seemed touchingly melancholy and vulnerable—in effect, very much like Sasha herself. But when her listener, René, asks if she and the girl made love, Sasha's response is immediate: " 'No, of course not. [. . .] Certainly not.' " The vehemence in her statement implies that any actual sensual contact would be unacceptable to her—possibly because a loving bond between women would represent too closely a fusion between daughter and mother, which is rejected elsewhere and more overtly throughout the narrative. Sasha produces as follow-up and justification of her distaste a memory of the bordello girl hurrying to align herself with the other whores circling a male customer and vying for his attention. She thus makes the point that her own " 'sentimental thoughts' " were misplaced (160) and, by extension, that any same-sex eroticism must be kept in the realm of fantasy—both because its enactment would be unpalatable and because the reality of one's object of desire is bound to disappoint.

9. Martien Kappers-den Hollander offers another view of the autobiographical underpinnings of both Ford's and Rhys's novels that disputes an intertextual reading and stresses, instead, that the authors had in common the impulse to link their actual lives with the fictive presentations of themselves.

5   *GOOD MORNING, MIDNIGHT*: A STORY OF SOUL MURDER

1. Thus I take issue with readers who would assert that this novel displays Sasha's always-conscious strategies of control. Paula Le Gallez, e.g., sees in her narration an accomplished "bifurcation" of voice as well as capacity for intentional "detachment" and "theatricality" of self-presentation (114; 137). In contrast, Mary Lou Emery has noted Sasha's "dream logic" and use of condensation (167) but does not develop her argument in the direction of an analysis of how Sasha's narrative sheds light on unconscious processes.

2. Among the more persuasive dismantlings of the notion that diverse readers will produce consistent responses to the same text, see Norman Holland's analysis of how individual predilections and prejudices determine readers' interpretations; Stanley Fish's discussion of "interpretive communities" as these shape readers' understandings of texts; and Judith Fetterley's critique of the many ways in which female readers are coerced into reading against their own gendered experience.

3. In his study of child abuse, Leonard Shengold clarifies his use of the term "soul murder," from which he takes the title of his book, as a "dramatic designation for a certain category of traumatic experience: instances of repetitive and chronic overstimulation, alternating with emotional deprivation, that are deliberately brought about by another individual" (16–17). He further traces the history of the concept from the first usage he can find, in the 1832 narrative *Kasper Hauser* by Anselm von Feuerbach; to its appearance in works by Ibsen and Strinberg in the late nineteenth century and in the *Memoirs* (1903) of D. P. Schreber upon

which Freud drew for a famous case study; and in its influence through the middle and late twentieth century in chronicles of the mistreatment of children by such analysts as Ferenczi (1933) and Masson (1984) (17–23).

4. Although other commentators have noted that this novel references Sasha's father, the discussions of how he is presented and the sexually loaded content of his daughter's responses avoid any specific consideration of the effects of incestuous desire on the psyche of the individual. Emery, e.g., notes the symbolic correspondence between Sasha's dream of a father and the eerie *commis* who stalks the pages of *Good Morning, Midnight*, a correspondence that my argument also cites; but Emery's concern is to demonstrate how Sasha's experience of these male figures reflects societal pressures that women capitulate to "a nameless and questionable patriarchal authority, demanding submission to tabooed relations [. . .]" (152). Peter Wolfe offers a fleeting observation on the treatment of paternal themes in Rhys's work: "Now father-figures in Freud excite lust," he comments. "The number of much-older lovers and husbands in the Rhys canon reveal a Freudian strain [. . .]" (135). Wolfe's only elaboration is that because Rhys's oeuvre reflects predominantly failed sexual engagements, this "strain" is less apparent than it might be, in *Good Morning, Midnight* and elsewhere.

5. Even in rare instances, as in Shelley's *Frankenstein*, when the text begins with a sympathetic presentation of the "double," other figures in the narrative insist on perceiving the character as malign. Frankenstein's monster obligingly accommodates their vision by story's close, devolving into a force of death that opposes their self-righteous sanctification of life. Shelley thereby suggests a deep need within the human community to locate an identifiably uncanny figure who will carry the burden of what others have repressed.

6. In a letter of 1956, Rhys commented on her use of time in the final portion of *Good Morning, Midnight* : "I wanted Sasha to enter the No time region there. 'Everything is on the same plane.' " With characteristic self-deprecation, she added, "I tried and rewrote and rewrote but no use" (*Letters* 138). As my argument is intended to establish, she did herself an injustice in diminishing the impact of an extremely disorienting temporality that is established at her novel's close.

7. In a biographically informed reading, Carole Angier interprets this passage as a veiled reference to the episode to which I allude in the introduction to this study, in which Rhys experienced, at about age fourteen, a sexually charged engagement with a much older man who took her on long walks, briefly experimented with fondling her, and then enticed her into listening to an increasingly sado-masochistic series of narratives in which she figured as his ever-compliant sexual slave (26–29). Rhys's retrospective sense that she had allowed him to elaborate on this theme—that in fact she had been fascinated with it—suggests her feeling of complicity in the sexual abuse; and it underscores the guilty renditions of Oedipal desire for a father figure in *Good Morning, Midnight.*

8. For instance, *The Ego and the Id*, Freud's most explicit discussion of the "complete" Oedipus complex with its "positive" (i.e., heterosexual) and "negative" (homosexual) components, centers entirely on boys (28–39).

9. Alan Karbelnig, who generously read this chapter in draft form, called my attention to the link between Sasha's reliance on alcohol and the desire for the mother's milk in the oral stage of childhood development.

10. The groundbreaking work of Nancy Chodorow in recasting the feminine Oedipal narrative has been the basis of numerous subsequent studies and clearly informs the more contemporary treatment of this material to which I refer here.

11. The other "author" Rhys conjures is the eponymous character Lotus in a late short story. Lotus comments that she has been advised to avoid recording subject matter that may be depressing but nevertheless longs to " 'write down some of the things that have happened to me, just write them down straight, sad or not sad' " (*Collected* 212). The contempt leveled at her by a female neighbor, who also appears to be jealous of her boyfriend's relationship with Lotus, underscores the particularly isolated, misunderstood, and melancholy plight of the woman who chooses the life of a writer.

12. Coral Ann Howells reads the conclusion of *Good Morning, Midnight* as a comment on the "misognyny" of masculinist configurations of feminine existence and a stark contrast to the bliss expressed by Molly Bloom (92; 99); Le Gallez cites the "grim irony" of this echo of Joyce in a novel that closes, in her view, on a desperate note (140); Arnold E. Davidson offers a summary of differing critical responses to the Joycean ending of the text before proposing a rather baffling, upbeat argument that Sasha's words, like Molly's, are entirely affirmative. Sasha, he explains, is now able to embrace "a different kind of love, one that depends entirely on her" in her acceptance of the man who comes in through her door (95–96; 111).

13. Rhys's own statements about the hiatus were generally elusive and abbreviated; after *Good Morning, Midnight*, as she noted in an interview, "I didn't write for a long time. And then I wrote some short stories. And then there was this thing about doing *Good Morning, Midnight* on the BBC radio. And then I started *The [sic] Wide Sargasso Sea*" (Vreeland 234). Her remark about the radio broadcast refers to a production that was mounted by the actress Selma Vaz Dias, who had placed an ad in the *New Statesman* trying to locate Rhys at a time when the public seemed to believe that she was dead. She emerged from obscurity to grant Vaz Dias permission to adapt *Good Morning, Midnight*, and she was buoyed up by the renewed general interest in her work although she did not complete *Wide Sargasso Sea* for another decade. In commenting on the period during and immediately following World War II, Rhys characteristically minimized both her personal agency and the writing that she was in fact producing in piecemeal fashion. She was plagued by many kinds of difficulties during this time, as Angier's treatment of her "Lost Years" from 1939 to 1966 delineates (411–567); but I am concerned with the specifically artistic determinants that kept her from publishing another long narrative until *Wide Sargasso Sea* appeared in its completed and revised form in 1966.

6   *WIDE SARGASSO SEA*: THE TRANSFORMING VISION

1. Along these lines, see Gayatri Chakravorty Spivak's comment: "Rhys makes Antoinette see her *self* as her Other, Brontë's Bertha [. . .] the so-called ghost in Thornfield Hall [. . .]" (269).
2. Gregory H. Hallidy discusses this first forest dream of Antoinette's as it follows from her day at the bathing pool with Tia, and in light of Freud's association between water symbolism and phantasies about intrauterine life. Thus Hallidy's interpretation of the dream: "The heavy footsteps which Antoinette hears 'coming closer' are the heartbeats of her mother growing louder as she goes into labor" (9).
3. Various explanatory paradigms may be used to understand Antoinette's way of relating to and handling herself. In an overview of psychoanalytic discussions of internalizing processes, Thomas H. Ogden recollects Freud's initial assertion that one response to a lost object is to replace it with a part of the self modeled on the object. As Klein developed this idea, emphasis was placed on the relation among internal objects, as much of my study has shown. Fairbairn saw the mind as composed of formations that had the ability to create meanings and act on their own motivations. Because, as Ogden asserts, the ego usually makes splits as it internalizes at a very early stage of existence, "the identification with the object is of a poorly differentiated nature. The experiential quality of the identification is one of 'becoming the object' as opposed to 'feeling like' the object" (150). Furthermore, "[. . .] a dual split in the ego is required for the establishment of an internal object relationship. One split-off aspect of the ego is identified with the self in the original object relationship; another is thoroughly identified with the object" (*Matrix* 164–65). Thus I would argue that for much of her experience Rhys's Antoinette lives her internal world both as the self who was figuratively left in the cold by a withdrawn mother as well as the object who coldly turned away from the small child who needed her.
4. See Deborah Kelly Kloepfer for an insightful account of how Rochester's desires traverse both Oedipal and pre-Oedipal terrains; in the forest, his statement, "What I see is nothing," replicates "the castration contract. But even he knows that there is something else there which, though unseen, is not missing, is not lack, is 'not nothing.' " Here, as she argues, it is the primal space of the maternal for which he longs (151).
5. This proclivity for denial infects everyone on the island; as Charles Sarvan points out, the Creoles have collectively forgotten how the town of Massacre was named, and thus express their own "flight from remembering" (60).
6. Commentators on the novel are divided in their assessments of Rochester's and Antoinette's respective powers as speakers of the text. Lori Lawson claims that Rochester "preempts Antoinette's voice with his own. Already himself a bastion of the symbolic order, he assumes his culturally endorsed position as speaking subject and speaks *for* her" (24). Conversely, as Kathy Mezie observes, Rochester's hold over the narrative is tenuous at best; with Antoinette's "invasion

of his narration" (206), Rochester loses dominion in Part Two, a view that my argument supports.

7. Despite the terrible sadness of Antoinette's presentation throughout the text, and the highly ambiguous quality of the conclusion, Rhys's readers generally choose a single, uplifting interpretation of the last pages of her narrative in Part Three. Liz Gunner, e.g., sees Antoinette's madness in contrast to her mother's "as a resistance of the imagination [. . .] an enabling process which allows for both the subversion of the male power of the husband/coloniser and an assertion of the undefeated self" (143). Elizabeth Abel views Antoinette's suicide as an active rejection of her mother's passive imprisonment and thus a way to free herself by demanding selfhood (174). Such readings point to a pervasive critical discomfort with the multiplicity of meanings upon which Rhys's texts, in their evocations of the processes of the unconscious, insist.

8. In a brief but clearly pertinent discussion, R. McClure Smith draws on Winnicott's theory "of that 'transitional space' of artistic creation as the area where texts blur, dissolve and separate" as way to describe Rhys's use of Brontë's work (126). I do not, however, align myself with Smith's conclusion that *Wide Sarasso Sea* speaks of Rhys's "masochistic aesthetic" insofar as it ultimately expresses "merger and transcendence through suffering [. . .]" (130). Although Rhys certainly struggled in her relationship with Brontë and Brontë's text, I read her own progress, finally, as the narrative of a literary daughter beginning a positive movement away from the splitting processes that characterized her earlier novels and toward an integrative, balanced experience of the object world.

9. Of the many critical responses to Rhys's relationship with Brontë's text, Ellen G. Friedman's account of how Rhys disrupts nineteenth-century conventions by adopting conspicuously twentieth-century attitudes with which to revision *Jane Eyre* is particularly perceptive (119). Judith Kegan Gardiner offers the foundational argument that Rhys is "validating her forebear's prior importance at the same time that she wishes to displace it. [. . .] Rather than being overwhelmed by the sense that it has all been said before, she tells us what has never been said or said falsely" (*Rhys* 125).

Works Cited ✑

WORKS BY JEAN RHYS

Rhys, Jean. *After Leaving Mr. Mackenzie.* 1930. New York: Norton, 1997.
———. *The Collected Short Stories* [incl. *The Left Bank, Tigers Are Better-Looking, Sleep It Off Lady*]. 1927–1976. New York: Norton, 1987.
———. *Good Morning, Midnight.* 1939. New York: Norton, 1986.
———. Jean Rhys Papers. Department of Special Collections, McFarlin Lib., U of Tulsa, Tulsa.
———. *Letters, 1931–1966.* Ed. Francis Wyndham and Diana Melly. London: André Deutsch, 1984.
———. *My Day: Three Pieces.* New York: Frank Hallman, 1975.
———. *Quartet [Postures].* 1928. New York: Norton, 1997.
———. *Smile Please: An Unfinished Autobiography.* New York: Harper and Row, 1979.
———. *Voyage in the Dark.* 1934. New York: Norton, 1982.
———. *Wide Sargasso Sea: Backgrounds Criticism.* Ed. Judith L. Raiskin. 1966. New York: Norton, 1999.

ADDITIONAL WORKS CITED

Abel, Elizabeth. "Women and Schizophrenia: The Fiction of Jean Rhys." *Contemporary Literature* 20.2 (1979): 155–77.
Altman, Leon. "The Oedipal Conflict and the Dream." *The Dream in Psychoanalysis.* Madison: International UP, 1975. 209–30.
Angier, Carole. *Jean Rhys: Life and Work.* Boston: Little, Brown, 1990.
Athill, Diana. Introduction. *Jean Rhys: The Complete Novels.* New York: Norton, 1985. vii–xiv.
———. Jean Rhys and her Autobiography: A Foreword. *Smile Please: An Unfinished Biography.* New York: Harper and Row, 1979. 5–15.
Balint, Michael. *The Basic Fault: Therapeutic Aspects of Regression.* London: Routledge-Taylor & Francis, 1979.

Balint, Michael. "Early Developmental States of the Ego. Primary Object-Love." *Primary Love and Psycho-analytic Technique.* 1937. Ed. Michael Balint. London: Routledge-Taylor & Francis, 1979. 90–108.

Benjamin, Jessica. *The Bonds of Love: Psychoanalysis, Feminism, and The Problem of Domination.* New York: Pantheon, 1988.

Benvenuto, Bice, and Roger Kennedy. *The Works of Jacques Lacan: An Introduction.* London: Free Association Books, 1986.

Berry, Betsy. " 'Between Dog and Wolf': Jean Rhys's Version of Naturalism in *After Leaving Mr. Mackenzie.*" *Studies in the Novel* 27.4 (1995): 544–62.

Bollas, Christopher. *Ideas in Psychoanalysis: Free Association.* Cambridge: Icon, 2002.

———. *The Shadow of the Object: Psychoanalysis of the Unthought Known.* New York: Columbia UP, 1987.

Bowen, Stella. *Drawn From Life.* 1940. Maidstone: George Mann, 1974.

Brontë, Charlotte. *Jane Eyre: An Authoritative Text: Contexts Criticism.* 1847. Ed. Richard J. Dunn. New York: Norton, 2001.

Caper, Robert. "Early Stages of Oedipal Conflict." *Immaterial Facts.* New York: Aronson, 1988. 203–16.

Chodorow, Nancy. *The Reproduction of Mothering: Psychoanalysis and the Sociology of Gender.* Berkeley: U of California P, 1978.

Cixous, Hélène. "Castration or Decapitation?" Trans. Annette Kuhn. *Signs* 7.11 (1981): 41–55. Rpt. in *Contemporary Literary Criticism: Literary and Cultural Studies.* Ed. Robert Con Davis and Ronald Schleifer. 2nd ed. New York: Longman, 1989. 479–91.

———. "The Laugh of the Medusa." Trans. Keith Cohen and Paula Cohen. *Signs* 1.4 (1976): 875–93. Rpt. in *The Critical Tradition: Classic Texts and Contemporary Trends.* 2nd ed. Ed. David H. Richter. Boston: Bedford, 1998. 1,453–71.

Curtis, Jan. "Jean Rhys's *Voyage in the Dark*: A Re-assessment." *The Journal of Commonwealth Literature* 22.1 (1987): 144–58.

Davidson, Arnold E. *Jean Rhys.* New York: Ungar, 1985.

DeKoven, Marianne. *Rich and Strange: Gender, History, Modernism.* Princeton: Princeton UP, 1991.

Delany, Paul. "Jean Rhys and Ford Madox Ford: What 'Really' Happened?" *Mosaic: A Journal for the Interdisciplinary Study of Literature* 16.4 (1983): 15–24.

Emery, Mary Lou. *Jean Rhys at "World's End": Novels of Colonial and Sexual Exile.* Austin: U of Texas P, 1990.

Fairbairn, W. Ronald D. "On the Nature and Aims of Psycho-Analytical Treatment." *International Journal of Psycho-Analysis* 39.5 (1958): 374–85.

———. "The Repression and the Return of Bad Objects (with special reference to the 'War Neuroses')." 1943. *An Object-Relations Theory of the Personality.* New York: Basic Books, 1954. 59–81.

Felman, Shoshana, ed. *Literature and Psychoanalysis: The Question of Reading: Otherwise.* Baltimore: Johns Hopkins UP, 1980.

Fenichel, Otto. "Specific Forms of the Oedipus Complex." *International Journal of Psychoanalysis* 12 (1931): 412–30.

Fetterley, Judith. *The Resisting Reader: A Feminist Approach to American Fiction.* Bloomington: Indiana UP, 1978.

Fish, Stanley. *Is There a Text in This Class? The Authority of Interpretive Communities.* Cambridge: Harvard UP, 1980.

Ford, Ford Madox. *The Good Soldier: A Tale of Passion.* 1915. New York: Penguin, 1999.

———. Preface: Rive Gauche. *The Left Bank and Other Stories by Jean Rhys.* 1927. Freeport: Books for Libraries P, 1970.

Freud, Sigmund. *The Ego and the Id.* 1923. Strachey 19: 3–66.

———. "Female Sexuality." 1931. Strachey 21: 225–43.

———. "Fragment of an Analysis of a Case of Hysteria." 1905. Strachey 7: 13–146.

———. *The Interpretation of Dreams.* 1900. Strachey 4: 1–338.

———. *New Introductory Lectures on Psycho-Analysis.* 1933. Strachey 22: 5–182.

———. *An Outline of Psychoanalysis.* 1940. Strachey 23: 144–207.

———. "The Return of the Repressed." *Moses and Monotheism: Three Essays.* 1939. Strachey 23: 124–27.

———. "Some Psychical Consequences of the Anatomical Distinction between the Sexes." 1925. Strachey 19: 248–58.

———. "Two Encyclopedia Articles." 1923. Strachey 18: 233–59.

———. "The Uncanny." 1919. Strachey 17: 217–56.

Friedman, Ellen G. "Breaking the Master Narrative: Jean Rhys's *Wide Sargasso Sea.*" *Breaking the Sequence: Women's Experimental Fiction.* Ed. Ellen G. Friedman and Miriam Fuchs. Princeton: Princeton UP, 1989. 117–28.

Gardiner, Judith Kegan. *Rhys, Stead, Lessing, and the Politics of Empathy.* Bloomington: Indiana UP, 1989.

———. "Rhys Recalls Ford: *Quartet* and *The Good Soldier.*" *Tulsa Studies in Women's Literature* 1.1 (1982): 67–81.

Gornick, Vivian. "Jean Rhys." *The End of the Novel of Love.* Boston: Beacon, 1997. 53–63.

Grosskurth, Phyllis. *Melanie Klein: Her World and Her Work.* New York: Knopf, 1986.

Gunner, Liz. "Mothers, Daughters and Madness in Works by Four Women Writers: Bessie Head, Jean Rhys, Tsits Dangarembga, and Ana Ata Aidoo." *Alif: Journal of Comparative Poetics* 14 (1994): 136–51.

Hallidy, Gregory H. "Antoinette's First Dream: The Birth-Fantasy in Jean Rhys's *Wide Sargasso Sea.*" *Notes on Contemporary Literature* 21.1 (1991): 8–9.

Harrison, Nancy R. *Jean Rhys and the Novel as Women's Text.* Chapel Hill: U of North Carolina P, 1988.

Hemingway, Ernest. *The Sun Also Rises.* 1926. New York: Scribner-Simon and Schuster, 1954.

Hite, Molly. *The Other Side of the Story: Structures and Strategies of Contemporary Feminist Narrative.* Ithaca: Cornell UP, 1989.

Holland, Norman N. *5 Readers Reading.* New Haven: Yale UP, 1975.

Hollander, Martien Kappers-den. "Measure for Measure: *Quartet* and *When the Wicked Man.*" *Jean Rhys Review* 2.2 (1988): 2–17.

Holtzman, Deanna, and Nancy Kulish. "The Feminization of the Oedipus Complex, Part 1: A Reconsideration of the Significance of Separation Issues." *Journal of the American Psychoanalytic Association* 48.4 (2000): 1,413–37.

Howells, Coral Ann. *Jean Rhys.* New York: St. Martin's, 1991.

Hughes, Athol, ed. *The Inner World and Joan Riviere: Collected Papers: 1920–1958.* London: Karnac, 1991.

Hulme, Peter. "The Locked Heart: The Creole Family Romance of *Wide Sargasso Sea*—Art Historical and Biographical Analysis." *Jean Rhys Review* 6.1 (1993): 20–36.

Irigaray, Luce. *This Sex Which Is Not One.* Trans. Catherine Porter and Carolyn Burke. Ithaca: Cornell UP, 1985.

Jacobs, Fred Rue. *Jean Rhys—Bibliography.* Keene: Loop, 1979.

Jacobus, Mary. *First Things: The Maternal Imaginary in Literature, Art, and Psychoanalysis.* New York: Routledge, 1995.

James, Louis. *Jean Rhys.* London: Longman, 1978.

Joyce, James. *Ulysses.* 1922. New York: Vintage, 1986.

Karbelnig, Alan. Personal communication. March 2003.

Kineke, Sheila. " 'Like a Hook Fits an Eye:' Jean Rhys, Ford Madox Ford, and the Imperial Operations of Modernist Mentoring." *Tulsa Studies in Women's Literature* 16.2 (1997): 281–301.

Klein, Melanie. "A Contribution to the Psychogenesis of Manic-Depressive States." 1934. *Contributions to Psycho-Analysis, 1921–1945.* London: Hogarth, 1950. 262–89.

———. "Early Stages of the Oedipus Conflict." 1928. *Contributions to Psycho-Analysis, 1921–1945.* 186–98.

———. *Envy and Gratitude: A Study of Unconscious Sources.* New York: Basic Books, 1957.

———. "Notes on Some Schizoid Mechanisms." 1946. *Developments in Psycho Analysis.* London: Hogarth, 1952. 292–320.

———. "The Origins of Transference." 1952. *Developments in Psycho Analysis.* 201–10.

Kloepfer, Deborah Kelly. *The Unspeakable Mother: Forbidden Discourse in Jean Rhys and H. D.* Ithaca: Cornell UP, 1989.

Kraf, Elaine. "Jean Rhys: The Men in Her Novels (Hugh Heidler, 'The Gigolo,' and Mr. Mackenzie)." *The Review of Contemporary Fiction* 5.2 (1985): 118–28.

Kurzweil, Edith, and William Phillips, eds. *Literature and Psychoanalysis.* New York: Columbia UP, 1983.

Lacan, Jacques. "Aggressivity in Psychoanalysis." 1948. *Écrits: A Selection.* Trans. Alan Sheridan. New York: Norton, 1977. 8–29.

———. "The Function and Field of Speech and Language in Psychoanalysis." 1953. *Écrits: A Selection.* 30–113.

———. "The Mirror Stage as Formative of the Function of the I as Revealed in Psychoanalytic Experience." 1949. *Écrits: A Selection.* 1–7.

———. "The Signification of the Phallus." 1958. *Écrits: A Selection.* 281–91.

Lawson, Lori. "Mirror and Madness: A Lacanian Analysis of the Feminine Subject in *Wide Sargasso Sea.*" *Jean Rhys Review* 4.2 (1991): 19–27.

Le Gallez, Paula. *The Rhys Woman.* London: Macmillan, 1990.

Loewald, Hans. "The Waning of the Oedipus Complex." *Journal of the American Psychoanalytic Association* 27 (1979): 751–76.

Melltown, Elgin W. "A Bibliography of the Writings of Jean Rhys with a Selected List of Reviews and Other Critical Writings." *World Literature Written in English* 16 (1977): 179–202.

Meltzer, Donald. *The Apprehension of Beauty.* Perthshire: Clunie, 1988.

Mezei, Kathy. " 'And It Kept Its Secret': Narration, Memory, and Madness in Jean Rhys' *Wide Sargasso Sea.*" *Critique* 28.4 (1987): 195–209.

Miller, Alice. *Thou Shalt Not Be Aware: Society's Betrayal of the Child.* New York: Farrar, Strauss and Giroux, 1986.

Mitchell, Juliet, ed. Introduction. *The Selected Melanie Klein.* New York: Free P, 1986. 9–32.

Mitchell, Stephen A. "The Origin and Nature of the 'Object' in the Theories of Klein and Fairbairn." *Fairbairn and the Origins of Object Relations.* Ed. James S. Grotstein and Donald B. Rinsley. New York: Guilford, 1994. 66–87.

Morris, Mervyn. "Oh, Give the Girl a Chance: Jean Rhys and *Voyage in the Dark.*" *Journal of West Indian Literature* 3.2 (1989): 1–8.

Nebeker, Helen. *Jean Rhys: Woman in Passage.* Montréal: Eden, 1981.

O'Connor, Teresa F. *Jean Rhys: The West Indian Novels.* New York: New York UP, 1986.

Ogden, Thomas H. *The Matrix of the Mind.* Northvale: Aronson, 1986.

———. "On the Nature of Schizophrenic Conflict." *International Journal of Psycho-Analysis* 61.4 (1980): 513–33.

Plante, David. *Difficult Women: A Memoir of Three.* New York: Atheneum, 1983.

Raiskin, Judith L., ed. *Wide Sargasso Sea: Backgrounds Criticism.* By Jean Rhys. 1966. New York: Norton, 1999.

Riviere, Joan. "Hate, Greed and Aggression." 1937. Hughes: 168–205.

———. "Jealousy as a Mechanism of Defense." 1932. Hughes: 104–15.

———. "The Unconscious Phantasy of an Inner World Reflected in Examples from Literature." 1952. Hughes: 302–30.

———. "Womanliness as Masquerade." 1929. Hughes: 90–101.

Rutter, Peter. *Sex in the Forbidden Zone: When Men in Power—Therapists, Doctors, Clergy, Teachers, and Others—Betray Women's Trust.* New York: Fawcett Crest, 1989.

Sánchez-Pardo, Esther. *Cultures of the Death Drive: Melanie Klein and Modernist Melancholia.* Durham: Duke UP, 2003.

Sarvan, Charles. "Flight, Entrapment, and Madness in Jean Rhys's *Wide Sargasso Sea.*" *The International Fiction Review* 26.1–2 (1999): 58–65.

Scharfman, Ronnie. "Mirroring and Mothering in Simone Schwarz-Bart's *Pluie et vent sur Telumee Miracle* and Jean Rhys' *Wide Sargasso Sea.*" *Yale French Studies* 62 (1981): 88–106.

Segal, Hanna. *Introduction to the Work of Melanie Klein.* New York: Basic Books, 1964.

Shelley, Mary. *Frankenstein.* 1818. Harmondsworth: Penguin, 1985.

Shengold, Leonard. *Soul Murder: The Effects of Childhood Abuse and Deprivation.* New York: Fawcett Columbine, 1989.

Sheridan, Alan, trans. Translator's Note. *Écrits: A Selection.* vii–xii.

Smith, R. McClure. " 'I don't dream about it any more': The Textual Unconscious in Jean Rhys's *Wide Sargasso Sea.*" *The Journal of Narrative Technique* 26.2 (1996): 113–36.

Socor, Barbara J. "The Self After Thought: An Object Relations Discussion of a Failure to Know." *Journal of Analytic Social Work* 1.1 (1993): 75–104.

Spivak, Gayatri Chakravorty. "Three Women's Texts and a Critique of Imperialism." *"Race," Writing, and Difference.* Ed. Henry Louis Gates, Jr. Chicago: U of Chicago P, 1986. 262–80.

Staley, Thomas F. *Jean Rhys: A Critical Study.* Austin: U of Texas P, 1979.

Steiner, John. "Revenge and Resentment in the Oedipus Situation." *International Journal of Psychoanalysis* 77 (1996): 433–43.

Sternlicht, Sanford. *Jean Rhys.* New York: Twayne-Simon & Schuster Macmillan, 1997.

Stevens, Wallace. *The Collected Poems of Wallace Stevens.* New York: Knopf, 2000.

Strachey, James, ed. and trans. *The Standard Edition of the Complete Psychological Works of Sigmund Freud.* 24 vols. London: Hogarth, 1953–1974.

Thomas, Sue. "Jean Rhys, 'Grilled Sole,' and an Experience of 'Mental Seduction.' " *New Literatures Review* 28–29 (1994–1995): 65–84.

Tustin, Francis. "Autistic Encapsulation in Neurotic Patients." *Master Clinicians on Treating the Regressed Patient.* Northvale: Aronson, 1990. 117–37.

Vreeland, Elizabeth. "Jean Rhys: The Art of Fiction LXIV." *Paris Review* 76 (1979): 218–37.

Weintraub, Harvey. Personal communication. June 2001.

Winnicott, D. W. "Aggression in Relation to Emotional Development." 1950–1955. *Collected Papers: Through Paediatrics to Psycho-Analysis.* New York: Basic Books, 1958. 204–18.

———. "Ego Distortion in Terms of True and False Self." 1960. *The Maturational Processes and the Facilitating Environment: Studies in the Theory of Emotional Development.* New York: International UP, 1965. 140–52.

———. "Living Creatively." *Home is Where We Start From.* New York: Norton, 1986. 39–54.

———. *Playing and Reality.* New York: Routledge, 1999.

———. "Primary Maternal Preoccupation." 1956. *Collected Papers: Through Paediatrics to Psycho-Analysis.* 300–05.

Wolfe, Peter. *Jean Rhys.* Boston: Twayne-G. K. Hall, 1980.

Index